DIGGING DEEPER

Sam Harris Adventure Series

Book 6

PJ SKINNER

ISBN 978-1-913224-06-6

Third Edition

Copyright 2019 PJ Skinner

Cover design by Self Publishing Lab

Dedicated to my friend Walter, without whose patience and stubborn insistence I would never have been able to say 'I have finished my novel' instead of 'I am writing a novel'.

Discover other titles in the Sam Harris Series

Fool's Gold (Book 1)

Hitler's Finger (Book 2)

The Star of Simbako (Book 3)

The Pink Elephants (Book 4)

The Bonita Protocol (Book 5)

Coming Soon

Concrete Jungle (Book 7)

Go to the PJ Skinner website for more info

www.pjskinner.com

Chapter I

'Diamonds are a girl's best friend. Are you planning to sleep with Black to get your share?'

Sam Harris looked across the scarred table at the drunken, dishevelled shell of a man sitting opposite her. She had waited a good hour for Pat Murphy to turn up at the hotel and he had barely acknowledged her presence when he arrived. Instead, he headed to a small serving hatch in the corner of the room which opened onto a bar at the other side. He had ordered a large whisky without asking her if she would like anything.

Murphy's hand shook as he raised his cigarette to his mouth, his fingers yellow and gnarled. *Had he really asked her if she was planning on sleeping with her new boss, Adrian Black, the CEO of Gemsite Diamonds? What sort of interview was this?* Maybe it was her tight suit, bought when she was one size slimmer? Being unemployed was fattening, all those chocolate biscuits in the kitchen. *Did she look tarty?*

She hadn't thought so earlier when she had squeezed into the dark grey interview suit and looked at herself in the full-length mirror. She hadn't worn the suit for a while and it only just buttoned up over the plumpness carried evenly on her athletic frame. Although she didn't think of herself as a beautiful woman, her vivacious green eyes and ready smile made her approachable and attractive.

She wasn't in the habit of wearing make-up but she applied some foundation to her unlined face for the interview. Then she experimented with her mother's mascara, but she decided she looked like a panda and took it off again. Her hair was growing out from a short cut but she managed to force it into a small bun, which left rebellious hairs dangling around her long neck.

She rummaged around in the bottom of the wardrobe for her only pair of high heels. They were too tight for her size-eight feet (10 American) but it was almost impossible to find shoes in her size. Having inherited a genetic predisposition for shoe purchasing from a mother who rivalled Imelda Marcos in that department, this was particularly galling.

Grabbing her handbag, she tottered down the stairs of her parents' house.

'Good luck, darling,' yelled her mother.

She came out from the underground station at Paddington already limping in her tight shoes. She checked the location of the hotel on her map and set off as fast as she could, not wanting to arrive late. The Lancaster Hotel sat in a none too salubrious back street behind the mainline station. The Victorian residence, which had been converted into a cheap lodging house, had seen better days.

The front door hung open and she entered a dingy passageway with a foxed mirror in which she checked her appearance. Frazzled and red-cheeked from exertion would not impress many people, but at least she hadn't arrived late. She tidied a few stray hairs back into the bun and headed for the battered reception desk on which perched an electric bell. Sam pressed it hard and it rang loudly, making her jump.

After a few seconds, a decrepit woman wheezed into view.

'Good afternoon,' said Sam. 'Can you please show me the lounge? I'm meeting someone there.'

The woman didn't answer, beckoning her forward and showing her into the room at the front of the hotel before shrinking back into the gloom like a character in a horror movie. The lounge did not invite relaxation. The filthy state of the carpet made Sam's skin crawl. She lowered herself gingerly into one of the greasy, stained armchairs and waited.

After Murphy had bought his drink, he dumped his luggage in the other corner of the room and came to sit opposite her. His demeanour suggested he was already drunk. She steeled herself for a tricky hour but he wasn't interested in asking technical questions. He leered at her in a suggestive way that made her feel sick.

She would not rise to the bait. Like a lot of people, Pat Murphy's interview technique probably deteriorated after the bars opened. He didn't know her from Adam.

'Can you tell me about Mr Black?' she said. 'I imagine he's an interesting man.'

'Adrian Black is an alcoholic, chainsmoking megalomaniac who is completely obsessed with diamonds and money. He hasn't a grain of pity or empathy in his entire being, and he likes girls who resemble boys.'

Murphy sat back looking pleased with himself. Sam refused to be intimidated. During fifteen years of working as an exploration geologist in remote sites, most of her bosses had been more than a little eccentric, so this was not exactly a revelation.

'What age is he?'

'Age? What's that got to do with it? About forty, I think.'

Common ground at last. Maybe he had similar tastes in movies or childhood television series.

'When will I meet him?'

'You're to travel out to Johannesburg and see him there before you fly on to Mondongo, the capital of Tamazia. He'll give you a briefing, and read you the riot act, as is his custom. You'll meet Marybelle too, I imagine.'

'Who is Marybelle?'

'His new wife. She's a Filipino cleaner who worked at Gemsite in the laundry before Black promoted her to girlfriend. She replaced his first wife, who produced female triplets. Not a good move when you're married to a man like that.'

He laughed at his own joke. Sam ploughed on.

'And what do you do at Gemsite, Mr Murphy?'

'I worked at Kardo, one of the company's diamond mines in northeastern Tamazia. It's a shithole. I won't be going back. I've been fired.'

'Fired?' Sam tried to sound shocked.

'That bastard Black said he wouldn't pay me what he owed in salary unless I interviewed you. That's the only reason I'm here. I don't know why he's employing a fucking woman. The other lads won't like it.'

This comment went right over the top of Sam's head. She always started from zero, whatever her role in an exploration company. No one was the least bit interested in her abilities or experience when she arrived on site. It was always her gender that concerned people until they got used to her, or had something more pressing to talk about. She had got better at not caring, but fighting alone was hard when you were far from home in dangerous and remote locations.

An almost full ashtray sat on the ancient table in front of her. She wrinkled her nose in disgust, pushing it as far away from her as she could.

'Oh, I'm sure they'll get used to me,' she said. 'I don't bite.'

'Why does he want you out there?' Murphy relaxed in his chair as if expecting a long explanation.

'They've hired me as the manager of their new projects. The position's based in Mondongo. I'll be living there most of the time. The lads won't see much of me.'

Thank God, she thought. Murphy looked her up and down with ill-concealed lust.

'I can't understand why a woman like you would go to Tamazia. Mondongo's a slum, and people in the rural areas are still fighting a low-level civil war.'

Sam crossed her arms over her breasts as if protecting them from his lecherous gaze.

'I've been told that the capital's quite safe,' said Sam. 'I'm taking my tennis racket.'

The bravado sounded hollow, even to her. There was no disguising the fact that this interview was an act of desperation on her part but she had no intention of telling a drunken Pat Murphy about her humiliating circumstances. She had been out of work for a year and had been forced to move back in with her parents, despite being nearly forty, to protect her meagre savings. She wanted to put a deposit on a house, and this job paid well, if she could stomach the conditions.

Being jobless on a regular basis was par for the course as an exploration geologist, but even when there was work available Sam still got the tail-end jobs in the remotest sites with the worst pay as a result of her gender. The job in Mondongo was like manna from heaven.

Murphy snorted. 'Tennis? Ha! You'll be lucky. It's not a holiday camp, you know. Don't speak back to Black if you want to survive. He appreciates subservience, and I should know. I've got to go to bed now.'

'What if I have any questions about the job?'

'Call the London office. They'll know most things.'

He threw a filthy business card on the table and staggered out of his seat over to the bar, dismissing her without a backward glance.

By the time she got home, her parents had gone to bed but their bedroom light crept out under the door. They would want a report on the interview. She gave the door a light knock and went in. Her parents were both sitting in bed, reading glasses balanced on the ends of their noses. They both peered at her over the top of them like quizzical owls.

'How did it go?' said Bill Harris. 'You were there for ages.'

'Um, well, the man arrived an hour late,' said Sam.

'Honestly,' said Matilda Harris. 'What is wrong with people these days? Was his plane delayed?'

'He didn't say. His manners left a lot to be desired, to be honest. And I think he was drunk.'

'That's annoying. Do you think there was any point to you going?' said Bill.

'Apparently I have the job,' said Sam. 'I don't know whether to be thrilled or horrified.'

'That's great, darling. A job's a job.'

'How can you say that?' said Matilda. 'It sounds like Sam will be working with another bunch of rude drunks to me. And even worse, in a country approaching civil war.'

'I need the money. I promise to do six months and come home. I can always leave if it gets too dangerous.'

'That's the spirit,' said Bill. 'You should be able to look after yourself by now, after all those other jobs you've had.'

Sam smiled. Her parents had been fed a severely censored version of her working life. There didn't seem to be any point to worrying them about stuff that had already happened. Anyway, as her mother had said, she could come home any time she wanted.

Chapter II

Before going to Tamazia, Sam flew to Johannesburg to meet her new boss, Adrian Black. Normally she would have been buzzing with the prospect of starting a new job, but she had been unable to shake the feeling that working at Gemsite would be an ordeal, especially if the other expatriates resembled Murphy. She was going to a country at war with itself, but this represented only one of the pitfalls to the job. None of these had been apparent when she first replied to the advertisement searching for a new projects manager for a diamond mining company in Africa.

This was not a new dilemma. The initial conundrum hadn't changed since she had first graduated. Whenever she tried to stay in England she felt out of place. No matter how hard she tried, she just didn't fit in. She would rather take a dodgy job with the chance of adventure than sit in a suit at a desk, mute with the fear of alienating yet another person. How many pubs had she lurked in, dying to tell her companions about the time someone put a snake in her bed, knowing that to do so would not make things better but worse? The ability to trump anyone's story was not an advantage. It made her a pariah.

So, she always took any job that was offered,

because, despite the casual misogyny rampant in remote sites, at least she could talk freely when she was with other misfits like her, people who had years ago forsaken a normal life to have an adventure instead. Being a woman complicated matters, and she always had to fight for recognition as one of the team, but she was used to it. She lived for the day gender would be irrelevant but she loved her career. Working on remote sites was the lesser of two evils as far as she was concerned.

A hand touched her tense shoulder making her jump. The stewardess placed a plastic tray in front of her.

'I'm sorry. We only have chicken left. What would you like to drink, madam?' she said.

'Can I have an apple juice please?' said Sam.

The aircraft landed on such a thick blanket of fog she wondered if she had gone to the Antarctic instead of Johannesburg. The chilly morning air sat damp on the airport tarmac. It was winter in South Africa. *Have I got the right gear for Tamazia?* She had tried to find out from the London office, but they had been vague about the climate, unwilling to commit themselves. According to the data she had dug up at the library, the ambient temperature in Mondongo was about forty degrees all year round.

She cleared customs, emerging out into the fog-filtered sunlight, staggering under the weight of her cases. A driver organised by the London office picked her up outside the airport terminal. He drove her at breakneck speed through the foggy suburbs which were almost free of traffic at that hour. The car entered Sandton, one of the wealthier suburbs in Johannesburg. The driver headed for a modern hotel with a covered marble entrance. He dropped her off at the reception and left with a cheery wave.

'Passport, please.'

The receptionist at the check-in desk examined the document and sniffed. Turning her back on Sam, she marched into an office behind the desk. She came back holding what looked like an old cigarette packet.

'I've got something for you, Miss Harris.'

The receptionist handed the packet to Sam with undisguised disgust. The packet smelled of stale smoke. Sam opened it, and noticed Adrian Black's name and telephone number scribbled on the inside in blue pen. Putting it into the front pocket of her rucksack with her passport, she signed the check-in form and took her room key.

She made her way to the identikit room, following the buttons carrying her luggage. He staggered in an exaggerated manner, looking for a big tip.

'What you got in here?' he said. 'Gold bars?'

She gave him a dollar and shooed him out. Her bed looked inviting, as she hadn't slept much on the flight due to her neighbour snoring like a tractor. She decided to call Black before taking a nap in case he had a tight schedule. She sat on the bed and got an outside line from the hotel operator. Then she dialled the number written inside the cigarette packet. The telephone rang and rang but nobody answered.

Just when Sam was about to hang up, a sleepy female voice answered the telephone.

'Hallo?'

'Can I speak to Mr Black, please?' said Sam.

There was a long pause. Grumpy voices in the background. The woman came back on the line.

'Mr Black won't be up for several hours yet. Is that Sam Harris?'

'Yes.'

'He'll call you when he wakes up.'

The woman hung up the phone before Sam had a chance to say anything else. Having heard Murphy's description of the extent of Adrian Black's bad manners, which clearly extended to his companion, this reception did not faze her. She hung up the telephone and was soon asleep herself.

Later that afternoon, the phone rang, its shrill tone waking her with a start. Groggy, she reached for the receiver and put it to her ear. Black did not waste words.

'Is that Sam?'

'Yes, Sam Harris here.'

'This is Adrian Black. I'm staying at the Crown Hotel in Sandton. I'll wait for you here at seven in the downstairs bar.'

'How will I recognise you?' said Sam.

'Just look for a guy in a scruffy sweater.'

The tone did not invite any more questions. Sam rang reception to make sure she had changed her watch to the correct time. Then she ordered a taxi for six-thirty. She took a shower, and dried herself watching cricket on the television to distract herself from the nerves that bubbled up tightening her chest. *Surely, he couldn't be that bad?*

She dressed in a khaki uniform of chinos and a short-sleeved shirt. Before leaving, she examined herself in the full-length mirror on the wardrobe door and smiled. The transformation was complete. She looked like a geologist without a beard.

Going downstairs, she got into the taxi, which whisked her across Sandton to a similar hotel to the one in which she was staying. Her hands sweated, and her stomach did flips on the journey. Her reaction was exaggerated by the fact she had not signed her contract yet. *Could Black still change his mind about employing her?*

Her last conversation with the London office had not reassured her about their administrative competence.

'Sam? I'm Sally from the Gemsite London office. I'm calling to tell you that you got the job in Mondongo. You'll be going via Johannesburg to meet Mr Black in two weeks' time.'

'Really? That's fantastic. Can you send me the contract please?'

'I'm sorry, but I haven't been able to get a copy. You'll have to sign it in Mondongo. The phone lines are atrocious and the fax in Mondongo isn't working.'

'Can you at least confirm my living conditions?'

'Senior management are entitled to single accommodation and their own vehicle in town. There's a canteen on site for meals but you can eat elsewhere if you want to. Mondongo is prohibitively expensive so you'll probably eat in the canteen most of the time.'

Why would a shithole, if she believed Murphy's hyperbole, be so pricey? That didn't make any sense, but she had already made her decision to go.

'Okay. Please fax me the details of the hotel in Johannesburg and so on.'

'I'll send you the itinerary and let you know the address of the travel agent in London where you can collect the tickets for the flights,' she said. 'Ah, I almost forgot. You are entitled to send two boxes of possessions by airfreight under your contract. Just let me have them here at the office before you go.'

'Excellent, thank you. Do you have a list of things I'll need to bring with me?'

'I'm afraid not. Just pack for the Ark. There isn't much you can buy in Mondongo except beer and mangoes.'

'I will.

'Don't forget malaria tablets and a good quality net. It's rife out there. And get all your jabs up to date.'

'Thanks. I won't forget.'

'Good luck Sam, and be careful in Johannesburg. That place is really dangerous.'

Sam had been amused that Sally had apparently confused Johannesburg with Mondongo but she hadn't commented. Now she wasn't so sure. Although the area they were passing through appeared prosperous, with wide avenues and nice detached houses, a high wall with barbed or electric wire around the top surrounded every property. Most houses also had a small hut outside with an armed security guard in it.

'Why are the houses surrounded by walls and electric fences?' she asked the driver.

'Because there are a lot of violent criminals in Johannesburg,' he answered. 'If they get inside the house, not only do they steal everything, but they quite often murder the inhabitants too for no reason. You won't meet many people here who don't know someone who was murdered by robbers or muggers.'

Sam sat back in her seat, astounded by this revelation. *How could anyone live here? It was like being in prison.* No wonder Sally considered Johannesburg to be more dangerous than Mondongo.

The taxi pulled up at a hotel resembling the one she had just left. After being assured she was not on *Candid Camera*, Sam paid the driver and approached the reception desk to ask for the location of the bar, which turned out to be in the basement. She descended the spiral staircase into the bar, which had a counter running along the back wall. Bottles of spirits lined the walls behind the counter, glinting in the reflections from a disco ball.

Peering around in the gloom, she couldn't spot any lone man in a sweater. There were several groups of businessmen in suits sitting around tables covered in beer glasses and smoking cheap cigars. The only man who fitted the description given to her was accompanied by an attractive, slim, tall Asian girl with waist-length hair that swished like a curtain when she turned her head to observe the new arrival. Her expression of relief when she spotted Sam was almost comical.

Sam walked up to the man and stuck out her hand.

'Hello, I'm Sam,' she said. 'Sam Harris.'

He shook her hand with vigour, but not the macho squeeze she expected.

'I'm Adrian Black,' he said, 'and this is my wife, Marybelle.'

He did not elaborate. Marybelle looked Sam up and down, and offered the tips of her fingers for Sam to shake. They were sweaty and slipped out of Sam's grasp like a bar of soap.

'Pleased to meet you,' said Sam.

They sat at the knee-high table and surveyed each other. Sam wondered if she should speak or wait to be spoken to. The table dug into her knees as she leaned forward in anticipation.

Before they could start a conversation, Black's mobile phone rang. He stood up and walked across to the far side of the room gesticulating to Sam and mouthing '*Mondongo office*'. Whatever they had to say, it did not please Black. He shouted into the brick-like cellular phone, a harangue that went on for about fifteen minutes. Swearing punctuated every sentence, and veins bulged on his forehead and neck.

Sam took the opportunity to inspect her new boss

at close quarters. Despite being the same age as her, he had a second-hand air about him, as if he had been reincarnated from a former life, and someone had forgotten to give him a new shell. He had a rotund body balanced on sturdy looking legs. Round lenses as thick as bottle ends in his oversized glasses made him resemble a cross owl with a hangover. His right forearm had an open sore near his elbow. The skin around the sore was red and weeping, and made Sam feel quite ill. The index and forefinger of his right hand were stained yellow from nicotine.

After her initial visual examination of Sam, Marybelle had relaxed. If she had come to this meeting to check Sam out as possible competition for Black's affections, it was clear Sam's drab outfit ruled her out as a threat. Black hadn't given Sam a second glance so she relaxed too. *He might be a philistine, but only my abilities are being assessed.*

Marybelle produced a map of Tamazia and the women looked at it together, with Marybelle pointing out the locations of the different mines and the capital Mondongo on the coast. She had a stoned look about her, with a big sleepy smile she directed at Black's shouting figure from time to time, like a mother tolerating a toddler's tantrum.

When he finished his call, Black returned to the table and explained his plans for her stay in Tamazia in the manner of an army sergeant barking orders. There was no pretence at politeness. He chainsmoked, screwing up his eyes to glare at her through the fug on his filthy glasses. *Tread with caution. This man is a despot.*

'You'll be spending your first two months in the Kardo Mine, which is located in the northeastern province of Tunde Norte.'

Although taken aback by this revelation, Sam tried not to show it. The relative safety of the capital had been a major factor in the decision to go to Tamazia in the first place. *Wasn't Tunde Norte MARFO country?* Sam remembered the advice given to her by the awful Murphy and she didn't interrupt Black despite her panic. Black didn't notice her reaction, or if he did, he ignored it.

'For the time being, you'll be working with Jim Hennessy, the manager of Kardo, learning the ropes before you can visit the other projects owned by the company. You can take over for a month when he goes on leave, if you're ready. Once I'm satisfied, you can take on the Mondongo job as the manager of new projects.'

'When will I go to Kardo?' said Sam.

'The day after you arrive in Mondongo.'

Sam's heart sank. The baggage she had sent by airfreight from London had preceded her to Mondongo, but not by much. Nearly all her field gear was in those boxes, as she had expected to be based in Mondongo for a while before she visited the mines. She would be going to Kardo without it. Not only would she be new, and female, but she would look like an amateur in her smart office shirts. She nodded.

'You realise, of course, there's no hope of the local people following any orders you give them? The combination of African and Portuguese cultures is a fucking trainwreck, and they have no respect for women. You'll also have lots of attention from the white men in camp. Most of them haven't had any contact with a woman for six months so they're not fussy about women. They replace sex with alcohol and get pissed a lot,' said Black.

'I'm sure I'll be okay,' said Sam.

This tirade did not worry Sam. All mining and exploration camps had their quota of bitter drunken misfits whose wives *'didn't understand them'*. Gemsite probably hadn't had a woman in senior management before, so in reality, Black could have no idea what the reaction would be. The fact that he had hired her at all suggested that he thought she would be able to do the job despite any prejudice she might encounter.

Sam had extensive previous experience of other people's perceptions. When she went to work in South America, rumour had it that Latin workers wouldn't work for a woman either, but she had never had any problems with the locals. Expatriates were another matter. It was a constant fascination for her to watch the reactions of the incumbent white male population to her arrival at a project.

There were two groups: those who told her to her face that they thought women shouldn't be allowed in mining camps, and those who burbled on about how nice it would be to have a woman around. After two weeks, the former would have overcome their prejudices and be working with her, and the latter would have realised that she was more competent than decorative and would be looking for ways to stab her in the back. She didn't doubt that Gemsite would be similar.

Black hadn't finished his diatribe.

'I want to make it crystal fucking clear that things will be done my way only, no matter what bleeding objection or doubts you may have. You are not entitled to any opinions in your first six months. If that doesn't suit you, you can fuck off now.'

No wonder Murphy had warned her about Black. This relationship could get rather interesting considering how opinionated she was. She nodded again. Black looked pleased and pointed at his chest.

'You have only one boss. That's me, and you will report directly to me and to no one else. You will report everything that goes on including any dissent or rebellion amongst the staff. Any questions?'

Sam wasn't at all sure she liked the change of venue but the chance of running diamond production for the first time was too tempting to turn down. She reminded herself that she could leave whenever she wanted to if it got too dangerous.

'No.'

She had millions of questions but Black was not the person to ask. He beamed, a weird expression on his owl-like face.

'Okay, tomorrow you'll travel to Mondongo. Jorge Ramos, the mining engineer and a new metallurgist, Dirk something, will be on the same flight as you. You'll meet them when you get there.'

Black gave her a brief nod of approval and threw back his drink. She'd managed to hold her tongue, but only just. She would find a way to communicate with Black on another occasion.

Before they left, Black insisted on buying her a whisky.

'Here's to a successful partnership,' he said, draining his glass.

Sam did the same. The neat whisky burned its way down to her empty stomach, which growled in protest. She noticed that Marybelle didn't drink hers, setting it down on a table behind a flower vase.

Black drove her back to her hotel at high speed, ignoring the traffic lights. Whether this was to avoid muggers or because Black was tanked up, she didn't know. He chainsmoked in the car, filling it with noxious fumes. Sam wound her window down a fraction but he noticed immediately.

'Wind that window up. The muggers here are ferocious. By the way, you can't leave the house in Mondongo by yourself, and you'll have to bring a guard with you when you go outside. The police force mug people in broad daylight,' he said.

'At least you can spot the muggers by their uniforms,' said Sam.

This fell on stony ground, and she got the feeling that Black did the jokes.

Back in the hotel, Sam reflected on her meeting with Black. She felt a bit guilty about her parents and their reaction to her taking the job in the first place. They had tried to be encouraging but their fears had been transparent.

As the date for leaving England drew near, they had got more nervous. They seemed calm on the surface but Sam could tell that they had been talking about her and it was obvious that her mother was concerned. Matilda Harris was from a generation of women who had worked as secretaries in the hope of marrying the boss. It wasn't easy for Sam to explain why she needed more than that to a woman who had been happily married for forty years and saw no need for women to be 'liberated'.

'But why don't you get a nice secretarial job in London, darling?' said her mother. 'I can't understand why you need to go rushing off to Africa when you could have a perfectly good job at home.'

'I know you're worried, but being offered such a good position in a producing company is a first for me. I can't turn it down. They're going to pay me really well and I need the money to save for a deposit on a house. I'm ready for a job like this.'

'I'm sure you're ready, but none of your other jobs have been in such a dangerous place. Your father and I worry about you.'

'You don't need to worry. I'll be fine. I've had some tough jobs in remote places but I get to see some really amazing things.'

'But there are amazing things to see in London: theatre, ballet, cinema.'

'How could a job in London compare to this? Could you imagine me in an office? I won't be a prisoner in the job. I can leave if it gets too dangerous.'

Her mother threw up her arms in despair, knowing she was beaten.

Sam kept her departure as low key as possible, receiving a stiff hug from her mother and a warmer one from her father before she got into the taxi to the airport. She still felt guilty for worrying them but not enough to stop her.

***

Back at his flat, Black was also getting ready for bed while Marybelle hung up his clothes and made sure he was packed for his trip to London. He puffed on his last cigarette of the day, stubbing it out in the ashtray only when it reached the filter and burned his fingers. He sniffed to attract Marybelle's attention.

'What did you think of Sam?' he said.

'She's pretty ordinary looking, isn't she? Did you see what she was wearing? What a frump. She certainly hasn't got any dress sense,' said Marybelle.

Black grunted irritably.

'That's not what I meant. What did you think of her as a person? Did she leave any impression on you?'

'She's quite clever, I think.'

'But she didn't say anything.'

She smiled. 'That's what I meant.'

Chapter III

Sam rose at dawn to go to the airport. She loaded her luggage into one of the hotel taxis and the driver set off through the silent streets in the soft light. As with her arrival, check-in was quick, and she spent a pleasant hour or so drinking tea and reading the newspapers in the business-class lounge. Several Europeans waited there with her, some of them middle-aged women in Laura Ashley flowery dresses.

The dresses looked old-fashioned compared to the chic clothes worn by some other occupants of the lounge, but there was something reassuring about the unflappable colonial relics. These expatriate wives turned up all over the world and organised drinks parties and *Hash House Harriers*, more drinking but with running, for the foreign communities in remote or developing countries. Some of Sam's apprehensions melted away. *If they were going to Tamazia, it couldn't be that dangerous.*

The flight to Mondongo took about three hours. She tried to sleep, but lurid images of rebels and robbers invaded her thoughts whenever she shut her eyes. The inflight magazine contained an article about some actress she'd never heard of, and her perfect life with her film star husband in their ideal home. She snorted. *He was probably a womaniser and she looked like she hadn't eaten for a month.* Suddenly self-conscious about her plump stomach, she pulled her khaki shirt down and smoothed it out.

She came out into the arrival hall, pushing her overloaded trolley and squinting in her effort to find her welcoming party. Nervous again, her heart rate increased when she couldn't spot anyone from Gemsite there to greet her. Crowds of passengers and families thronged the terminal, making it difficult to spot anyone holding a card with her name on it. Taxi drivers tugged her sleeve looking for a dollar fare. Sweat ran down her back in the sweltering heat.

After searching the inside of the arrival hall twice, she went outside. *Maybe they had parked nearby and couldn't leave their car.* Stepping through the airport doors, she was hit by a wall of heat and laser-bright sunshine. Blinded, she fumbled around in her rucksack for her sunglasses. As her vision returned, she examined the vehicles parked at the kerb for a logo or some sign that they belonged to Gemsite. They were just the normal mixture of taxis and family cars surrounded by people with luggage and beeping their horns in frustration at not being able to get in or out of their parking spaces.

She tried to disguise her nerves and keep an eye on her luggage, glancing at every new arrival. An airport security guard lounged against the wall smoking with his eyes closed.

'Excuse me, sir,' said Sam, in her rusty Portuguese. 'Do you know a company called Gemsite? They are supposed to meet me here.'

The guard opened his eyes and blew smoke in her face.

'Gemsite, of course, everyone knows them. The

driver's gone to eat. He'll be back soon.'

He shut his eyes again and took another drag of his cigarette.

Taken aback by this piece of news, Sam sat disconsolately on her luggage outside the terminal. She didn't think much of the driver's casual attitude. *I've arrived in a war zone, and no one has bothered to meet my flight.*

The Gemsite driver turned up after about half an hour and found her still sitting on her suitcase.

'Hello,' he said. 'Are you Sam?'

'Where have you been?' said Sam. 'I thought you had forgotten me.'

'I'm sorry. They should've warned you. I was collecting lunch for some of the airport staff. They get tiny salaries, which are often paid late. We need to help them if we want them to help us.'

She had misunderstood what the security guard had told her. It was a good reminder of how rusty her Portuguese was. She had only worked in Brazil for three months, and while she found it easy to understand, as Brazilian Portuguese had many similarities to Spanish, the Tamazia accent was different. It was a good lesson. She would try not to jump to any more conclusions.

The driver showed her to the Gemsite minivan. He gave her some brochures to read from some loony Christian sect so beloved of many Africans she had met. This one appeared to be searching for handmaidens for the high priest. Not the sort of job description she craved.

'I'm going to look for Jorge Ramos, the Kardo project engineer. He should have been on the same flight as you. He should be with the new metallurgist who is also arriving today,' said the driver.

He disappeared back into the heaving airport, leaving Sam melting in the heat. She tried sitting in the van but it was even hotter in there. A tiny patch of shade under a balcony in the airport welcomed her into its warm embrace. It was over forty degrees in Mondongo, and Sam could feel the damp waistband on her trousers digging into her stomach. Her T-shirt clung to her back, and her bra straps were too tight in the heat. *Those damn biscuits had a lot to answer for.*

The driver emerged almost an hour later accompanied by two men, one much younger than the other. By then Sam was pretty sure she didn't want to join the church of Saint John of the Virgins or contribute any of her hard-earned cash to their cause.

'Sorry about that. One of the bags was delayed by customs and they wouldn't let any of us leave,' said the driver.

Sam shook hands with the two men.

'Hello, you must be Sam,' said the older one. 'I'm Jorge Ramos. I work at Kardo with Jim Hennessy.' He shook her hand with a broad smile, and struck her with his open, honest manner.

'Hi,' said the other younger man. 'I'm Dirk Vetter. This is my first shift at Gemsite. I'll also be working at Kardo. Where are you based?'

Blond with a lantern jaw, which didn't detract much from his handsome face, his sturdy muscular body also caught her eye. *Far too young for me.* She banished all impure thoughts.

'I'm starting at Kardo, and then later I'll be based in Mondongo head office. Is it your first time in the country?'

'Oh no, I've been here before. I'm from South Africa. I did my national army service in Tamazia. Our brigade fought with MARFO and had a strong alliance with them.'

'I had no idea that MARFO were once the good guys,' said Sam. 'You must feel pretty ambivalent about that.'

'Yes, it's really weird, but I told Black about my past, and he doesn't mind. He needs a metallurgist. He doesn't care about politics or wars.'

Sam could believe that.

They squeezed into the minivan, and drove into the centre of Mondongo along streets packed with traffic. Most of the surfaces had been damaged and many were under repair. The resulting road works and lane closures created traffic jams that emitted a cacophony of horn blasts.

A medley of strong smells assailed Sam's nostrils; sewage mixed with coffee, cooking and traffic fumes. The fact that most of the cars were modern reduced the traffic pollution, but public transport consisted of ancient Hi-Ace vans spouting acrid black smoke, which stopped and started at every corner, causing chaos behind them and making the irate drivers sound their horns in fury.

It took forever to get to their destination, a combined caravan compound, storage depot and garage in the centre of town. Located on a derelict site one block from the offices of Gemsite, it acted as a staging post for people returning to and leaving the mines in the Tunde Norte province. The compound consisted of a row of ancient caravans parallel to a line of storerooms and garages. The staff canteen sat on top of the storerooms where the food was kept before it was shipped out to the projects.

'The technical office is up there,' said Jorge, pointing above the stores to some filthy windows obscuring an interior which was dark and appeared to be empty. The entrance was up a separate set of stairs with metal gates at the top and bottom with huge padlocks on them. The whole compound had an air of neglect, much like the city itself.

They descended from the van to be greeted by the accommodations manager who allocated Sam one of the six caravans in which to stay. The group dispersed and mounted the stairs to their allocated caravan. *Talk about small.* There was barely room to squeeze between the tiny bed, which stretched from end to end of the room, and the wall. Sam hadn't enough room to swing her arms, let alone the proverbial cat.

Sam went upstairs to the canteen where she would be having all her meals in Mondongo. A horrible grubby room with Formica tables and a dirty floor met her disgusted glance. From the look of the kitchen behind the counter, the food would match the room. She drank a cup of vile coffee in the canteen.

'I'll take you down the street to the Gemsite office,' said the accommodations manager. 'You need to hand in your cash and valuables and sign your contract.'

'Why do I need to hand in my valuables?' said Sam.

'Employees are not allowed to have cash on site in Kardo to reduce the incentive for the locals to rob them. Also, it prevents any Gemsite staff from buying diamonds.'

'Buying diamonds?'

'Yes, it's illegal to buy diamonds in Tamazia. Local miners try and swap diamonds for money, crates of beer, or any electrical goods going. The penalties for being caught with an illegal diamond in Tamazia are draconian. Gemsite fires anyone who gets caught buying one and hand the culprit over to the police.' He shuddered. 'I wouldn't recommend a stay in a Tamazia jail. They are dangerous and overcrowded. Even so, there is always some idiot who thinks they can get away with it.'

'I don't like diamonds,' said Sam. 'I won't be tempted.'

'Excellent. Let's go then.'

He walked as far as the office building which occupied a corner of a shabby street five minutes from the compound.

'Good luck,' he said, and headed back to the compound, leaving her to fend for herself.

She pushed open the glass door and entered the gloomy interior of the Gemsite office which had far too many desks in it, jammed up against each other with minimal space in between. A man came out of a small corner office as she entered and, spotting her, he signalled for her to join him.

'I'm John Collier, the office manager. You must be Sam.'

'Yes, hello, nice to meet you.'

'It's all a bit of a rush around here but can you read and sign your contract, please? We need it completed before you fly to Kardo.'

She took the document from him and sat at an empty desk to review it. After her conversation with Black, it did not surprise her to see that the conditions of service did not match those she had been offered in London. She knocked on the door of John's office.

'Can I ask you some questions about my contract, please?' she said.

'Sure, what's the problem?'

'Well, it says here that due to the shortage of suitable accommodation in Mondongo, I will be sharing living quarters with other people. This is not what I agreed to in London.'

'Ah, yes, unfortunately our London office is about as much use as a condom in a nunnery. Tamazia has been at war for twenty years. There are almost no habitable buildings still standing, none that are available for rental. That's why this office is full to bursting.'

'I had noticed,' said Sam, gesticulating at the chaos.

'We are building an annex at the Villa Alice staff house. It should be ready in about six months. Until then, you'll share the house with some other expatriate staff. I'm afraid you'll have to use whatever bedroom is free as all are already allocated to someone, but there is always one person on leave, so you should have a bed at least. Anyway, I understand you're going to Kardo, so this shouldn't be a big issue for you, right?'

The challenge in his voice irritated her.

'And my car?'

'One of the purchasing agents is using your car. But you won't need that yet either, will you?'

The casual 'take it or leave it' attitude got right up Sam's nose but a feeling of inevitability about the arrangements prevented her from discussing them. Going with the flow appeared to be her best option until she figured out how to get what she wanted.

She added a handwritten note to the bottom of the contract saying that she had been offered private accommodations in Mondongo, but that under the circumstances, she would accept shared accommodation for the first six months.

She was concerned that both her job relocation and her downgraded accommodation might mean a lower status in the company, but she decided to wait and see what transpired before making any decisions about staying. None of her previous jobs had been perfect, not by a long shot. Sam signed the contract.

'By the way,' said John, 'you're leaving for Kardo tonight.'

'Tonight? Black said I was due to fly out tomorrow.'

'No, your flight is tonight,' said John.

Sam remembered her airfreighted belongings.

'Have any boxes arrived for me from England?'

'When did you send them?'

'Two weeks ago.'

'Ha! Not a chance. They'll take that long to clear customs. We'll send them up to Kardo when they arrive.'

'Can you let me know when they get here please?'

'Will do. By the way, we issue soap, toothpaste and toilet paper to our staff once a month. It has to last until the next consignment. Sometimes, the projects in the field run out of these and other basics, like tea, coffee and rice, and they have to wait for the next shipment from South Africa before they can have any more. Have you brought any supplies from home?'

Sam's travels in various countries worldwide had taught her that Tamazia was unlikely to have drinkable tea. So, she had brought about a year's supply of tea bags with her in her luggage and freighted boxes. She had also packed shampoo and other nice treats, as she knew from experience that most mines only stocked the most basic provisions like harsh soap and dandruff shampoo. The luggage she had brought with her also contained part of these supplies.

'Don't worry about me. I could open a shop,' she said.

'You should get ready for your lift to the airport. Good luck, Sam.'

'Thanks. I've a feeling I'm going to need it.'

As evening fell, Sam left for the airport with Jorge and Dirk who were also going to Kardo, and despite her uncertainty, her anticipation rose. It was like being in one of those old Hollywood films where the stars set out on safari. She half-expected that Clark Gable would get on the flight with them and drink dry martinis.

The speed of events had been startling, but she was glad after all that she didn't have to hang around in Mondongo. When they got to the airport, a tall, dark, handsome man approached the minibus. *Maybe Clark Gable reincarnated?*

'Hi guys,' he said when they drove up, 'I'm afraid the flight has been cancelled and the flight crew has gone home for the night.'

'Is there any chance we'll be flying tonight?' said the driver.

'No chance. I'll advise the office around midday tomorrow when we get new flight times.'

Her feelings of anticipation evaporated and were replaced by one of anti-climax. They turned around and drove back to the compound through the glacier-paced rush-hour traffic.

'Does this happen often?' said Sam.

'All the time,' said Jorge.

They went to the canteen for dinner but Sam took one look at the food on offer and returned to her caravan without eating. She hung her mosquito net over her bed and got underneath it. Lying in the darkness, listening to the whining and buzzing of thwarted insects, she mulled over her luck. *What had she done to deserve this? Why couldn't she get a job with a major mining company and stay in cushy hotels with room service and cable television?*

Chapter IV

The next morning, breakfast started early and the rations were sparse. The bread was so stale it could have been used as missiles for MARFO. Sam dunked her bread in her tea and hoped this was not an example of the general standard of Gemsite cuisine. Breakfast was essential to Sam's humour and drive. Without a decent one, she would be toast for the rest of the day.

She hung around all morning in the office with Dirk and Jorge waiting for news of their flight and getting in the way in the confined space.

'Do you want to borrow a car and driver for a trip down to see the bay and beaches of Mondongo?' said John Collier. 'You won't be leaving for a few hours yet.'

'Yes, please,' said Sam.

'The driver is South African, so he speaks English.'

'Can I come too?' said Dirk.

'Sure. Jorge, do you want to come with us?' said Sam.

'No thank you, Sam. I have to do some paperwork in the office.'

'Okay, let's go then.'

The streets of Mondongo were lined with decrepit old colonial houses painted in faded pastel colours like ghosts of their former selves. These were interspersed with the same breeze-block houses with zinc roofs that made South American cities so ugly. Here and there, Sam spotted Art Deco buildings with fantasy ironwork on their balconies. Gaps in the streets were filled with makeshift accommodation such as shipping containers. Pools of green sewage festered in the large gaps between the pavements.

The seafront buildings also suffered from neglect, the Central Bank of Tamazia the only exception to this. It stood on the boardwalk, huge and magnificent with a palatial entrance and cupola. Newly painted in pink and white, it made a striking contrast to the decrepitude all around it. All of the legally mined diamonds passed through the doors of the bank, and the bank profited from its association with them.

The car swept them along the promenade in black, pink and white brick that lined the edge of the bay, crossing a bridge to a long, thin strip of land running parallel to the shore, creating a lagoon between itself and the town. There were two ugly oil rigs standing in the lagoon. The white sands running on both sides of this thin sliver of land made up the main beaches at Mondongo.

'This part of town is known as the Island,' said the driver. 'It is joined to the mainland by the bridge we just crossed. The huge oil rigs in the middle of the lagoon might spoil the view but they provide millions of dollars of revenue for the government.'

At the far end of the Island, there were a couple of half-decent cafés and beach bars. Many people had set up small stalls consisting of an umbrella shading a cooler box with a few cans perched on top. Small, bossy boys directed the parking and fought over the tips. Rich Tamazians of all races slumped in deckchairs, sporting huge gold chains and tiny bikinis.

'The town of Mondongo was originally built for a population of half a million inhabitants. Before independence in 1958 and the subsequent abandonment of the country by ninety per cent of its skilled white workforce, Mondongo was known as the Paris of Africa. Now, four million inhabitants, mostly refugees from the fighting in the countryside, have stretched the infrastructure past breaking point, and huge slums sprawl out in all directions from the central part of the city,' said the driver.

Despite this, the old heart of the town still retained a genteel air and a Mediterranean feel, and Sam relaxed as they drove around in the dry heat with the windows down. On the way back to the compound, they passed through an area where a massive renovation program was creating a stunning pink mini-city of large colonial buildings up on a hill.

'These houses will serve as the parliament and the President's house when they are finished. Jose dos Manos, the President of Tamazia, is one of the richest men in the world.'

'The International Finance Corporation claim that he and his cabinet skim one billion dollars a year from the petrol receipts,' said Dirk.

'From what I see, he can't be spending any of it improving the conditions of the population. How can he sleep at night knowing that children are dying every day from lack of basic amenities while he salts away more money than he could ever spend?' said Sam.

'His nickname is Tres Manos, or three hands, because he has one right hand, one left hand and one in the till,' said the driver.

Far away in the docks, Sam could see an extraordinary tall, odd structure pointing up into the sky, like something out of Star Wars, towering over the city.

'What's that?' she said, pointing at it.

'That, my lady, will be the mausoleum of Tamazia's first president, Pedro Fernandez. It is known as Pedro's Rocket. It contains the embalmed remains of the poet and writer who became independent Tamazia's first head of state. He died in Moscow, and his body was left in a morgue until it was discovered twelve years later in a drawer. It has since been repatriated but had rotted so badly that it had to be buried rather than put on show.'

'Like Lenin,' said Sam.

'Yes, that was the original intention. Since the mausoleum is still in construction, I think the chances of the present incumbent of the presidency being buried in a finished monument before the next century are not good,' said the driver, who laughed at his own joke.

Sam and Dirk arrived back to a mediocre lunch of a choice of nondescript looking curries in the canteen. Sam's hunger forced her to swallow some revolting lamb curry that contained so much chilli that it burned her tongue.

She went to her trailer to read, but Pedro, the handsome man who had talked to them at the airport the night before, turned up in his car and leaned out of the window.

'Hi. You're Sam, aren't you? Do you want to come to the beach and have coffee with me?'

'Maybe, but who are you?'

But Sam knew exactly who he was and had already noticed him in the gloom of the airport, especially his deep rumbling voice. Pedro looked like Mr Big from Sex in the City. Tall and dark, he had a naughty twinkle in his eye that she pretended not to see. He appeared to be quite well aware of his effect on women already.

'I'm Pedro, the head of logistics at Gemsite. I won't bite. I promise.'

They drove back out to the beach. Sam didn't bother telling Pedro that she had just been there. They sat at a cafe drinking strong Portuguese coffee and she had a custard tart, which restored her good humour as the sugar entered her bloodstream. Relaxed and charming, he offered the possibility of fun times when she got back from her training period at the Kardo Mine.

'I've worked with the company for five years, but I don't know how much longer I'll be here,' he said.

'Oh, and why is that? Have you got another job?' said Sam.

'I punched someone from the accountant's office and I'm on my last warning. I might be more careful if you are going to be around for a while.'

Sam blushed. She wanted to know why he had punched the accountant but she didn't want to break the mood. It had been a while since she'd had a handsome man all to herself. Boyfriends and long rotations away from home didn't mix. She changed the subject.

'Is the food in the canteen always revolting?'

'I don't think it's revolting.'

'I mean is the food always curried? I hate curry.'

'Yes, it is. The chef at the Mondongo canteen is Pakistani so two or three of the four choices in the canteen at mealtimes are always curries. However, it is not because he doesn't know how to cook anything else. He's an expert at using the strong flavours of the spices to cover up the rotten taste of the meat.'

'Why is the meat rotten? Don't they have fridges?'

'The meat's rotten because all the food for Gemsite is imported from South Africa in containers that sit in the port for days waiting to clear customs. Mondongo's average temperature is forty degrees. The combination of the two factors mean that most of our meat is eaten rotten.'

'Why doesn't John Collier buy meat in Mondongo instead?'

'The civil war in Tamazia has obliterated the agricultural and food industries. The presence of so many landmines has put a stop to any farming activity, and the lack of working infrastructure prevents any produce from reaching the capital. He simply isn't able to buy enough produce to feed the mines, and Black won't let us pay bribes to get the food out of customs.'

'Isn't that your job?' said Sam. 'To rescue the food from customs?'

Pedro stiffened.

'You have no idea how difficult it is to get anything out of customs. Besides, the officials do it on purpose. They hate Gemsite because we won't pay them any bribes. They do everything they can to delay the food until we get desperate and have to negotiate. Once I get it released, any food that escapes the clutches of customs sits in freezers prone to power cuts. That's why you have to eat curry every day.'

'I was kidding,' said Sam. 'I've lived in many places where the customs are a nightmare. Blackmail is their favourite sport.'

Pedro relaxed again but Sam made a note to be wary of him. He hadn't liked the dig about customs and had been unable to take it as a joke. He was not as easygoing as he pretended to be.

'I heard you had coffee with Pedro,' said Jim Collier, when she went back to the office. 'He goes out at night dancing and drinking and womanising. You need to watch yourself where he is concerned. He punched one of the accountants the other day.'

'Why did he do that?'

'I think the guy insulted his macho pride in some way. These Portuguese guys are sensitive to any perceived slights, you know.'

Sam could not imagine how Pedro went out every night in Mondongo, one of the most expensive cities in the world, but she held her tongue.

The driver turned up to collect the Kardo passengers in the late afternoon and loaded them into the minivan to take them back to the airport. When they got there, the cargo company, TransTamazia, said that the flight had been delayed until later that night by a fuel shortage, so they went back to the trailers again.

There was a lot of swearing. Nerves were fraying, even amongst the returning staff who were used to these aborted flights. Sam felt sick from the amount of adrenaline that was surging around her system. She bought a carton of cigarettes and a couple of lighters from the store shop under the canteen. She didn't smoke at home in London but what she had seen so far persuaded her she might need something to distract her.

Finally, the fuel was obtained from somewhere and the flight was ready for take-off so they took yet another trip out to the airport. A plane was sitting on the tarmac in the gloom of the humid night, waiting to leave for Kardo. An ancient Boeing belonging to TransTamazia, it contained diesel in two large tanks for the project.

They entered the plane up a ramp through the rear

door and stowed their bags behind the fuel tanks. Then they had to leave the aircraft again and sit in the van beside the TransTamazia offices for half an hour while the final permits were dealt with.

'Why do we need permits to travel in country?' said Sam.

'Anyone travelling in Tamazia, especially expatriates, have to fill out all sorts of papers and permits for each journey,' said the driver.

'How long do the permits last?'

'I'm afraid that they have to be renewed each time you want to travel. They like to make things difficult in Tamazia. More chances to demand bribes.'

Since Gemsite was using the cargo section of the airport, there were no departure halls for the passengers. They sat in the car on the tarmac beside the plane and waited. It was dark, and various officious types rushed around with a gun in one hand and a clipboard in the other. *Thank goodness their driver was dealing with all the paperwork involved.* Sam didn't fancy her chances of getting through the red tape alone.

When the passengers were finally allowed onto the plane again, they climbed up the ramp at the back of the aircraft and into the gloomy, oily, cargo bay. They filed down the fuselage on a narrow walkway between two large fuel tanks. The floors of the vessel were slick with diesel, and the dim lighting flickered, illuminating the filthy, ancient seats in a row at the front of the cargo bay. Sam, Jorge and Dirk strapped themselves in with oily seatbelts. So much for the dry Martinis. Sitting in front of the huge diesel tanks, Sam felt as if she were strapped to a liquid bomb.

The cabin went dark and the plane took off at last. The noise in the aircraft was at an eardrum-splitting level. Some dim lights came on after the plane levelled out, but no one spoke. It would have been pointless, as it was impossible hear anything above the din. As they rose to cruising height, the temperature in the cabin plummeted and Sam shivered in her cotton shirt. She made a mental note to bring a jacket next time.

They flew in silence for an hour and a half, alone with their thoughts. It was tempting to chicken out and demand to go home, but Sam was more afraid of being thought a coward than facing whatever awaited her in Kardo. The presence of the other two men reassured her. *Why would they be going back if it was that bad?*

Suddenly, the plane started dropping down into the darkness. The cabin lights went out again, and the passengers sat in pitchy darkness. There were some tiny filthy windows in the fuselage, but nothing was visible through them. Sam couldn't see a runway, and the plane landing lights had not been switched on.

They sat in the blackness, falling through the air in their flammable torpedo. There was something more than a little bizarre about the way they just sat there and no one said anything. Sam had seen many movies in which the women started screaming and the men leapt out of their seats in the same situation. In real life, passengers sit there in grim silence and hope it's not the last thing they do.

Just before plane hit the ground, the engines throttled down and the pilot turned on the outside lights. Simultaneously, the runway lit up only tens of feet below the plane. It landed in the same instant with a kidney-crushing bounce. *Luckily, she had good sphincter control.*

The plane came to a full stop, grinding to a halt on the gritty red runway. Sam turned to Jorge, who was calmly undoing his belt.

'Why did the pilots land like that? Was there a

problem?' she said.

'There is always a problem with landing in MARFO territory. Blacking out is done to avoid being shot down by a shoulder-launched missile. The guerrillas need a visual on the plane to fix an approximate direction for the heat-seeking missile to home in on its target, so the plane has to land blind.'

What on earth had she got herself into? The level of danger had risen to the point where she had serious doubts about the wisdom of accepting her changed job description and coming to Kardo. There wasn't much she could do about it at two in the morning, so she kept her thoughts to herself.

Deafened and shaken, they tottered down the steps of the plane onto the gravel and carried their bags across the sandy apron to the customs post. The airport buildings consisted of a zinc hangar for aircraft with a brick hut attached to one side which served as the arrivals area. Drunken customs officials caroused with local girls in its shadowy interior. Sam staggered into the hangar with her heavy bags, her rucksack sliding down her arm and impeding her progress.

'Papers, please. All visas and flight permits must be shown,' said a jaundiced-looking security officer. He fussed about, trying to find something wrong but his heart wasn't in it. Eventually, the lateness of the hour defeated him, and the Gemsite workers were allowed to leave with minimum hassle.

They got aboard another Hi-Ace van and drove to the compound. Sam's spirits rose as they entered Kardo project and drove down a road lined with sturdy brick bungalows with zinc roofs. The streets were empty, and all the houses had padlocked outer doors. Huge mango trees weighed down with swollen fruit grew between the houses. Sam loved mangos.

'This looks pretty civilized,' she remarked to Jorge.

'Yes, it's a bit run down but it's not bad. It's a Portuguese mining village from the 1950s arranged on a grid system.'

'Who lives in the bungalows?'

'Those are for senior staff like you, Sam.'

He laughed at her expression.

'The more junior staff members live in prefabricated housing blocks contained in the same grid. The more junior the position, the more people there are to a room.'

The driver dropped Jorge and Dirk off at one of the nicer looking prefabs and then Sam was taken to one of the bungalows near the canteen.

'This is Murphy's old house,' said the driver. 'I understand you met him.'

'I had that pleasure,' said Sam, trying not to laugh.

Sam got out of the car and the driver handed her some keys. There was a padlocked outer door to get through before entering the house through the also padlocked inner door, which was a clear illustration of the level of crime around the village. Sam struggled to open the locks swearing and feeling stupid.

'Why have the padlocks got metal sleeves on them? Doesn't that make them more difficult to open?'

'It's to prevent people shooting them off,' he said.

Great. I feel a lot better.

However, as she finally managed to open the inner door to the house, she could see what looked like a coffee table on a cheap Persian-style rug in the middle of the first room. A stereo system blinked at her, and she immediately regretted sending her music CDs by freight to Mondongo. The driver, who had waited patiently until she had locked herself into the house, left with a wave.

The house was spacious and looked comfortable despite being sparsely furnished. A quick tour assured her that she was the sole occupant. She found the main bedroom at the back of the house and sat on the bed to set her alarm clock. Then she put up her mosquito net and slipped underneath it.

Chapter V

Sam crawled out of bed a few hours later and stripped off in the bathroom, intending to shower. There were no towels in the bathroom and she couldn't find any in the rest of the house. She had a shower anyway and dried herself with a T-shirt. The mirror had been smashed by a blow to the centre and she struggled to put in her contact lens using her reflection in a shard still sticking out of the frame. *I bet Murphy punched the mirror.*

She got dressed and sat on the sofa in the front room waiting to be picked up by Jim Hennessy or whoever he would send to find her. Despite the early hour, the nylon covers made her sweat. When he didn't turn up, she snatched a nap sitting up, but it wasn't restful, as she kept waking up. *Has he forgotten about me?*

Just when the heat in her house became stifling, a man arrived outside the house in his jeep and beeped the horn. She tried to hurry out but the number of locks made that impossible. Opening the padlock on the outer gate from the inside was difficult due to its protective sleeve. *I hope I don't have to leave in a hurry. At least it would be as hard for any assailant to get in.*

Flustered by the delay, she composed her face when she finally snapped the padlock shut on the outer door and turned to face the jeep.

The man leaned out of the window and grimaced, shaking his head.

'Those locks are a bit of a mission I'm afraid. I'm Jim Hennessy and you must be Sam.'

A Belfast accent you could cut with a knife.

'Yes, they are. Great to meet you.'

'So, you got here in one piece then? How did you like the transport? Not what you're used to, I suppose?'

'I missed the inflight safety briefing, and spilt my gin and tonic on landing,' said Sam. 'But I'll get over it.'

Jim laughed. *I bet he's got a quick Irish temper.* He was a small, neat man with a bristling moustache and a ready smile. Sam took to him immediately. Maybe her stay at Kardo wasn't going to be so bad after all.

Jim took her straight over to the management office at the other side of the compound. Sam would have killed for some breakfast but she didn't want to ask and break the mood. The office buildings were set on a ridge with a view over the valley of the Chimbo River. They were basic in the extreme, with cement floors, and cheap desks and chairs. Sam could only see one computer in an office to the right of the main room.

'Whose office is that?' she said.

'That's the office of the site geologist, Fred. He's always off somewhere when you don't want him to be,' said Jim. 'I don't think he works more than a couple of hours a week. He's responsible for controlling the material that gets mined on site and for collating the information about the diamonds recovered from the mining operations. The only time you are likely to come across him is in the canteen. He never misses a meal.'

'I don't see any other computers in the office,' said Sam. 'Do you have email?'

'Ha! Black won't let us have internet. It's too expensive.'

'So how do we communicate with our families?'

'You'll have to book time on the satellite phone if you want to make a call. You get thirty minutes a week on a line that cuts off every two minutes.'

'Is there any television?'

'Yes, there's one in the staff room where we get the sport channels on satellite television. Apart from that, the only news of the outside world comes from the Mondongo office or on the BBC World Service radio.'

Several of the senior staff members had already arrived at the office but Jim left her standing in the middle of the room and wandered off without introducing Sam to them. To make it worse, none of the men left their desks to introduce themselves or even appeared to notice her wavering.

Shy by nature, Sam forced herself to make an awkward circuit of the desks, shaking reluctant hands, and trying to catch mumbled names.

'Hi, I'm Sam Harris.'

'Bob Norton, Engineering.'

'Sam Harris.'

'Brian Lynch, Security.'

She got the distinct impression that they weren't happy to see her. The only person unaffected by this reluctance was Jorge. He arrived at the office shortly after her and shook her hand effusively, chatting in Portuguese and beaming at her. He was not a handsome man but he was attractive in a healthy, swarthy way. He struck her with his open manner and the way he accepted her at face value.

Sam noticed the sullen looks their conversation was causing and asked Jorge in his language, 'Am I the only manager who speaks Portuguese?'

'Yes, no one else can be bothered. Some of them have worked here over ten years.'

'I see,' she said. 'Well, I'm happy to practice with you as I'm not fluent yet. We can speak Portuguese whenever you like if you don't mind my mistakes.'

Jim reappeared at Sam's elbow. 'Let's go then.'

'See you later,' said Sam to an office of unsmiling blank faces. *They are just waiting for me to step out so they can discuss me.*

***

No sooner had Sam, Jorge and Jim set off for the diamond fields than work in the office came to a halt.

'Well, there you go lads. There's the new spy. Black must think that we're a bunch of complete tossers.'

'I couldn't believe it when Pat Murphy called me and said that Black had hired a woman to spy on us. Do you think she's for his own personal use?'

'Don't be an arsehole all your life. Black doesn't like fat women like that. He likes them more like boys—Filipino style.'

'I wouldn't say she was fat. She didn't seem too bad. Maybe it's not true about her spying for Black. Murphy isn't the most reliable source, you know. He's bound to be paranoid with all the booze he puts away.'

'Of course it's fucking true, you moron. Don't go soft on me at this early stage. Didn't you see her showing off and speaking Portuguese to Jorge? We were told she had a job in Mondongo. Instead she's here to spy on us all and report back to Black. It's up to us to force her out as soon as possible. She won't last a month by the time we've finished with her.'

***

The first stop on their tour of the Gemsite project was the small headquarters of Greys security force where Potty, the aptly named head of the regional security unit, gave Sam a safety briefing.

'Greys patrols the licence area and keeps the MARFO rebels away. It's a Mondongo-based joint-venture company run by General Fuego, a famous Tamazian soldier,' said Jim.

'General Fuego's a hero of the Tamazian revolution, and their independence from Portugal. He played football with Eusebio at Benfica Football Club in Lisbon, before running away to Cuba to join Che Guevara and Castro,' said Jorge.

'Why did he leave Benfica?' said Sam

'The police came to arrest him for involvement in conspiracies to separate Tamazia from Portugal. He fought in the Cuban Revolution as well. After Tamazian independence he was nominated as the head of armed forces and the lead negotiator on the peace agreement with MARFO. He's Tamazia's US ambassador and has a house in Washington,' said Jorge.

'He set up Greys to profit from the precarious security situation in the diamond mining areas. He hired several South African mercenaries, who work at Kardo. They are ex-South African army and fought alongside MARFO in the early days but now they are fighting against them,' said Jim.

No wonder MARFO thought that the West had betrayed them, if their former allies were now fighting against them. Sam inspected the mercenaries as they went about their business in Greys compound. Most of them were large, handsome South African men with broken noses, brutal eyes and shark smiles.

'Our job is to patrol the area, and prevent incidents with garimpeiros, the illegal diamond miners, and MARFO. We used to shoot garimpeiros who tunnelled under the gravel to steal diamonds from the concession. The government decided we should stop killing them unless we had to, even though it is quite legal to do so,' said Potty.

Potty's detachment was chilling. He talked about shooting people like it was an inconvenience.

'You need to be ready to leave at a moment's notice at all times. Have you prepared an emergency rucksack?' said Potty.

'No, I'm afraid I haven't. I didn't realise I would need one,' said Sam.

'You must do it tonight. The rucksack should contain emergency supplies of water, malaria tablets, a mosquito net and repellent. You can add other things if you like. I put chocolate in mine.'

'Okay, I will do the same. And some tins of tuna.'

'Don't overdo it. You may have to carry it miles if anything happens.'

He indicated a fat, bald fellow with strands of yellow hair stuck across the top of his head and a beer belly on which she could have balanced a couple of pints of beer.

'If there is an attack, Frik here is your designated security man. He will find you and take you to safety. You must always have your emergency rucksack ready. You won't have time to pack if something happens.'

My luck with men even extends to this? Could this

man run at all? He'd be impeded by his stomach. She made herself a promise that if he couldn't keep up, she wasn't waiting for him. She smiled at Frik and said, 'Excellent. I feel safe knowing that.'

Frik beamed. Potty nodded and went back to work.

After the visit to Greys, Sam, Jorge and Jim drove through the village of Kardo, which was built along the road into the compound. The tattered mud huts with roofs made of palm leaves followed the local road until they petered out into the red dust.

'What's the pipe for?' said Sam.

'That's our water supply,' said Jim.

'Where do the villagers get their water from?' she said.

'The women carry water up from the Chimbo River for cooking and they wash their clothes in the river.'

'Why don't Gemsite provide a standpipe for them? It would be simple to do and create a lot of goodwill, not to mention freeing up time for the women of the village to do something more useful.'

'That's naïve thinking. If you give them water, they'll demand electricity. If you give them electricity, they'll want something else. Anyway, about twice a month, someone from the village breaks the pipe so that they can have water in the village without having to trek down to the river. The compound endures two days without water whilst it's replaced, which means we have to wash using water stored in barrels. It's a pain in the arse.'

Sam did not agree but she didn't say so. Gemsite policy was sure to be causing resentment in Kardo but no one appeared to care. Black was certainly no politician.

'Well, that was Kardo,' said Jim. 'Ten thousand

garimpeiros, who sneak onto our excavated sites and mine out the high-grade areas.'

'Isn't that illegal?' she said.

'Is the Pope a Catholic? One hundred garimpeiros recently stole a big patch of pre-stripped high-grade gravel at night from the rich terrace Gemsite had been exploiting. Black almost had a coronary.'

'How did they know where to dig?'

'The local diamond pickers in the sorting house are a direct source of information for the garimpeiros. When there are a lot of diamonds coming out, the pickers tell the garimpeiros who bribe the truck drivers to tell them from which separation plant they had collected their diamond concentrate. It's not rocket science to work out which of the terraces being exploited is nearer the separation plant with the best concentrate. It's impossible to police. We just have to get the material before they do.'

'And why don't the night shift guards stop them?'

'Ownership of the AK-47 is ubiquitous around here and they know how to use it. Guards just take their share of the booty rather than a bullet.'

They descended from the village of Kardo down into the valley of the Chimbo River.

'Are there any animals in the river?' said Sam.

'Of course. We don't use any chemicals in the process so the river is clean. It is full of hippopotami, crocodiles and tiger fish. Swimming is forbidden. It's too dangerous.'

Jim gave Sam a tour of the various worksites in the Kardo mining concession starting with a quick summary of each location and its place in the operation, and Jorge added asides in English and Portuguese.

'Where does Gemsite mine most of the

production?' said Sam

'The diamonds are buried in the river terraces, which are formed of gravels eroded from Kimberlite rocks over millennia. The terraces are mined using excavators and trucks, and the richest hauls tend to be at the base of them. That's why only vehicles and people who work for Gemsite can use the roads within the concession boundaries,' said Jim. 'To stop the villagers sneaking in and stealing the bottom gravel at night.'

'But I've seen several women on the road carrying large baskets on their heads,' said Sam.

'The women of Kardo are an exception to the rule. The company has tried to prevent them from going to the river, on the pretext that they were stealing the diamonds, but this was ludicrous and untenable, so we allow them in and out without a fuss. They plant cassava tubers, which are the staple diet of their families, all over the concession area. They come at dawn, carrying their laundry on their heads in big metal basins. At the end of the day, they walk out again with the basins filled with clean laundry, firewood and cassava. They can carry the most extraordinary weights balanced on their heads, but the hard work ages them. Those tiny old ladies who you'll see tottering in to Kardo in the evenings are only about fifty.'

Fresh material and footprints around some of the garimpeiro pits in the terraces where they were walking, indicated that the illegal miners were close by. This was not a comforting thought. Standing exposed on a mound of gravel in bright sunlight, Sam wondered just how easy a target she was for a disgruntled garimpeiro with an AK-47.

The sun punished the terraces from a crystal-clear

sky. Sam struggled to adjust to the punishing temperature. Puce and sweaty, strands of her hair escaped from her bun and stuck to her pink cheeks. She sucked water from a two-litre bottle, trying to stay hydrated.

The local dirt roads were covered in a thick layer of fine red dust. Jim's car had a severe mechanical problem and slid from side to side as it shot down the shimmering roads at speeds reminiscent of a rally. In some places, the car lost all power as it ploughed through the dips in the road filled with this red flour. There was no air conditioning in the battered jeep, so they drove with the windows down. Soon, all of them were coated in the red dust.

'Are we in a hurry?' said Sam in the vain hope of alerting Jim to the fact that he was driving too fast. Even Gloria, the original manic driver, would have been impressed.

'Ah, the speeding. We all drive this fast believing if we drive fast enough over a landmine, it will blow up behind us. In reality, more expatriates die in car crashes than by landmines, which defeats the purpose somewhat.'

He grinned at her. *Hardly reassuring. What landmines?*

'There are landmines on the roads?'

'Well, not during the day. The rebels bury them in the night and the security services hunt for them and dig them up at dawn. There are some roads on the concession that aren't used often. You need to ask for these roads to be reviewed by security before driving down them. The security patrols check constantly in case a new landmine has been laid, but sometimes they miss one.'

'Why do they do it?'

'To kill us, of course. They're trying to force us to leave.'

Sam tensed each time the car went over a bump. *How could she get used to it? What happened when security missed one? What am I doing in this place?*

They visited the worksites along the length of the river covered by the mining concession. The countryside had a blanket of predominantly red soil and dried out vegetation which looked as if it were dead, but during the rainy season, the slopes would turn verdant and the roads to quagmires.

The land was pockmarked with old mining works and strewn with abandoned mining machinery. Even the machinery currently being used on the mine was so old Sam had only seen some of it in historic mining texts from the nineteen fifties, half of it broken down or working at a glacial pace. The draglines were the most ancient of them. They had a crane-like structure, which tossed a big scoop out onto the gravel and then dragged it back again filling the bucket with sand and gravel. There were some modern hydraulic excavators, too, but in a pitiful state. They needed to be put down like old, worn-out animals.

They got back to the office about mid-afternoon. The air conditioning had conked out, and the heat made Sam queasy. She tried to look at some turgid scientific papers about diamonds, but she was flagging. No one else showed any sign of wanting to associate with her so she made tea with a couple of her bags and brought one in to Jim.

'Tea? Where did you get that? It's like gold dust.'

'I brought some with me. This is a free sample but you'll have to pay me in kind. I'm going to need some help.'

'Have you worked in a diamond mine before?'

said Jim, catching Sam unaware. Risking ridicule, she told him the truth.

'I've worked on alluvial gold projects before, but I don't have any diamond experience. I'd be grateful for a summary in case there are any major differences I should know about.'

Jim raised an eyebrow.

'If you have any questions, it would be better if you come to me, or Ramos. We all had to start somewhere but the other lads are not as understanding.'

'They didn't seem too enthusiastic to have me on the team.'

'No, well, they're a difficult bunch. Give them time. Let's start with the basics. Alluvial diamond mining's a simple process once a deposit containing diamonds has been located. The diamonds originate from kimberlite pipes, tubes of material, which come up from deep in the earth's crust during explosive volcanic activity. These pipes erode at the surface over millions of years, and the diamonds are liberated from the kimberlite rock and washed into the river valleys. I'm sure you know that much?'

'Yes, I did kimberlite geology at university.'

'Okay, so, once an area is targeted for mining, it's drained of water. Then the hydraulic excavators and draglines clean off the barren top sands and gravel, and dig out the basal or bottom gravel, which contain the diamonds. This gravel is transported to the dense media plants along the river. The diamonds and some of the heavier materials in the gravels are separated from the lighter materials for transporting to the diamond recovery plant where the final concentrate is obtained. The diamonds are handpicked from the final concentrate in the picking cabinets.'

'Where's the recovery plant?' said Sam

'It's just outside Kardo. I'll take you there soon so you can observe the picking process.'

'I'd love to see that,' said Sam. 'I didn't see much geology going on in the office. Is there a separate building for that?'

Jim gave her a pitying glance and laughed.

'We don't have one. All of the production is done on the basis of the old Portuguese geology maps. Black doesn't believe in exploration.'

'That's not great news for a geologist,' said Sam.

'I'm one too. I feel your pain. Black decides where we are going to mine by listening to his balls. If they start to itch as he walks over a terrace, then there are diamonds under his feet and we must mine there. What do you think of that?' he said, with a wry grin on his face.

'I'm afraid I'm not familiar with genital technology,' she said.

Jim roared with laughter.

'We're going to have a great crack together,' he said.

Jorge appeared and put his head around the door. Seeing Sam already there, he made a sign that he would be back in five minutes and left again.

'Jorge's pretty important around here, isn't he? Is he senior management?' said Sam.

'No, he's one of the engineers. He's a special case at Kardo. His long service and friendship with Black have earned him privileges way above his position in the hierarchy of the mine. He started out in Tamazia on a contract building roads for the government in Tunde Norte but was tempted over to the dark side by Black. Jorge's coming up to retirement and his wife's desperate for him to come home to Portugal. Black is trying hard to make him stay.'

'How long have you been manager of Kardo?'

'I started as a geologist but I caught Black's eye. He promoted me after six months. I'm now acting as interim general manager because Murphy was fired by Black. You met Black in Johannesburg, didn't you? What do you think of our lord and master?' he said.

Not sure if she could trust Jim yet, Sam tried to be diplomatic.

'I don't know yet,' she said.

He laughed.

'Have you had the "you must follow my orders to the letter" lecture yet?'

'Yes, I have.'

'Did you notice that sore on his arm?' said Jim.

'Yes. What happened?'

'It's self-inflicted. A mosquito bit him and it became infected, but he never let it heal and he chews on it when he's agitated.'

Sam made a face. If the comment was calculated to make her shudder, it had the desired effect.

'That's disgusting.'

Kardo was located close to the equator so it was dark outside by six o'clock. Jim dropped her back to the house and she had a closer inspection of its contents. She found an old washing machine in the back room and filled it with dirty clothes. The machine switched on but would not fill with water until she opened the valves on the water pipes. The circuits blew when she plugged in the kettle. And she had to wait until the washing machine had finished before switching on the air conditioning.

The next morning, she used the state of the wiring in her house to open a dialogue with her colleagues in the office, figuring they would have that in common with her, but their reaction was not what she hoped for.

'If you can't cope, we can give you a tent down by the river,' said Bob, the maintenance manager.

Barbed comments had been common since she had arrived on site. The management team didn't disguise their hostility at her presence. Her unexpected arrival seemed to have upset them, but she couldn't fathom why and Jim wouldn't elaborate.

After the morning production meeting, Jorge took her to see the latest river diversion.

'The river has changed course over the years and some of the best diamond terraces are now found underwater in the present river channel,' said Jorge. 'I divert the river into a new channel so these deposits can be mined. It is a tricky technical operation and the dykes are prone to collapse if not built correctly.'

'Jorge is so enthusiastic about the quality of his diversions that he needs to be reined in before he also builds a marina and a large pleasure pier to go with the dykes,' said Jim.

The creaking, groaning and wheezing of the vintage machinery they were using to dig the diversion made them seem like geriatric dinosaurs. *Maybe they operated on a tight budget? But why were the salaries so high if they didn't have any money?*

At lunchtime, Sam went to the canteen and filled her plate with food resembling that served at boarding school (overcooked meat, watery vegetables and soggy chips). As the only woman in the room, she attracted a certain amount of attention. She dithered with her plate as she didn't know where to sit. People appeared to be grouped according to their rank and department. As Manager of New Projects, she didn't belong to a particular department and the other managers had made it clear she wasn't welcome at their table.

Then, she noticed a pair of sky-blue eyes on a handsome young face staring right at her. Dirk, the metallurgist, gestured at the seat opposite him and raised his eyebrows in question. Never one to resist a challenge, she picked up her tray and sat right beside him. He was sitting with the other metallurgists and the staff from the diamond recovery facility. He looked her straight in the eye and winked as she sat beside him, and she almost fell over the bench as she caught the suggestive message in his glance.

'Hi, Sam, nice of you to join us. This is Sam. She's the new projects manager, who will be based in Mondongo but has come to work with Jim for a few weeks.'

They greeted her in a friendly manner which made a nice change. Dirk's scrutiny made Sam blush. She wasn't good at being the centre of attention. She avoided having relationships with fellow workers as it led to all sorts of complications, although the odd liaison had slipped through her defences. She told herself to behave and finished her lunch.

That afternoon, Jim called her into his office.

'I'd like you to do a diamond run to Mondongo for me,' he said.

'A what? I have no idea what that is.'

'It's pretty simple. You take the diamonds to Mondongo with the government officials who come here to collect them, and you deliver them to the central bank. You don't have to do anything, just tag along as the witness to the transaction.'

'When will I have to do it?'

'I will let you know in a week or so. It depends on how much production we have. It's not safe to keep too many diamonds on site with MARFO about. First we have to get you into the diamond sorting house so you can see the procedures involved.'

On the way home from the office, she noticed a large monkey sitting on an outhouse in the backyard of the house across the street from her. He was sitting on his bottom with his hands on his open knees, looking down from his perch on the wall like an eastern Buddha. She presumed that he was tied up, although she couldn't see any chain or cord. He looked oddly human sitting serenely on his perch. *I wish I felt that calm. This place is a madhouse.*

Despite her willingness to get involved with production, the other senior staff had made it clear that she was not wanted on site. She hadn't managed to determine why, but only Jorge and Jim talked to her at all. She was finding it hard to sleep as the power plant couldn't cope when the air conditioning was switched on in all the residences and often conked out at night. When she got home, she found that her dirty clothes had been washed and were folded in a neat, clean pile on her bed.

Sam listened to the news on the BBC World Service on her radio as often as was practical. The station only broadcast during certain hours of the day and she hadn't managed to establish which they were yet. The news about Tamazia was not good. MARFO had suspended cooperation with international observers monitoring the Tamazia peace process. This had heightened the escalating tensions between MARFO and the government which had tangible effects on the operations at Kardo.

'I can't ask the control tower at the airstrip when the cargo flights are due because they are not allowed to tell me over the radio,' the logistics manager told her.

'That must be pretty inconvenient.'

'You have no idea, but this is a protective measure against MARFO. They listen to our radios. If they don't know when the flights are coming in, it's harder to organise an attack.' The thought of flying to Mondongo and back again to do the diamond export gave her palpitations, but Jim had not given her a choice.

Chapter VI

As part of her training before moving to Mondongo, Sam had to spend time with Fred Allen, the geologist, to learn how the diamond data were entered into the computer. Fred was a big, fat lad with piggy eyes and a Walter Mitty complex.

'You know of course that I have the only computer on site? I'm the person Black trusts with the data on diamond production,' he told Sam. 'Black's paranoid about anyone finding out what the production is. He doesn't trust computers at all and is avoiding getting internet for the site, even though it is available from our satellite provider.'

Fred was not willing to befriend Sam, and incur the disapproval of the other expatriate staff, but she flattered him enough to get to look at the famous graphs and figures.

'You see this table? Diamonds are divided up by shape, colour, clarity and size. The production from Kardo is of excellent quality in all of these facets. Fancy coloured diamonds also turn up from time to time, which increases their value even more.'

After several frustrated attempts, she was given a permit that allowed her to enter the diamond sorting plant and see the real thing.

'I'm annoyed it took so long to get you the permit. You're senior management and it should have been a formality,' said Jim, blowing his cheeks out. 'The men in the internal security section are a law unto themselves and don't associate with the other people on the mine to maintain their impartiality.'

'Why did they obstruct it?' said Sam.

'I suspect someone in security, maybe Brian Lynch, is responsible. He's a professional security man and a real stickler for protocol. He's also one of the original crew here.'

'What's his background?'

'He was in the British army for many years and spent a lot of time in Northern Ireland.'

'How did he finish up here?' said Sam.

'He went into security when his commission ran out but found doing the security for shopping malls a little tame compared to what he was used to. His attention to detail and experience in conflict means he's a natural for working abroad in mining security, and he quickly rose to management level. He runs a tight ship at Kardo, which is vital when dealing with a product that is so easy to conceal. He's responsible for the strict security in the diamond recovery room and the periodic lie detector tests conducted at random on all of the staff. You should be careful of Brian Lynch,' said Jim. 'That man is always plotting something. He's a vindictive character. He likes to play people off against each other by spreading false rumours and other methods.'

'Thanks. I'll remember that. Can I ask you a question?'

'Sure, as long as it's not about macramé.'

'I'm still having a tough time with the other management members. They ignore me or treat me like shit. Is there something I've done wrong?'

'God, no. They're a bunch of old wankers who think they own the place and they don't like you because you're not one of them. Even worse, you're a woman and they think you're Black's spy.'

'Black's spy? Why would they think that?'

'Because Murphy told Brian Lynch that you must be a spy when he heard that you were living in his old house here.'

'When did he do that?'

'Just before you arrived, he called to organise the shipping of his stuff from Kardo to the UK. Brian told him you were coming here and were going to stay in his old place. Murphy now thinks you were involved in some sort of plot to get him fired, even though you weren't hired before Black threw him out. He told Brian that you pretended you were going to work in Mondongo.'

'Wow. Now that explains a lot. I was told that I was working in Mondongo by the London office, you know. I had no idea that I was coming to Kardo when I spoke to Murphy. And what do you think?'

'Me? I think he was fired for being a useless drunk wanker. Have patience. The boys will soon get used to you. It's quite a slow business teaching new tricks to old dogs. Anyway, you'll be getting a break soon. I need you to go to Mondongo with the diamonds as soon as possible.'

As soon as Jim could organise it, she went to visit the diamond recovery plant with him. On their arrival, Sam and Jim first had to sign in at the guard's office. Next, they passed through a fortified revolving door and down a long passageway back out into the stifling heat of the inner compound, which was surrounded by a high razor-wire fence. Large Alsatians patrolled the fence with their minders.

They went through another gate with a security hut where they had to sign in again and were accompanied to the plant. There was a slight disagreement about her entering the premises as the security guard hadn't seen her pass which had been left with the first guard, and the other copy which had been left at the security hut. This was soon sorted out, and then they entered the plant followed by eight people: four security guards and four observers.

They were locked into the building, the metal door slamming behind them and reverberating in the cavernous space.

'Is that it?' said Sam. 'I was expecting strict security measures.'

Jim laughed. The building had a tin roof and no air conditioning, making it like an oven. Squadrons of mosquitoes sailed around in the hot air. Sam had not been allowed to bring anything to drink with her, not that she wanted anything to drink. There were no toilets that she could see, and she had not been warned about the lack of facilities before drinking three cups of tea in the office. Her bladder was already uncomfortably full.

Brian Lynch, the head of security, gave her a tour of the premises. Already large by design, he carried too much extra weight. He panted if he went up more than four or five stairs, and the exertion showed in his face.

They were watched by a phalanx of the guards and observers. Sam didn't like people supervising her. All those eyes boring into her. She resented feeling under suspicion even though it was the same for anyone who wanted to enter the plant. *This is ridiculous. No one is more honest than me.*

They reached the door to the picking room along

a narrow walkway with chain-link walls. Four large padlocks secured the door. The four guards each had a key to one lock only. They unlocked their own padlock and then let the next keyholder squeeze past to open his. It was a bit of a challenge to squeeze past each other in such a confined space with their large guts and it produced a considerable amount of extra huffing and puffing. Sam tried not to giggle.

The diamond picking was done in a Perspex cabinet, which consisted of a long table covered in a transparent box formed of panels stuck together with silicon seams. The panels had arm-holes along its length. Long leather gloves extended into the cabinet from these holes. The gloves had seen better days and were dark with sweat. Sam shuddered. *I don't fancy putting my hands into them.*

The material that had been transported from the DMS plants at the river had been concentrated further before being passed through a Sortex machine to separate the diamonds from the heavy minerals by irradiating the concentrate with ultraviolet light. The diamonds fluoresced under ultraviolet light, and this fluorescence triggered an automatic jet of air, which blew the diamond off a conveyor with a small amount of concentrate into the picking fraction. The picking material was then conveyed through a pipe and dropped into the cabinet through holes in the top.

There were local diamond pickers seated alongside the cabinet. They put one of their hands into the gloves and the other arm up on the Perspex to steady themselves. They picked the diamonds out of the concentrate using tweezers and put them into a metal bowl. This was a tricky operation.

Picking diamonds up with tweezers while wearing heavy leather gloves is an art. The diamonds bounced all over the place if they were dropped. The larger the grain size of the concentrate, the bigger the diamonds found in that fraction. The diamonds were large, and some of them had perfect shapes. *No wonder people were fighting over the right to mine these lands.*

When the fraction had been searched and all the diamonds removed, the pickers were sent home to Kardo village, and the sorters took over. They started by sieving the diamonds into size fractions. At the far end of the bench, more gloves were employed for use in weighing and sorting the diamonds into envelopes.

Once the diamonds were sorted into sizes, they were removed from the recovery table and placed in a huge safe at the back of the room. The safe room had two doors leading to an inner room with another safe in it. There were strong boxes in the inner safe, which acted as temporary storage for the diamonds until they had to be moved.

The diamonds were still in their natural rough state, so they weren't inspiring to look at.

'I've never seen unpolished diamonds in bulk before,' said Sam. 'They're not glamorous, are they? They look like the glass from a car crash.'

'Their appearance is deceptive. These diamonds are gem quality with a large size and minimal flaws, meaning they sell for high prices at auction. That's why Gemsite can afford to pay big expatriate salaries and cargo costs,' said Jim.

They left through security and out to the front room again where they had to insert their hands through a rubber sleeve into a sealed iron box full of balls.

'Put your hand into the rubber sleeve and pull out a ball,' said Jim.

'Why do I have to do this?' said Sam.

'This box of balls acts as a filter for randomised security checks. You have to pull a ball out of the box and show it to the security guard. If you pulled out a black ball, you can go. If the ball is white, you have to empty your pockets and so on for the guards to check. A South African guy was made to strip and bend over the first time he went through, as a joke. He was on his own and didn't know any better.'

Sam was glad that she wasn't alone. She was relieved to get a black ball and leave with her dignity intact.

The next day, they returned to the diamond plant to re-weigh the diamonds and bottle them in hydrofluoric acid (HF) for cleaning. After boiling the diamonds in ceramic saucepans to give them an initial clean, they were decanted into plastic bottles. HF was poured into the bottles on top of a table in a small, unventilated room full of observers and security men.

Sam found it bizarre to see HF handled with such abandon. It was a corrosive acid, and if spilt on skin, caused a horrible death by eating through the flesh. It could not be washed off with water. Only special creams prevented it from burning right through flesh, and there was only one small tube. There was a fume extractor in the room, but it wasn't being used.

When Sam was at university studying geology, she wasn't allowed to use HF at all. Since no one asked her to handle the acid, Sam kept her worries to herself. With landmines buried all over the concession by MARFO, HF was obviously not considered dangerous in comparison. She also knew that people would sneer at her if she voiced an opinion, so she swallowed her objections. The idea of Brian Lynch getting a nasty burn was not such a bad option.

Sam was looking forward to running the mining

operations when Jim went away on leave for a month at the end of August but she had to be ready to take over the operation by then. Jim had been generous with his technical information, and she was absorbing it all like the proverbial sponge. *Perhaps if I work hard enough, the barriers preventing my entry to the management team will begin to crumble.* She had acclimatised to the heat and dust but the isolation was harder to take. Mondongo might be fun when she returned there. She quite fancied a long flirty lunch with Pedro.

A loud bang, somewhere in the house, woke Sam around midnight. Her heart almost shot out of her mouth and thundered against her ribcage for hours afterwards. She grabbed her emergency rucksack from beside the bed and sat there hugging it. She was supposed to wait for Frik, the security guard, and to run off into the bush and hide with him for a couple of days to avoid being raped or murdered by MARFO forces. Knowing her luck, she would get eaten by a crocodile before she was rescued.

She sat in bed forcing herself to be logical. The sound was coming from the kitchen or maybe the laundry room. *Why would someone be thrashing about in the laundry room?* There was nothing to steal there. She got up, despite her terror, and forced herself to go and look. She switched the light on in the kitchen and shoved the laundry room door open.

The main pipe from the outside water tank to the laundry had burst free from its bindings and was swinging around in a circle bashing the washing machine and walls and filling the utility room with water. She looked around the kitchen for the key to open the padlock to the back door. Finally finding it, she opened the lock and the door. The water rushed out into the dust. The pipe was still spraying gallons of water all over the electric circuits of the hot water tank, washing machine and pump.

Something would short. This normally happened at the slightest excuse, but when she wanted something to happen, it invariably didn't. She tried to re-attach the pipe and was saturated with cold water. Then, she spotted the switch for the water pump. Praying not to get an electric shock, she pushed the switch. Nothing. Again. Nothing. She grabbed a big piece of wood and poked the switch box hard. No result.

She couldn't leave the water running all night, so she threw on some clothes, and after negotiating the padlock, ran out into the road. She didn't know what else to do. Despite being senior management, Sam had not yet been allocated a radio because they were in short supply and she always drove around with one of the senior team, who all had radios. The internal phone service didn't work and looked like it hadn't worked for years.

She had no idea where anyone lived. They disappeared from the office at the end of the day or went to the bar beside the canteen. Apart from Jim, and Jorge who was nice to everyone, no one had shown the slightest interest in working with her or talking to her.

She ran to the prefab that housed the Filipinos at the back of the canteen, ringing the doorbells of several houses on the way that went unanswered. She found two nonchalant Tamazian security guards having a cigarette on the steps of the prefab.

'Excuse me, there's a water leak in my house. Can you help me, please?' said Sam.

They failed to grasp the urgency of the situation and carried on smoking and chatting and ignored her. She went right up to within inches of one of them and tried again.

'I need you to go inside the prefab to wake up a plumber and an electrician, who can come to the house and fix the damage.'

One of the guards turned around and looked her up and down. She glared at him as fiercely as she could.

'Okay, wait here,' he said.

Five minutes later, Sam was walking back to her house with the electrician and the plumber, a couple of jolly Filipinos who didn't seem at all fazed to be dragged out of bed in the middle of the night.

'They should've told you about the washing machine,' said the plumber.

'That place is a death trap,' said the electrician.

It took them an hour to fix the problem and for Sam to sweep the rest of the water out of the kitchen and utility room. She was shattered and grumpy by the time they left. To her amazement, she managed to get to sleep again but she woke up knackered.

'Oh, that's always happening,' said Bob, who as the maintenance manager was in charge of fixing that sort of thing and resented it for taking away from the heavy machinery. The ancient wiring and plumbing in the compound caused constant problems. Sam wondered why Bob couldn't figure out a way of preventing it from happening if he had so much practice, but she didn't comment. She spent the afternoon out and about with Jorge and Jim. That night, she slept like a baby but turned the water off at the mains just in case.

Chapter VII

On her way out of the canteen after lunch the next day,
two small boys, who looked like brothers, begged her
for food. They were thin almost to the point of
emaciation and covered in red dust. The older boy held
on to the younger boy to stop him from reaching out
and touching Sam.

'I haven't got any food today,' she said in
Portuguese.

They appeared startled to hear her speaking in their
language. The smaller boy tugged his brother's T-shirt
and whispered in his ear. Sam smiled reassuringly but
just then Fred lumbered into view and stepped towards
them shaking his fist. They cowered from him under
the eaves of the canteen.

'Bugger off. Go on,' he said. 'Those little bastards
are always trying it on. We're not allowed to give them
any food, so don't go getting all bleeding heart about
it.'

'Message received,' said Sam. 'Next time,' she
said in Portuguese to the small boys and winked. They
ran off giggling and glancing back at her with their
huge brown eyes.

'You've got to make more of an effort to fit in,'
said Fred, sighing.

'You may not believe this, but I'm doing my best,' said Sam.

'Can't you wear normal clothes? You look as if you're working in London.'

'My field gear hasn't arrived yet. I don't know how to expedite it.'

Fred sighed again.

'Go to the administration office. They should be organising it.'

Before she had a chance to thank him, he had turned on his heel and headed for his accommodation block.

It wasn't as if she wanted to wear her silk shirts in the field. No one in the laundry at Kardo has ever seen silk before, and they had thrown Sam's shirts into a normal wash. They now looked as if they were used for fieldwork after all, as they were faded and streaked. Still, she could be able to afford new clothes if she survived six months in Tamazia.

She went straight to the administration office to inquire about her air freighted luggage.

'Your luggage? Oh, yes. I believe it arrived in Mondongo airport a few days ago,' said the clerk.

'Has anyone been to collect it yet?'

'No, I don't think so. Are you waiting for anything in particular?'

Sam bit back a complaint.

'Well, not really, but the laundry here is ruining all of the silk shirts that I had intended for office wear in Mondongo. All of my field clothes are in those boxes. I would be really grateful if you could organise their collection before my office clothes are ruined forever. I know this is a trivial request, but I would be so grateful.'

'I am busy, but let me see what I can do,' said the

clerk.

'Thank you,' said Sam, giving him her best smile.

As if by magic, she got news from Mondongo on the flight which arrived at Kardo a couple of hours later. Dirk was the bearer of the glad tidings. He arrived at her house with a couple of tapes that had arrived on the flight from Mondongo. He had obviously offered to bring them so that he could see her. He was standing on the steps outside shifting from foot to foot.

'Hi, Sam. Someone sent you these tapes from Mondongo.'

'Really?'

'There's a note, I think. Yes, here it is'

Sam read the spidery writing. It was from Pedro. Her luggage had been collected from customs in Mondongo airport and awaited her in the Villa Alice. *Perhaps begging had its place.*

'Thank you,' she said. 'Do you want to come in?'

'Sure, it would be nice to hear some new music.'

He made her nervous. She tried not to get involved with anyone at work in the field, as it caused problems. Being senior made it worse. Since she spent most of her working life in exploration camps, this cramped her style a lot. She distracted herself by putting on the tapes. Pedro had sent her some middle-of-the-road tunes normally reserved for elevators. After a short while pretending to enjoy the music, she caught Dirk's eye.

'Well,' she said, 'the tapes are a nice gesture, but not something I would ever listen to, being a rock and roll sort of chick.'

'They are a bit crap, really.'

'Ghastly.'

They both laughed.

'Shall I put on something else?'

'That would be great. Have you got any Led Zeppelin?'

That evening, after Dirk had gone, a huge rainstorm hit the compound, heralding the start of the rainy season. At first, Sam was alarmed by the thunder in the distance. She hadn't been expecting rain and it sounded like a MARFO attack. However, as the storm rumbled nearer and nearer, the origin of the noise became obvious. The lightning was continuous. The rain came in waves, which reminded her of being in a car wash. It flung itself against the roof in the most violent manner, louder and louder.

The water poured off the roofs outside in torrents. *I hope this damn jinxed house won't collapse.* It was phenomenal. She expected the power to go any minute. It reminded her of working in the high-altitude rain forests in Sierramar. She never thought she'd ever see more rain than that.

The storm lasted only an hour or so. She fell asleep but was woken at about two a.m. by a drunken Jim ringing her doorbell.

'Hi, Jim. What's up?'

'No water or electricity in my house. Can I come in?'

He tottered and righted himself, swaying outside the gates. Sighing, she stepped through the mush of leaves and mud between her front door and the gates, and forced open the padlocks. Jim pushed past her into the house, and she shut the gate, first glancing up and down the street to see if it might be a trap or a prank of some sort.

'Got a beer?' he said.

'No, I haven't been to the bar yet.'

'Don't you drink? You should come to the bar. The

lads don't like it.'

The lads didn't like anything she did but she didn't say so. She was still half asleep and wondered why he was at her house instead of one belonging to another manager. He wandered around looking uncertain for a while, as if he wanted to say something, but wasn't sure how to start. He smelled like he had rolled in beer. Sam guided him to the spare bedroom, went back to her room and shut her door.

Jim left early in the morning, and it occurred to her that the rather vicious gossip machine in camp could have got the wrong idea about why his car was outside her house. But when she thought about it, *what was he doing at her house anyway? He didn't need any light or water to go to sleep, so why her house?* He had been paralytic with drink so maybe he got confused. She gave him the benefit of the doubt.

Anyway, living in remote sites for long periods away from their families was tough. She had seen even the most faithful succumb to the temptations offered by all the nubile young local women throwing themselves at expatriate wallets in other companies where she had worked. The fact that these women were not fussy about who they slept with had its own problems. They didn't have access to condoms, and they were riddled with venereal disease, including HIV in some cases, which put some of the more intelligent men off. This also meant that any non-local woman was bound to get lots of attention, whether they wanted it or not. Sam, the spy, was an exception.

Aside from Sam, there was only one British female in camp, Jean, who worked in the canteen as the assistant administration manager, and was going out with Bob. Half a dozen girls from the Philippines washed the laundry and ministered to senior management. Black's girlfriend Marybelle had graduated from their ranks. The girls got transferred from camp to camp as their 'boyfriends' got bored and made a swap.

Following this incident, Jim Hennessey became irritable with Sam. He blanked her and made her feel even more isolated. He could be seen scowling and muttering. *Was it something to do with his drunken visit to her house?* She hadn't been welcoming but then he hadn't been forthcoming either. She decided to try and find an opportunity to ask him.

The other members of the management team seemed only too pleased that he had joined them in ostracising her, so she was surprised when she was invited to join them for a drink in the bar one night. She didn't like beer or enjoy drinking in the bar, but she did understand that drinking was an important part of life for these men and in order to fit in, she had to drink too on occasion. Maybe the ice was melting a bit after her frosty reception. She walked to the bar and mounted the steps to find the whole crew had arrived before her, and they were standing up chatting in a big group.

'Get yourself a beer,' said Bob.

She went to the bar and signed a voucher. Taking a deep breath, she turned around smiling and approached the group. Almost imperceptibly, they moved closer together, forming a tight circle. She stopped about two metres away, her smile frozen on her face. She stepped forward, and they shuffled closer together. Nobody looked at her.

She stood there with the cold beer in her hand, condensation dripping onto the floor, trying not to get upset. A couple of metallurgists, who were not in the group, looked up from their table and looked back down again. She went back to the bar and sat down on a stool with her back to the group. She gulped back a sob. The barman looked like he might be about to say something, but she gave him a shake of the head. She forced herself to drink the freezing liquid and put her glass down on the bar.

'Thanks,' she said. 'Enjoy your evening.'

She walked out as slowly as she could bear. She felt the rush of gloating laughter follow her out of the bar, and she could hear their jeering as she stumbled down the steps. By the time she turned onto the road, tears were streaming down her face. Drowning in the misery of the rejection implied by the planned ambush, she ran home and struggled with the padlock on the outer door, swearing and crying and kicking it. She got through the two doors into her house and sat down in the dark, swallowing hard to muffle her sobs. She stayed like that for a long time.

***

Back in the bar, the men were congratulating each other on the success of their plan.

'That'll teach the stupid bitch,' said Brian. 'Who the fuck does she think she is anyway? Did she really imagine we wanted a drink with her of all people?'

'Black did it on purpose. He shouldn't have sent a fucking woman in here to spy on us,' said Bob.

'Fucking bitch,' said one of the engineers.

'We'll break her soon. No one can take this for long,' said Brian, who knew a thing or two about breaking new recruits. 'Let's liven things up a bit. Why don't we take bets on her?'

'On her leaving?'

'No, she'll be leaving soon, that's too easy. Let's bet on who will have her first. She'll be looking for comfort after tonight. Someone should cosy up to her and pretend to like her. You can bet on someone else or on yourself.'

'Brilliant. I'm in.'

'Me too, but I'm betting on Dirk. I'm occupied,' said Bob. 'Jean wouldn't be happy if I was seen flirting with Sam.'

He also had a grudging respect for Sam, but he wouldn't have admitted that to any of these men. He didn't like to stand out from the crowd.

'Me too.'

'Hmmm. Dirk is a good bet. Maybe we should all bet on Dirk and how long it will take him. I've seen her look at him. That's not a work-related glance, lads,' said Brian, who prided himself on knowing all about women and their needs.

'Fucking right.'

'Okay, I'll run the book. You tell Dirk he's nominated.'

'What if he won't play ball?'

'He's new. He'll play ball if he wants to be one of the lads.'

'Brilliant. That'll be a bit of fun. Whose round is it anyway?'

'Get them in, Bob. It's your turn.'

They went back to the serious business of getting drunk.

Chapter VIII

Sam struggled through the next few days at Kardo. The management office went quiet every time she entered, and no one replied to her greetings. Jim still imparted his wisdom about mining alluvial diamond deposits but he, too, seemed distant. It had become a battle of wills, not one Sam intended to lose. *They won't force me out. Someone will break ranks eventually.*

The only bright spot had been her growing friendship with Dirk, who, being new, and relatively junior, did not belong to the clique. She sat beside him at most mealtimes and he came to sit on her porch for a beer in the evening. She confided in him about her failure to break into the team, and he listened in silence without giving her advice. He told her about his home in South Africa and his interest in parrots. This prompted her to tell him about the African Grey she had indoctrinated in Simbako, making him roar with laughter.

The discovery of a new pothole raised everyone's morale and Sam came into an office full of smiles and excited conversations. They even forgot to give her the cold shoulder for once.

'They found a big pothole in the riverbed of one of the new diversions I engineered,' said a jubilant Jorge.

Jim slapped him on the back.

'You found it, Jorge.'

'Is that the same as finding one in an alluvial gold deposit?' said Sam.

'Exactly the same. These potholes can act as diamond traps because diamonds have a high specific gravity like gold. This means that they tend to sink to the bottom of the river gravel and into any crevice or pothole that exists on the riverbed. The best news is that finding a pothole often means a production bonanza and one hundred per cent bonuses all around,' said Jim.

I'm supposed to be thrilled the bastards in the management team are getting massive bonuses? At least that includes Jorge.

'Wow, that's great news,' she said.

'The bad news is that the quantity of diamonds being extracted means it's time to move some of them to Mondongo. I need you to do the export tomorrow as you aren't vital to production,' said Jim.

Not vital to production. That summed it up. She tried not to mind, and instead concentrated on the upcoming experience. She was unsure what she was required to do as diamond courier, except to be there as a witness. As with other procedures in Gemsite, it was all word of mouth. They assumed she knew what to do and she didn't want to invite more ridicule by asking in front of them.

On the positive side, she needed to get away for a day or two after her humiliation in the bar, and this was ideal. It would be a relief to escape from the nasty management team and have some fun. Her boxes of freight were another incentive to go to Mondongo. The thought of all that chocolate made her mouth water.

'No problem,' she said. 'Glad I can do something

useful for once.'

Jim smiled in relief. 'Be outside the recovery plant at five.'

When Dirk turned up at her door that evening, she sent him away, but not before he made her promise to bring him a carton of cigarettes from Mondongo. As part of the management team she was entitled to two cartons a month and there was no way she would smoke them all. He gave her a kiss through the bars of the outer gate and winked. She watched him walk away, dying to call him back, but knowing it was a bad idea.

Sam got up before dawn and struggled to the plant half-asleep and starving. The canteen didn't open until five-thirty, and no mercy was shown to earlier risers. Sam and the security officers were outside the plant at five o'clock sharp, but they had to wait over an hour for the SDM delegation to arrive from the airport. The men from SDM, the government diamond agency who supervised all transport and deposits of diamonds in Mondongo had arrived on a special flight. Their plane stayed on the runway waiting to take them all back to the capital with the diamonds.

Crabby and jumpy, Sam kept quiet, as she didn't want anyone to know how nervous she was or that she was prone to verbal diarrhoea. When the men from SDM arrived at the plant, they all went through the usual routine in the dark passageways and entered into the gloom with the managers and the team from MLS, the Tamazian partners in the concession. The diamonds were still being soaked in hydrogen fluoride for cleaning, so they needed to be taken out of the acid, washed and sorted into size fractions for weighing and counting.

They had to be weighed three times, first by the

Gemsite management and then by SDM and by MLS. Sam tried to look interested but her enthusiasm soon flagged and she counted mosquitos to keep her awake. She yawned and one of the SDM men did too. They smiled in complicity. *Jim didn't warn me how tedious this would be.*

After the checking process was completed, the diamonds were loaded into a portable safe and then placed in the boot of a new Toyota jeep, which had been driven to the door of the recovery plant. Jim came up to Sam and shook her hand.

'Okay, have fun and see you tomorrow. All you have to do is follow the safe to the bank and sign it over. Don't look around, but the guy on your left is Eduardo. He was a garimpeiro not so long ago. I expect he will ask you to lunch. You may go if you fancy it, but whatever you do, don't give him any information about the production or our operations at Kardo.'

As she hadn't been allowed anywhere near the production figures, Sam didn't think there was a big danger of her telling Eduardo anything useful, but she nodded and sneaked a peak while pretending to look at something else so she would recognise him. It was the man who had yawned in sympathy with her. *Was he just faking it to make a connection?*

'The government is desperate to know our real production figures and Black is just as determined that they won't learn them. So be careful,' said Jim.

She got into the car with the SDM representatives, a tight squeeze. The big black men were squashed up against the windows like liver in a jar. They drove through Kardo behind a truckload of heavily armed police, who sat at the back of their pickup thundering along the bumpy road with their machine guns pointing at the vehicle they were supposed to be protecting. *I hope their safety catches are on.* It must have occurred to more than one of the police how easy it would have been to kill all the people in the car and run off with the safe. She hoped the escorts were changed regularly so they never got friendly enough to plot together.

They roared through the town with the horn blasting, being thrown about in the jeep by the big potholes. Dogs, pigs and chickens scattered before them. People shook their fists at the convoy. It all called attention to the fact that there was a couple of million dollars' worth of diamonds in the jeep. It was also pointless, as the diamond pickers in the sort house were local men. They knew when there was an export to Mondongo planned, so MARFO must have known, too. *They'd be quite happy to shoot down the Gemsite plane and kill everyone inside it to get the cargo.*

At the airport, the plane was on the runway with the engines running, a nice change from Sam's last experience with TransTamazia. They were shooed straight up the back steps of the cargo jet and took off immediately for Mondongo. The men from SDM were solicitous of her wellbeing, ushering her to her seat and strapping her in. Then, after the plane took off, they gave her a tin of a fizzy pineapple drink. Despite being warm, such was her thirst that it tasted like nectar.

Next, a small soft package wrapped in tissue paper was pressed into her hand. She had no idea what to expect. She unwrapped it. A small whole fish, not gutted, lay there, cold and grilled with its mouth open in protest. Sam didn't want the fish, but she couldn't refuse, so she ate it, avoiding the copious bones and the intestines. The brown flesh turned out to be delicious. Sam licked her fingers and finished off the pineapple juice. *A weird breakfast but so welcome.*

The plane landed at Mondongo, and the passengers

transferred directly into a large four-wheel-drive vehicle waiting on the tarmac for them. The safe containing the diamonds was loaded into a small security van in front of them. A pickup truck full of soldiers armed to the teeth pulled in front of them, and another appeared behind them. All four vehicles had removable sirens on their roofs. These were switched on, and the convoy took off at high speed on a wave of sirens heading for the National Bank of Tamazia through the chaotic streets of Mondongo.

They mounted pavements, barged traffic off the road, shotguns in the air and called attention to the fact that they had two million dollars' worth of diamonds in the convoy. *Why not sell tickets?* The convoy got separated from the front truck of soldiers a couple of times by cars crossing in front of them. Any of these could have been set-ups and Sam's guts churned with fear each time it happened. She tried to ignore the traffic and focus by holding on to the seat in front of her.

'Are you scared?' said Eduardo.

'Scared? Of course not,' said Sam. 'How could I be afraid with five tough bodyguards looking after me?'

They lapped it up, beaming at her and each other. She wasn't a woman in a man's world for nothing and flattery always worked.

After what seemed like eternity, their car pulled into a courtyard and up to the back entrance of the Central Bank. Two security guards emerged and marched to the back of the vehicle, where they were handed the safe by the SDM representative. The security men took the safe into the bank and disappeared from view. Sam was nonplussed. *Shouldn't I be going in with it?* She tried to follow the safe but Eduardo shook his head and indicated she should follow him.

They walked around the pink marble building and entered by the main portal. Sam had to show her passport and sign a registration form at the reception desk to get an ID card to enter the diamond zone. This took ten minutes. By the time she got past internal bank security and through the maze of corridors to the handover point again, the safe had already been processed and taken to the vault for safekeeping.

Eduardo handed her a form to sign. The contents gave her a sinking feeling. It certified the delivery of the diamonds. After the elaborate and tedious security measures in Kardo, where each diamond was weighed four times and six men watched her every breath, the lax procedure struck her as improbable. She hadn't even seen the handover. She could just imagine the resulting scandal if the diamonds went missing. *Bloody stupid woman. That's the last time we hire one to work with Gemsite.*

Sam signed it anyway. There was nothing she could do at that juncture, and no one seemed fazed by the absence of protocol. In fact, they seemed in a hurry to get away. They had arrived at the Central Bank in the nick of time to deposit the diamonds just before it closed for lunch, and eating trumped diamonds in their list of priorities.

'It would be my honour if you joined us for lunch,' said Eduardo. 'I know just the place.' Sam almost laughed. Jim had been right. Eduardo intended to try and grill her for information on Gemsite operations. She accepted the invitation anyway, as she enjoyed a bit of cat and mouse, and she was still starving.

'Thank you. It would be my pleasure,' she said.

Eduardo led Sam to a nice car with leather seats,

which she suspected belonged to someone a lot more senior. They drove off leaving the other men behind them.

'Aren't your colleagues coming with us?' said Sam.

'No, they're not invited,' said Eduardo, pretending to concentrate on his driving.

Sam wanted to ask why, but she decided to go with the flow and see where it led her.

They pulled into the pavement outside an old-style bistro on a backstreet in central Mondongo. A tattered green awning offered respite from the punishing sunshine. Cracked green gloss flaked from the door but the view through the window showcased Mondongo's upper class relaxing at tables with starched white tablecloths. Sam eyed her shabby field gear with dismay. *Too late now.*

A uniformed parking attendant opened Sam's door and beckoned her inside. They stepped out of the searing heat of midday and through double doors into the cool darkness. The restaurant was packed. *Would they even be able to get a table?* As she stood in the entrance, conscious of dark looks at her dishevelled appearance, Eduardo had a word with the maître d. As if by magic, his look of disapproval changed to one of warm welcome, reserved for special customers.

They were ushered to a private booth in the corner, which was made of dark mahogany and lined with faded burgundy velvet. Eduardo fiddled with the cutlery and made no attempt to order. Every time the door opened, he leapt to his feet. Sam had already chosen something to eat and found his behaviour bizarre.

'Are we waiting for someone?' she said.

Suddenly, there was a commotion at the front door.

All the clients in the restaurant stopped eating and gazed towards the entrance. The sunlight streamed in, lighting up the dust particles in the air. A small, neat figure stepped into the light and was chaperoned towards their booth by at least four members of staff. People were standing up and greeting him with something approaching reverence.

The man was shorter than Sam, stocky but not portly, with a pencil moustache on his lip. He had short, cropped curly hair and a spring in his step. He exuded a strange raw power. Eduardo almost pulled off the tablecloth in his haste to stand up and receive him.

'General, you're here. What a pleasure. You look fantastic,' he gushed.

A look of irritation flashed in the General's eyes.

'Yes, yes, yes. Thank you, Eduardo. Are you going to introduce me to the lady?'

'Of course, my General. This is Sam Harris. She's working at Kardo with Gemsite.'

'Thank you.' He turned to face her. 'I've heard a lot about you. My name is Antonio Sanchez Magalhaes, although I am better known in Tamazia as General Fuego.'

Sam's jaw dropped. *Was this the General Fuego she had heard so much about at Kardo?* He was a legend in Tamazia. How did he come to be having lunch with her, a lowly geologist and a foreigner to boot? She felt embarrassed by her dusty trousers and baggy shirt. She hadn't looked in the mirror before dawn when she got up to go to the diamond sort house, so she had no idea what she looked like, except that it must be pretty bad. She regrouped and offered him her hand.

'It's a pleasure, General. I've heard all about you, too.'

The General tilted his head and looked her right in the eye. His own eyes twinkled with mischief as she held his gaze.

'Your Portuguese is terrible,' he said.

'Oh, is it that bad?' said Sam, blushing.

'Pretty bad. Do you speak Spanish?'

'Yes. Better than Portuguese, anyway,' she said.

'Ah, then let us speak Spanish,' he said, changing in mid-sentence. 'I learned to speak it in Cuba with my first wife Carmen.'

'I'd like that.'

The other diners were staring at them, forks still in the air between mouthfuls. The General turned to glare at them, and everyone's heads dropped back to their plates. Eduardo gestured to Sam to sit, and the General slid into the booth so that he was sitting in front of her. 'Thank you, Eduardo,' he said, and just like that, Eduardo melted away, leaving Sam and the General in their velvet booth.

Sam sank into the velour seat, and spread the napkin over her knees to cover her stained trousers. She felt as if she'd been tricked into this. *But why would a man so important want to lunch with her?* It must be for the same reason as Eduardo. The same rules would apply.

She picked up one of the menus and pretended to be choosing.

'Are you hungry?' said the General.

'Famished. I'm always hungry,' she said.

Hardly surprising considering the revolting food served at the canteen in Kardo. Her trousers were in need of a belt as a result. The General beamed.

'Excellent,' he said. 'Lunch is on me. Let's eat.'

Despite her original misgivings, Sam enjoyed a lovely lunch with the General. He insisted on ordering lobster and helping to break into the more recalcitrant shells for her. He ordered lemonade to drink, so she did the same. Amusing and self-deprecating, he didn't appear to have any other motive than to meet the gringa he had heard so much about, although from whom she couldn't tell. She garnered gossip for Jorge.

'Where did you meet your first wife Carmen? Were you living in Cuba during the revolution?' said Sam.

'Oh, yes, I acted as an advisor to Che Guevara and the Castro brothers. I met my wife under a table during a battle.'

'Really?'

'Yes, really. There I was, trembling like a baby, and this ferocious warrior dived under the table and saved me. I love strong women.' He winked. 'She was the daughter of one of the leaders of the revolution. We had a passionate relationship but it could not last. It burnt out after the peace.'

'Did you come back here after Tamazian independence?'

'Yes, President Jose Dos Manos asked me to help him set up the government. I ended up marrying his sister, you know.'

No wonder the other diners were so deferential. I'm having lunch with the President's brother-in-law.

'So why is MARFO still fighting? I thought there was a ceasefire.'

'MARFO felt cheated after the election. They had not realised that the people who lived in the cities wanted democracy and not communism. They couldn't believe only people in the countryside had voted for them after they had won independence from Portugal. I have negotiated with them many times myself. I feel kinship but I can't give them power.'

'That's sad,' said Sam.

'And you? How are you doing at Kardo? I imagine it's pretty tough down there.'

'Yes, it is. I am struggling a bit I admit.'

'I am acquainted with your boss, Mr Black. Have you met him yet? I know that he is out of the country this week.'

Sam smiled and tried not to catch his eye.

'Yes, Mr Black and I met in Johannesburg. I couldn't say that I know him yet, though.'

'How is production? I hear things are going well?'

Tread carefully. This is a fishing expedition.

'I really have no idea,' said Sam. 'I haven't been there long enough to find out yet.'

The General looked thoughtful but didn't inquire further.

Long after most of the other clientele had left, the General was still arranging salt cellars and breadsticks across the table to demonstrate the battles he had fought with his men in the fight for Tamazian independence. Every now and then, he would shout 'boom' to the consternation of the waiting staff. Sam was enchanted by his exuberance and charm. *I wonder if all Generals are like this. Probably not.*

Finally, the General looked at his watch.

'Oops,' he said. 'Can't keep the President waiting.'

As they stepped outside, Sam noticed Eduardo was waiting for her. *Had he been there the whole time?* She turned to thank the General, but he was hurrying to his car with a bodyguard at either side.

'Thank you!' she called.

He turned and beamed at her. 'See you,' he said and then, 'Soon, I hope.'

And he was gone in a flurry of doors and dust.

∗∗∗

General Fuego was driven to the presidential palace, where he was ushered straight through to the President's private apartments. The President was waiting for him with undisguised impatience, his hands twisting in his lap.

'Cunhado, Bom dia.'

'Bom dia, Senhor Presidente.'

'How are you and your family?'

'Well, thank you, and yours?'

'Good also. How was the meeting with the gringa? Can we use her?'

The President's abrupt manner indicated to General Fuego that the usual niceties were not going to be observed. He was a man on a mission.

'Yes, Mr President, I think we can. She responded well to my irresistible charm.'

He looked the President in the eye and smiled mischievously.

'Don't lose focus here, Fuego. We need information on the real production numbers at Gemsite. I don't trust Black. I am sure he is cheating us out of tens or even hundreds of thousands of dollars in tax revenue. I want you to liaise with the Minister of Mines and keep him informed of anything that you learn. We have to find out how much those filhos da puta are taking out of the ground up there. I need taxes.'

General Fuego was fond of his brother-in-law but couldn't imagine what the President needed with more money, seeing as there was a rumoured billion dollars of petroleum income going missing annually, and he was pretty sure that the President had first dibs. However, he was not unhappy with his new assignment and had indeed been quite taken with the spikey young woman. It would be no hardship to have to spend some more time with her and her nice, round bottom.

93

Chapter IX

After Eduardo had dropped Sam at the Gemsite office, John Collier came to see her.

'Do you want some cash?' he said.

'I thought I wasn't allowed any,' said Sam.

'Not for Kardo, but as an official member of the Mondongo office, you are entitled to take out salary advances while you are here for your expenses over and above those provided. Most people eat out quite a lot.'

So that's how Pedro funded his exploits. Not surprising given the standard of the canteen. Somehow, she had ended up without a fixed workplace, but with the benefits of both. It made her laugh to imagine how annoyed the Kardo clique would be if they knew. She didn't need much money, as she was going straight back to Kardo the next day, but she signed a chit for twenty dollars in local currency and she went with one of the drivers to try to buy postcards to send home.

Chaos reigned in Mondongo. Armies of street hawkers besieged pedestrians and drivers alike. They soon surrounded the car selling shirts, car spares, carrycots, cigarettes, stereos, cassettes, sunglasses and cartons of juice.

'In Mondongo, you don't go to the shops. The shops come to you,' said the driver, gesturing at the women sitting on the sidewalks selling individual cigarettes from open packets. 'They give you your change in sweets or bubble gum because there are not enough coins circulating anymore.'

'What happened to the coins?'

'I suspect they have been melted down.'

The only physical shop Sam had seen in Mondongo was on the corner in the same office building that housed Gemsite's offices. It was filled with expensive vases and glassware. Its windows had a heavy iron grating protecting them. Sam watched people stand for ages outside this shop staring longingly in the window.

The women stopped and pointed out their favourite items, objects of intense desire. Objects they would never be able to afford. The women themselves had superb figures and were shaped not unlike some of the vases. They were slender with long, slim legs that an average British woman would die for. They had pretty faces and neat features. Scatters of beautiful children in their smart clothes accompanied them. Even the poorer women stood out in their tight wraparound skirts. The men were also slim and quite striking. There were a lot of protruding bottoms, which looked like ripe fruits in their tight trousers with their belts pulled tight to emphasise their figures.

After scouring the whole commercial district, Sam found eight identical slightly out-of-focus postcards in a little booth on the side of the road. They were leftover from pre-independence days and featured the fortress on the mainland side of the bridge to the island in Mondongo Bay. It overlooked the bay towards the National Bank of Tamazia. The fortress had once been used to protect the bay, but it was now being used to store confiscated MARFO weapons. The postcards cost one dollar each, despite their advanced state of decay. She wrote some lies to her family about having a good time, and gave them to the secretary at the Gemsite office so she could put Tamazian stamps on them. *Would they ever arrive in England?*

After buying the postcards, she was driven to Villa Alice, where she would stay the night before returning to Kardo. She was looking forward to seeing Sky News and catching up on the world outside. To her chagrin, interminable stories about Princess Diana monopolised the coverage on Sky. It was the fifth anniversary of her death in a car crash, and the media were making the most of it. Sam fell asleep on the sofa and woke only when the power cut out late at night. She wandered into an empty bedroom and fell into the soft bed with a sigh of relief to have a night away from Kardo.

The next morning, Sam collected the keys for the geological office above the garages in the compound from John Collier. Nearly a dozen different keys dangled from a keyring with a naked woman on the fob. John noticed her expression of bemusement.

'Sorry about the naked woman,' he said.

'Oh. I don't care about that. It's the number of keys.'

'You have to open three padlocks to get in and the drawers in the desk and filing cabinet are also locked. Black's paranoid about secrecy. No one's allowed into the office without a permit except Black himself and a few of the senior management including you, so it's going to be a bit lonely up there.'

Sam shrugged. *Being away from most of the people I've met so far isn't exactly tragic.*

'I don't mind working alone. I guess he has a lot

of secrets,' she said.

She climbed the stairs to the office and fought her way through the padlocks, forcing open the rusty hinges of the battered door. The interior was gloomy and filled with old computers, printers and a scanner covered in spider webs. An old-style telephone was nestled amongst the chaotic pile of files and screwed up pieces of paper which occupied the desk. Hardly daring to hope, she picked up the receiver and put it to her ear. A clear dialling tone trilled in her ear.

She dialled her parent's number and waited. Far away in London, the phone began to ring.

'Hello, Matilda Harris here. Who's calling?'

Her mother's voice made her emotional and Sam choked up.

'Hi, Mummy,' she forced out.

'Darling, are you okay? The line's so clear you sound like you're in London.'

'No, I'm still in Tamazia, in the office in Mondongo. How are you and Daddy?'

'We are both fine, sweetheart. How's the job? Have you met anyone at the tennis club yet?'

'The job's okay. I've not had a chance to go to the club yet. We've been pretty busy.'

She winced at the lie but she couldn't tell her mother that the club had probably been closed after independence.

'Don't work too hard. You need to have a social life too. Are there any nice people there?'

'I'm sure there are, Mummy. Just haven't met them yet.'

'Are you okay darling, really?'

'Still in one piece, I promise. I can't talk long. I don't know if I'm allowed to use this line. Give Daddy a hug from me, will you?'

'Okay, darling.'

'Oh, I might not call you for a while as I am going to visit the projects soon.'

'Look after yourself out there.'

'I will.'

Sam hung up the phone. She tended to be economical with the truth at the best of times when it came to her parents. This was no exception. There was no point in worrying them with things they wouldn't understand, like where she was really working and why. She hadn't been in any real danger yet, despite the constant fear of what might happen.

Despite the luxury of having her own phone line, there were disadvantages to her new office. It didn't take long for her to realise there was no toilet. She had to leave the office, lock all the doors, walk to the transit trailers and find an open one to access the toilet. *I hope I never get diarrhoea whilst in Mondongo.* Some of the pieces of paper covering the desk turned out to have confidential content about the production figures and Sam spent a happy couple of hours trawling through them. *No wonder the government was suspicious. The books were being cooked in a major way.*

Before lunch, she went to a spare trailer, where her precious boxes of belongings had been stored after they had been rescued from customs. She intended to divide out her field gear and supplies for taking to Kardo, but first she fished out a tampon and headed to the toilet. At that moment, Pedro turned up unannounced to drag her off to lunch. There was an awkward moment when he offered her his hand to shake and she had to kiss him because she had a tampon in her hand, and didn't want to give him a heart attack. *Most men aren't good with that sort of thing.*

Sam and Pedro went to a nice restaurant with an

oval bar around which people were eating and drinking. He flirted with her, turning on his practised charm.

'I can't wait for you to come to Mondongo to work. It's going to be a lot of fun,' he said.

'I don't think I'd call working in that isolated office fun,' she said.

'I'm talking about after work.'

'Oh, and who are you going to have fun with?'

'You, of course.'

'Me? Oh, I don't really like fun. I'm a serious person.'

'Not that sort of fun. You know what I mean.'

'No, I don't, would you like to spell it out?'

Pedro raised an eyebrow and smirked.

'I love it when a woman plays hard to get.'

'Impossible to get more like it.'

'Don't be mean, Sam. I know what I want.'

'You know what you think you want. You don't know me, Pedro, and I don't know you. You might not like me as much as you are hoping.'

'But we're going to be so good together.'

Does he think I fancy him after the tampon incident? However, she had to admit that she enjoyed being the focus of his attention. It was fascinating to watch a man work that hard at seduction. She wasn't a prime catch. She was less plump now but not in any way glamorous, as she was dressed in field gear ready for her flight.

It was amazing what the laws of supply and demand could do for a woman's sex appeal. Foreign women were like gold dust in Mondongo and were fought over by single—and not so single—expatriate men. Pedro had the Latin man's belief that no woman could resist him. He didn't seem to realise that just because he fancied a woman, it didn't mean that it was reciprocal. Sam wasn't immune to Pedro's charms but she wasn't keen on the assumptions he was making about the ease of the conquest in her case. She had no doubt she could outlast his enthusiasm, but it might be fun to play along until he got bored.

Later that afternoon, she did a round of polite handshakes in the office, and then she went to the trailers to get her boxes of goodies. Pedro dropped her at Villa Alice to sort through her things and select the stuff she needed for Kardo. She was sharing the house with two other people besides Pedro. Before he left for the office, he gave her a tour of the building site behind the house that would be her bedroom when it was finished.

The annex that was being constructed looked like a prison cell. It had no windows except for a tiny one about three metres up in the bedroom. Not much of a view. In its favour, they were installing an ensuite bathroom, so at least she didn't have to wait for anyone to shower in the morning before she got a look in. Also, it would give her some much-needed privacy. The sitting room in the main house had been tacked onto the back of the original house, and they hadn't bothered to brick up the bathroom window that overlooked it. The window did not have curtains which meant she had to sit down below the window to wash herself, or provide more interesting entertainment than the morning news.

The lack of privacy embarrassed her, but Sam had been refused many jobs during her career due to 'the lack of women's facilities,' so she wasn't about to start fussing now. She stuck a black plastic bag across the window in the bathroom with sticky tape and solved the issue like a Tamazian.

Sam watched the news and sorted through her belongings. Most of them would remain in Mondongo. The items she really wanted to take to Kardo with her this time were her music and books, and her vital supplies of tea and chocolate. She resealed the boxes containing her Mondongo articles, and put them in a storage room she found at the back of the kitchen.

When she was ready, she radioed Pedro as arranged and asked him to get someone to pick her up and take her back to the transit trailers for her flight to Kardo. He came personally, which surprised her, and then drove her to the airport when he must have had better things to do. On the way there, he said he'd miss her while he was on his leave. So smooth she almost believed it. *How could he miss her after one lunch and a cup of coffee?*

'Oh, I'm sure you'll get over it,' she said.

Pedro was not put out.

'Did you know that all the gossip about you was heating up the airwaves?' he said.

'It can't possibly compete with the stuff I've heard about you and your reputation,' she said. 'Perhaps you should stay away from me if you don't want to make it worse.'

John Collier had told her to watch out for Pedro. She considered the advice carefully. She would make her own mind up about Pedro. And then there was the General. He was a complete surprise. She might have made an unlikely conquest. She decided not to tell Jim, or the paranoid Black, about her lunch. It was probably a one-off after all.

***

The flight back to Kardo was uneventful, and the same hair-raising landing routine failed to arouse many emotions this time. What was odd was how normal it seemed. Sam found Jim at the airport waiting to drive her to the compound.

'So, how'd the trip go then?' he said. 'Any garimpeiro trouble?'

Sam mumbled something non-committal but he wasn't listening to her answer. He drove her back to her bungalow, and it was obvious that he had had a really bad day. She invited him in for a beer, which he accepted with alacrity. He quaffed the first in one, still standing up and opened the second before sitting down on the sofa, head in hands.

'Jesus, Sam, you have no idea how hard it is to work for Black. He's such a bastard. I don't know how I put up with it. I work my hands to the bone here, but all I get is grief. What does the man want?'

'I don't know. I haven't worked with him yet.'

'With him. Ha! For him, you mean. He wouldn't know how to work with someone. He's a tyrant. Fuck him.'

'Well, he does seem to appreciate you. He has promoted you, after all.'

'Only to annoy Pat Murphy. He never does anything for the right reasons.'

He ranted on for an hour or so in an unfocused sort of way. Sam wasn't sure what was expected of her, so she just listened and nodded. When he finally paused for breath, she tried a tentative question.

'Is something the matter? Can I help?'

'Don't be ridiculous, woman. No one can play Black at his own game.'

'Actually, I meant you have been pre-occupied lately, rude even. I hope it wasn't something I've done.'

Jim looked embarrassed. 'No, please forget it. I

was drunk. I don't know what I was thinking. I felt rejected.'

'Rejected? I had no idea you felt that way about me.'

'I don't—I mean, well, I was drunk and afterwards I was embarrassed. You know how it is.'

Sam, who had never used alcohol as an excuse for anything, didn't know, but she agreed anyway. There was a long silence. Finally, having finished her meagre supply, only more drink in large quantities would cure whatever was bugging him, so he stomped off to the bar.

Dirk also dropped by later for a drink and to collect the cigarettes she had brought him from Mondongo. It was tempting to invite him in. She would have liked to be physically close to someone to distract her from the fear she felt at night. She got the impression that Dirk might jump at the chance. After all, they were both single, as far as she knew, and they wouldn't be hurting anyone. No one would be able to invent stories about her and Jim, or anyone else, if she was with Dirk. Dirk made it obvious that he wanted to stay that night.

'Come on, Sam,' he pleaded. 'What's wrong with sex between two consenting adults?'

But Sam wasn't sure, so she was glad that she had her period as an excuse. For some strange reason, she felt like she was being watched. She didn't want the whole camp knowing about her business.

'Not tonight, Dirk. It's still my time of the month. I need you to go home now,' she said.

'But we could just share your bed and hang out together. We don't need to have sex, you know.'

'I know, but I'm several degrees hotter than usual due to my period, and we'll be uncomfortable. I promise to let you know when I'm ready.'

'You're just mean. You know how much I want you.'

But she turned him out into the dark, still protesting.

There was no water when she got back to her house from Mondongo and the water pipe in the utility room had started leaking again. She couldn't wash for several days, and she was on the verge of a sense-of-humour failure. The plumber arrived again, this time with Bob, who ordered the pipe changed, and a new plate made for the pump. Bob could hardly look Sam in the eye. He was trying hard to find something to chat about. He appeared determined to bridge the gap that loomed between them since the incident in the bar but Sam was not in the mood.

He commented that the plumbing arrangements had been a bit Heath Robinson. He wasn't kidding. One of the water tanks was stagnant and was acting as a breeding ground for mosquitoes, so they let the water out to kill the larvae. No wonder the mosquitos came in squadrons at night; they had their own hatchery in the backyard to replace casualties. It was like the Battle of Britain. Sam felt like she was in combat against the Luftwaffe and their deadly cargo of malaria.

Chapter X

The rainy season had set in with a vengeance, and the countryside was coated in thick red mud. The river banks were turning green where they weren't churned up into an impassable mud bath. Even the stunted bushes had new leaves and shoots. The villagers were gathering new palm leaves with which to roof their huts. At night, frogs croaked from the puddles, rendering sleep almost impossible when combined with the crickets. Some of the machine operators had stopped work because of the rain.

'It's so infuriating,' said Jim. 'Every man jack of them has been given a set of waterproofs for the rainy season, and they have all sold them in town or swapped them for beer. And then they have the cheek to moan about getting wet, and they stop work if not supervised.'

Sam had no rain gear, as the London office had told her that she wouldn't need any because it never really rained in Tamazia. The rainy season in Tamazia lasted for seven months. She found it hard to believe they didn't know that. Perhaps with Black as a boss, they were too frazzled to remember anything.

The next morning, Jim appeared at the office looking sheepish.

'Hi. What's up?'

'I've got some bad news for you. I wanted to tell you when you got back from Mondongo but I was too drunk and I thought I might change his mind. Black called me while you were away. He's changed his mind about you running the place while I'm away on leave. I'm sorry. I know you were looking forward to it.'

'Why?' She couldn't believe it. She had so been looking forward to taking on the production duties.

'Don't be too pissed off. He's famous for changing his mind. When he comes on a visit, you can use your famous charm to change his mind back.'

Jim looked mischievously at her, arching an eyebrow.

'So, who will run the operation, then?'

'Ewen Mackenzie, a man who hoards toilet rolls and manages the Gali mine next door, will take over. He usually does when I am away. You'll work with him.'

'A man who what?'

'He hoards toilet rolls. He has dozens of them.'

'To be honest, I don't think that's an odd thing to do, considering the erratic supply. Toilet paper, soap, toothpaste, coffee and tea are all running out.'

'That's true. The latest container of supplies is being held for ransom by the customs agents in Mondongo, and Black hates to pay a bribe. Anyway, Ewen's okay, really. He doesn't say much unless he's pretty drunk, and then he mumbles and his Scots accent gets worse. He's a big hit with the ladies.'

'Just my luck.'

'You'll have to move into a room in my house because Jorge's wife is arriving in Kardo to stay. They are going to move her into your house.'

'What?'

'Again, I'm sorry. The truth is that Jorge isn't entitled to his own house as a mining foreman, but his long service to the company and his indispensable talents have earned him favours with Black that annoy many of the other senior staff, not just you. Jorge's wife has decided that since Jorge is retiring soon, she wants to make sure that none of the girls get their claws into her husband at the last minute, robbing her of her pension. I don't blame her, but it means that you'll have to live with Ewen. To make matters worse for you, Black is due to arrive in Kardo shortly after I leave, so you'll be living with him as well, as his room is always kept ready in my house.'

Sam covered her horror at the change in her living arrangements with the best grace she could muster. She realised that it would only be until Jim came back and it wasn't his fault. Instead of going to the terraces, they stopped at the recovery plant so that Jim could gloat over the diamond production.

'I've got some news for you that may sweeten the bitter pill you've had to swallow. There were five-thousand carats in the picking cabinet. It is a new record production for one day's picking, and they hadn't even finished all the concentrate yet.'

'Wow, so that confirms one hundred per cnet bonuses for the staff of Kardo. That's great news.'

'Not just for them. The accounts have decided that since you're at Kardo, you will also receive a pro-rata bonus.'

Sam felt something approaching ecstasy. She could imagine the money stacking up in her bank account in London with great clarity, and that was motivation enough for her to keep trying to stick out the six months.

'Thank you, Jim. I'm so happy.'

'You're welcome.'

That evening, Sam was reading about Paul Theroux in Oceania when the doorbell rang. She had a delivery. It was one of the clerks from administration with her portable stereo and the rest of her music CDs sent from Mondongo. She hadn't managed to take everything with her the last time, but Pedro had sent Sam her stuff before going on leave. She suddenly felt much better. She got a note from Pedro. He said he'd miss her while he was on leave (again). *Okay, Pedro, one brownie point for the stereo.*

Lying on the sofa listening to music that evening, she got her first mosquito bite. She usually sprayed herself with repellent from head to foot in the evening because half of the mosquitoes in Kardo carried malaria. She was annoyed at herself for forgetting. The prevalence of malaria in the town was evidenced by the number of working days lost to it. No one else at Gemsite took any precautions against malaria at all. They all wore shorts, didn't take any medicine and slept without mosquito nets. Sam suspected that malaria was the only way they could get any time off work, so they didn't mind getting it. Almost the first thing that she was told when she got to Mondongo was 'You will get malaria. We all get it sooner or later.'

The only protection offered by the company was some useless low-grade repellent, issued to them when it was available, and that was all. It was worse than useless against cerebral malaria. Sam had brought some jungle grade repellent containing fifty per cent DEET from the UK, and she could almost hear the mosquitos veering away when they smelt it on her. She went to shower and watched the red dust run off her body like blood down the plughole. Hitchcock would have loved it.

After her shower, she managed to get decent reception of the World Service news broadcast. It did not make her feel any safer. MARFO's representative had been suspended from the Tamazian government, and the Tamazian military was attacking rebel bases not far from Kardo in the east of the country. This might make them safer, but it was still worrying.

In Kardo, all was peaceful and calm. Jim was the most relaxed general manager of the Gemsite mines when it came to free time. On Sundays when a lot of maintenance was going on, and the machinery had to be shut down, he often let the staff have a day off. The only choices for entertainment during their free time were drinking, watching the single television, or fishing. The television was used almost exclusively for watching sports, the choice of the football match being made by the most senior person present, often Jim, who supported Liverpool. This caused conflict with the South African crew, who preferred rugby.

Theoretically, no one was allowed to go fishing because it was thought to compromise diamond security, but Jim turned a blind eye. Fishing parties always contained members of the internal security personnel, so it was unlikely anyone would try to look for a diamond with that sort of supervision. Also, the chances of finding one were minuscule.

The first Sunday after she returned from Mondongo, Dirk and Sam borrowed a truck and went fishing at Gali. They stopped at one of the river terraces where hippopotamus tracks crossed the dykes. The sun burned off the few clouds that dared float by. The still lagoons at Gali were glistening gold and green. Long reeds stood stiff in the damp banks. Massive dragonflies flew through the air and settled on the banks, the reeds and each other, stacking up like aircraft outside Heathrow.

Sam sat on a stone and did some painting, while Dirk thrashed around in the undergrowth along the riverbank, casting with vigour and resembling the tigerfish he was trying to catch. After missing two or three bites, he caught a small tigerfish that she used as a model for a painting.

'Wow, that's very beautiful. It has a mouth like a piranha. They could bite through fishing line.'

'You don't know the half of it,' said Dirk. 'They can grow up to two metres.'

She placed the fish on a cooler and copied it on a piece of paper. She painted the sea-green, bluish sheen of its scales and its pearl white belly. She concentrated on getting the brown fins shading to strong yellow and then bright scarlet at the tips. She made the ragged ends of the fins look like those on Siamese fighting fish.

Dirk went further along the bank, and Sam did more painting. When she put down her brush, she focused on her surroundings. She was sitting on a mud beach at the river's edge. There were a series of crocodile prints in the mud underneath her seat, ranging from tiny cute ones to very big not-at-all-cute ones. *What if a big crocodile had crept up on her as she sat absorbed in her paintings and taken her into the water? Shit.*

She stood up and walked to the pickup truck. When Dirk came back carrying a small catfish, which was hissing and spluttering in fury, she was leaning on the bonnet smoking one of his cigarettes, ready to leap into the pickup at the slightest noise.

'You okay?' he said.

'Yes, I was sitting on a bank with some massive crocodile prints on it. Gave me a hell of a fright.'

'They do say that no one sees the crocodile that gets them.'

'That's not really very reassuring.'

'Ha! I know. I was just kidding.'

'Not funny.'

He grabbed her and gave her a squeeze. Sam was planning on consummating her platonic relationship with Dirk. It would be less difficult to sleep if she had a man in her bed.

It would be nice to have regular sex, even with someone she suspected would make love like a jackrabbit. She had to stifle a giggle the first time she thought about it. At least someone liked her. No need to put him off too. Being with Dirk would also chase away the isolation she felt in the office where she had almost nothing to do. Black had dropped her right in it by not giving her an official role at Kardo. She had no set duties and no status in the group, giving her colleagues ample opportunity to snub her attempts to get involved in production work.

As they got back into the pickup, two little boys appeared out of the reeds at the side of the road. They were thin and dirty with dusty hair. She called out to the boys, who were standing frozen in panic on the red dirt track.

'Bom dia.'

They both chorused it back, flashing big, scared smiles, but they looked like they were ready to run away at any moment. The smaller boy was tugging at the larger boy's arm in agitation. Sam now recognised them as the boys who often stood outside the canteen and begged for food. She had developed a habit of dropping food by mistake as she left after lunch. She knew they recognised her too, but they showed no inclination to approach.

'What's wrong with them?' she said.

'Nothing. Just scared.'

'But why?'

'They can get beaten for being on the concession area.'

'What are they doing here?'

'Jorge told me that the adults use them for mining the vertical tunnels or shafts into the bottom gravel where the diamonds are. The shafts bell out at the bottom to take the maximum gravel possible out of the same shaft. Being small makes it easier to excavate the gravel out to the sides of the vertical shaft and under the barren gravels.'

'Jesus. Isn't that incredibly dangerous?'

'The tunnels collapse all the time. Sometimes the kids manage to scramble out, and sometimes they're buried alive.'

'Poor little buggers. That's dreadful. They look so thin. Give me the fish.'

'Black doesn't like us to feed them. We could get in trouble.'

'I'll take the blame. Remember, I'm an ignorant newcomer and have no idea we can't give food to the locals.'

Dirk took the fish out of his bag and handed them to Sam. They had lost their colour and didn't look very appetising. The small catfish was still alive. It squirmed and hissed and almost wriggled out of her grasp. She proffered the fish to the boys. They looked suspiciously at them and took a couple of steps forward.

'For you,' said Sam in Portuguese.

The larger of the boys darted forward and grabbed the fish. They ran off a short distance and then stopped and looked backwards. She beamed at them and waved.

'Obrigado,' yelled the older boy, and they scampered off, their bare feet flapping in the muddy road, sending streams of red mud up their skinny legs.

***

In Mondongo, General Fuego had been summoned for a drink at the President's house. They met in the President's study with a view of the city stretching out below the window. The two men sat in leather armchairs, which had been designed for bigger men. They sighed in appreciation, even as they both struggled to reach their glasses of whisky perched on the glass coffee table between the chairs. General Fuego was the first to break the convivial silence.

'So, how can I help you, Mr President?'

'I still need those diamond production numbers. I want you to get me information about Gemsite from that woman. I'm sure she knows what the numbers are by now. She's a geologist, isn't she?'

'Yes, I believe so. I'm having a lunch party next weekend at my beach house. I believe that there is an export on Friday. Perhaps I can invite Sam to stay at the beach?'

'Now that's more like it. I don't know what possible objection she could have to staying at a nice house with high-class people and eating delicious food.'

'It'll be a lot better than the muck they eat at Kardo. That's for sure. I know she likes lobster. I'll buy some fresh ones.'

'And pour drink down her throat, Fuego. Flatter her, seduce her—I don't care how you do it. I want to know what those bastards are hiding. There is nothing honest about our Mr Black, and I want to know what's going on.'

'If Sam comes on Friday, I'll get Eduardo to pick her up from the bank when she deposits the diamonds.'

'Excellent. So how about another whisky? My wife has made some excellent cod stew for us too.'

***

A production party was held at the prefabs where the workers lived, to celebrate the one hundred per cent bonus earned for the diamond production achieved in August. Greys Security had run over a large crocodile which had crossed the road in front of them at Tunde the night before. They had to shoot it due to its injuries, so there were croc steak sandwiches in the bar that night.

When faced with the choice between a tender, if ripe, fillet steak and fried onion butty and a tough overcooked piece of ancient crocodile, Sam's hunger got the better of her curiosity. There were plenty of takers for the crocodile. Some people were still chewing when they went to bed.

The girls were organising silly games, including one in which they snatched carrots tied around the men's waists in a rude version of musical chairs. Everyone got drunk, and Dirk started to get jealous and grumpy when some of the drunker members of the management team forgot that they had to all intents and purposes sent Sam to Coventry, and started flirting and trying to get her to dance with them.

Sam called Dirk over and started to whisper in his ear. She was feeling horny and had decided they had procrastinated quite long enough. Dirk cheered up, and a smug expression appeared on his face. He tried to kiss her, but Sam moved out of the way. Public displays of affection were definitely taboo. She had started to feel good all of a sudden. Dutch courage was having its effect. Jorge had been watching her from one of the tables and came over in a determined manner.

'I need to talk to you. Now.'

'For God's sake, now is not a good time. Let's do this tomorrow, okay?'

Sam wasn't in the mood for a lecture and muttered 'tomorrow' in Portuguese a couple more times but Jorge would not be put off. He pulled Sam away from the party and sat her down on the steps to the porch of one of the nearby houses.

'Sam,' he said, 'I'm sorry to drag you away from the party, but I have to tell you something right now.'

'Can't it wait?'

'No, I'm afraid it can't. I wanted to tell you sooner, but I wasn't sure how far it had gone.'

'How far what had gone? What are you talking about?'

'It's Dirk. Have you slept with him?'

'No, but I was about to when you called me over.'

'You mustn't. It would be a mistake.'

Sam was not sober, and she totally misinterpreted Jorge's motives.

'I like Dirk, and I don't like you. Not that way, anyway. You can't stop me. I'm a grown-up.' She tried to flounce off. Jorge grabbed her arm.

'No, you don't understand,' he pleaded. 'I'm trying to stop you from getting hurt.'

'Hurt? I don't think it's any of your business.'

'Oh, it is. I have a bet on you.'

'What did you say?'

'They're running a book on who will sleep with you first and when. Dirk stands to win a lot of money if he sleeps with you. He doesn't really like you. He just wants to win the bet.'

Sam froze, and Jorge waited for her to talk. She sat down again, hard. She looked up at Jorge, tears filling her eyes. 'He has a bet on himself?'

'Yes, and he expects to win it tonight. He's been telling everyone who will listen.'

Jorge could hardly look Sam in the eye. Her hard-won confidence evaporated away like the water off a boiled egg. She stood up wobbling with drink.

'Thanks,' she said. 'Nice to know who your friends are. I'm going to give him a Glasgow kiss.'

'A kiss?'

'Not that sort of kiss, Jorge. You'll see.'

Sam stomped back across to the party. She pushed her way into a throng of people near the drinks table. Dirk was standing there talking to one of the local girls. He looked up, and a lazy smile crossed his face. He stumbled over to Sam.

'Are you ready to go now?'

Sam tried to headbutt him but swayed at the crucial moment and hit his shoulder with her forehead.

'Ow!' he shouted. 'What the hell?'

'You bastard. I thought you were my friend.'

He looked dazed. 'But I am.'

'No, you're not. You're a pig like all the others. I hate you.'

'But what have I done?'

Then the expression on his face turned from surprise to remorse just when Sam was wavering. 'Bastard,' she said again and dredged up the dignity to leave the field of battle without another word. Her withdrawal didn't cause any comment, as everyone was too drunk to notice what had just happened. Feelings of betrayal wrenched her guts. *I really fell for that old trick?* What an idiot. One thing was for sure now. She did have a friend in Kardo, but it wasn't Dirk.

They won't ever defeat me. Never, ever, ever.

Chapter XI

The next morning, Sam felt like she'd been hit by a train. The combination of the drink and the shame was not ideal, as she had to get up before dawn to go down to the recovery plant to do the diamond export to Mondongo again. She did not have much to do in Kardo, so sending her to Mondongo with the diamonds prevented one of the security men, who were in short supply, from going instead. She had to do whatever was necessary to stay in Black's good books. Everything she did got back to him. She also needed to get out of camp to avoid seeing Dirk.

'Jim, I'm a bit shattered. Do you think that I could take Saturday off in Mondongo to see the sights?' she said, as they hung around waiting for SDM.

'Sure,' Jim laughed. 'And you won't need a whole day for that.' he said. 'Off with you then, and don't do anything I wouldn't do.'

Sam didn't think there was much chance of that, seeing as her only hope for a bit of entertainment, Pedro, was on leave, and she didn't know when he would be back. However, the prospect of a nice day at the beach with some of the Villa Alice boys cheered her up.

The SDM representatives arrived on time, and they

finished the weigh-up and put the diamonds in the small safe for transportation to Mondongo. They all got into their respective vehicles in the convoy and shot off to the airport with the usual pandemonium ensuing. As soon as they got there, they were ushered onto the plane and strapped in, and the doors were locked.

The plane started taxiing up the runway for take-off. Sam felt the anticipation in her stomach and held on to the edges of her seat. Then the engines cut out, and the co-pilot came through the small door from the flight deck.

'We can't take off yet, I'm afraid. The President is at Mondongo airport on his way to South Africa. The airport is closed to other flights when the president is passing through because of the intense security surrounding him. We have to wait until they are sure he has left.'

A collective groan echoed around the cabin. The aircraft sat on the ground for an hour and a half, a sitting target on the runway at Kardo. There were no security guards at the airport. They had all left after delivering Sam and her companions to the aircraft. The plane was carrying more diamonds than usual because of the record production. *I hope MARFO rebels are not in the vicinity. This would be too tempting to miss.*

Her mood was not improved by the fact that they were being broiled in the airless cargo hold, and they had nothing to drink. At last, the co-pilot informed them that the President had left Mondongo and that the airport was once again open. The engines started up again, and they took off for Mondongo. It was a pretty bumpy flight, and the SDM man beside Sam almost lost his breakfast beers.

They arrived at Mondongo at midday to find that

the trucks of security men, who should have met them on the tarmac, had left to eat lunch. They stood on the ground with their cargo beside them for ten minutes, while the security guards were radioed to come back. Sam felt vulnerable and scared. There were a lot of armed men wandering around on the tarmac, and Sam and the SDM men had a safe at their feet. She didn't want to die for some crummy bits of broken glass. Diamonds may be a girl's best friend in theory, but in practice, she preferred her best friends to be less life-threatening.

The troops returned after a short time, but Sam was panicky by then. They all got into the jeep sandwiched between the pickups full of security men and set off in a convoy for the bank. By the time they arrived at the bank an hour later, the staff were all back from lunch. The handover of the diamonds at the bank went as planned, and soon Sam came out of the bank to find Eduardo waiting for her. He greeted her and said simply, 'The General is waiting for you on the Island. He would like you to stay the night with him and his guests.'

Sam was taken aback by the request. She wasn't big on protocol, and she was pretty sure Black would not have approved of this development, but she didn't see how she could turn down an invitation from the brother-in-law of the President. General Fuego was rumoured to have a nice colonial beach house on a private island. That sounded like heaven after Kardo. Besides, she might learn useful things that she could tell Black and garner brownie points if there were ministers amongst the guests.

'I would love to come. It would be an honour,' she said, and followed him to the car, which was air conditioned, and felt like chilly heaven compared to the sweltering streets of Mondongo.

'Can you please stop at the Villa Alice on our way out of town? I don't have any suitable clothing in my bag for a social weekend,' she said.

'Of course, my lady. Anything for you,' said Eduardo.

They soon pulled into the cul-de-sac where the villa was located. Sam didn't ask him how he knew where the Villa Alice was located. Eduardo seemed to know everything.

'I'll be about fifteen minutes,' she said, and dashed inside.

She knew just what she was going to wear on this escapade. She had stashed a bag of more glamorous city wear in a cupboard, which she now raided for a couple of summer dresses and a swimming costume. *No need to look like a geologist all your life*. She had a quick shower and changed into one of the dresses. She didn't have a mirror, but she could tell she'd lost a few pounds in Kardo by the ease with which the dress slipped over her hips.

Eduardo looked her up and down with approval when she emerged from the Villa twenty minutes later, her hair still wet and a tight cotton floral stretchy dress on. She beamed at his reaction. They drove down the coast for about an hour, and then they pulled in beside a small jetty opposite a low sandy island with a colonial-type house on the shore. Eduardo emptied the contents of the car into a motorboat moored at the jetty.

'Get in,' he gestured to Sam.

She hopped aboard, hesitating just a moment as she realised that she was going to be trapped on an island with lots of people she didn't know and a man whose motives she hadn't figured out yet. However, having worked with men-only crews most of her life,

Sam knew how to hold her own in a house full of testosterone. The lure of decent food was too much for her, having seen a lot of fresh produce being loaded onto the boat.

They flew over the top of the waves and soon pulled into an identical jetty on the small island parallel to the shore. Some members of the General's staff were waiting to help her up from the boat and show her to the house. The General was waiting on the steps to the porch. He gazed at Sam with her windswept hair and flowery dress like he was trying to recognise her. A twinkle appeared in his eye.

'Don't they feed you in that place?'

'Not much that I want to eat.'

'I hope we can tempt your palate this evening. I bought some fresh lobsters; I know you like lobster. I bought three just for you.'

'Three? Three for me? I don't think I can eat three.'

'I thought you were macha. Don't let me down now. I'm counting on you.'

Sam laughed. She was going to enjoy herself on a diet of lobster and flattery.

'The Ministers for Mining and Petroleum are here and they have both come with their wives. Two of my daughters are also with us, so you should have fun.'

She beamed at the thought of having some friendly women to talk to. The monosyllabic conversations she was having in Kardo, despite all her efforts, were wearing her down. The General told one of the members of his staff to show her to her room and left to entertain his guests.

Dinner was great fun. Sam sat down at the women's end of the table and joined in the banter with the daughters and wives. The husbands all sat at the other end of the table, trying in vain to have a sensible conversation but failing as the women made merry and flirted with them. Sam managed to eat two and a half small lobsters, which elicited a round of applause.

After dinner, the General invited Sam to have coffee with him at the end of the front balcony looking out over the sea. He offered her a Cuban cigar, which she refused, and a cigarette that she didn't. They sat looking at the waves breaking on the beach.

'So how is work?' said the General.

'Oh, pretty tough and lonely,' replied Sam with a big sigh.

She remembered with horrible clarity how close she had come to humiliation with Dirk and the nasty sneering the night they shunned her in the bar.

'I don't think they like me very much in Kardo,' she said.

Her voice broke, and she started to cry. Despite her embarrassment at this unexpected turn of events, she was unable to stop. The dam had burst. The General reached out and put his hand over hers, and waited until she managed to control her sobs, then he handed over an immaculate handkerchief, its pristine whiteness a testament to the quality of his laundry staff. Sam blew her nose into it.

'I'm so sorry,' she said. 'I wasn't expecting that.'

'Neither was I. My charm does not often have such a catastrophic effect on young ladies.'

'Do you mind if we don't talk about Kardo?'

Sam missed the fleeting look of irritation that passed over the General's face.

'What would you like to talk about?'

'Well, I hope it's not an imposition. You told me that you were in Cuba with Castro and Che Guevara. Do you mind telling me about it?'

'Not at all. You realise that Imelda, who you were talking to this evening, is the daughter of my Cuban wife Carmen?'

'No, I didn't know that.'

The General excused himself for a minute and returned with two large glasses, a bottle of scotch and some more cigarettes.

'We may be here for a while,' he said.

***

The next morning, Sam stayed in bed and was served a sumptuous breakfast with some coffee that she could almost stand a spoon in. She had no hangover, perhaps due to the quality of the whisky or all the food she had eaten. The Minister of Mines had been pretty impressed that she spoke Portuguese, even if her grammar was a bit ropey. She had noticed that he kept trying to steer the conversation around to the production in the mine, but Sam had been careful to keep her answers vague like Jim had told her before. The truth was that no one knew about production figures except Black, Fred and Jim. Only Black knew about the bottom line.

As far as she could remember, she hadn't gone into any details at all. Not even after a couple of whiskies with the General. The last part of the evening was a little murky, but she did remember him escorting her to her room and kissing her goodnight on the cheek. She blushed again as she remembered bursting into tears. No wonder they thought she was useless and weak at Kardo. The water pipes at Kardo were less leaky than poor old sensitive Sam.

***

Downstairs, the three men were having a quiet breakfast.

'I don't think she knows anything,' said the Minister of Mines.

'I'm sure she doesn't know anything about diamond production,' said the Minister of Petroleum. 'Did you get anything out of her, Fuego?'

The Minister of Mines snorted. General Fuego ignored him.

'No, I didn't. She burst into tears when I tried to find out more about the Kardo operation. Perhaps she's not as senior as we imagined.'

'I thought she was Black's direct employee. How come she doesn't know anything about the diamond production numbers? I'm sure she must see the figures.'

'Gentlemen, as we are well aware, Mr Black is paranoid. I don't think his girlfriend knows his first name.'

'What is his first name?'

'I don't know,' the General deadpanned.

'So did you get anything out of her or not, Fuego?'

'I don't know what you mean,' he replied and winked. Both of the other men guffawed.

'You dog, Fuego; I knew you weren't interested in production. She is kind of cute, though, in a gringa sort of way.'

'The President is going to kill me.'

They all mused on this as they drank their coffee.

***

The General crossed from the island with Sam in the boat and insisted on driving her back to Mondongo by himself at a never less than hair-raising speed. Sam tried not to notice, but she could see Eduardo wincing in the back of the car. When they reached the centre of town, they stopped at a little coffee shop near the Gemsite office, and Eduardo stayed with the car. The site not only had milky coffees made from UHT milk but also Portuguese custard tarts.

The General ordered six, telling Sam that if they didn't eat them all, she could take one on the flight as a snack. He asked her how she came to work for Gemsite and proved himself such a good listener that Sam found herself telling him about the Dirk debacle. She was so desperate for someone to talk to, and she didn't think talking about Dirk was a betrayal of confidence. The General waited for her to stop speaking and smiled gently at her.

'Ah, my dear, you have made the mistake of choosing a younger man. In my opinion, you should look at someone a little more mature.'

'You mean vintage, like a good wine?'

'Yes, that's exactly what I mean.'

He gave her a mischievous smile and told her that he had to go. Sam refused a lift to Villa Alice and kissed him goodbye.

'See you soon,' he said.

After the General had left, Sam walked around the corner to the office where she would find someone on duty. She needed to know when the flight was due to take off for Kardo. To her surprise, it was Pedro who came to the door. He had a face like thunder when he saw it was her. Sam was miffed that he didn't notice her dress.

'So, Pedro, welcome back. Did you enjoy your break?'

'I see you've been busy while I've been away.'

'Busy? What do you mean?'

'Are you the General's whore now?' He was

purple with rage and quivering with the fury of a man who imagined himself scorned.

'What? How can you even ask me that? Are you on drugs?'

'Don't play the innocent with me. I saw you cosy up to him in the café.'

'I was having a coffee, and I didn't cosy up, not that it's any of your business. Who do you think you are, anyway? The sex police?'

'I thought we had an arrangement.'

'An arrangement?'

'You know what I mean. I sent you your stereo.'

'My stereo? What's that got to do with anything?'

But it was becoming clear that Pedro was suffering from a dangerous fit of jealousy. He must have attached far more importance to sending her a note than she had. She stood her ground with her hands on her hips. Pedro was not finished.

'How could you be such a fool? Do you really think a five-star General has the slightest interest in a two-bit gringa like you? Are you an idiot? Your only value to him is as a spy. Black will be livid when he finds out. You'll be fired for sure.'

'I haven't done anything wrong. I don't have any access to that sort of information. Anyway, he didn't even ask me anything about diamonds. Why would Black want to fire me?'

But even as she said it, she knew he was right. She had been very foolish to accept the invitation. But the temptation of good food and company was too strong after the weeks of misery at Kardo. She didn't have any information for them. *But why else would they invite me to the island?* It's not like she was a friend of the family or anything. The Ministers did seem to ask a lot of questions she couldn't answer about production and operations at the mine. The General had even engineered that private chat with her to talk about Kardo, but she had ruined his plans by bursting into tears.

It was all pretty clear to her now. Another humiliation for Sam. Was she so naïve when she thought no one would mind if she went to the island if she didn't have anything to tell? She decided on damage limitation.

'What are you going to do? You're the only one who knows. Please don't tell anyone. I don't even like the General.'

'I thought you liked me.'

'I did. I do. I didn't feel I had any choice. I was practically kidnapped. How could I fancy an old man like that when I had you here in the office?'

She touched his arm to lower the tension. Pedro appeared to be mollified by this. He moved closer to her and lifted up her chin.

'I was thinking about you on my break. I thought we would be a couple when I got back. I brought you a present. Sorry I overreacted. Maybe if you come back to the Villa Alice with me, we could fill in the time before the flight. We could have a couple of beers and hang out in my room.'

Sam was trapped. He had her backed into a corner. If she refused, he would take revenge, and if she didn't, he might blackmail her from now on. She played for time.

'I thought the flight was at six o'clock? Maybe we could do it next time I'm in town with more time. We could do dinner?'

But Pedro was not to be denied.

'No fuel. It is delayed until eight. Come on. I'll give you a lift right now. You look hot in that dress, by the way.'

'Okay, I need to repack my things anyway.'

'I'll take off your dress for you.'

***

When they arrived at the airport, there was no plane on the tarmac. An aircraft taxied up half an hour later, and they filled the tanks with diesel for delivery to Kardo. To Sam's dismay, they also took the cover off one of the engines and started to do maintenance or repair work on it. They sat in the mini-van in a cloud of mosquitoes waiting until late evening when the cover went back on. There was no point trying to drive back to Villa Alice in the appalling traffic jams that characterised Mondongo's evenings.

Sam avoided speaking to Pedro by pretending to sleep through all this but on leaving the mini-van, she had to kiss him goodbye.

'See you soon, I hope,' he said.

'Not if I see you first,' she muttered under her breath, and she got on the plane, clutching the lurid pink teddy bear that Pedro had given her at the house, which proved that he had no idea who he was dealing with. There was nothing Sam hated more than fluffy toys, above all pink ones.

Sam had plenty of time to think on the cold cargo plane to Kardo. She felt dirty and used. How could she get herself in such a horrible situation? It was bad enough feeling forced to have sex with Pedro, who fucked her like a battering ram with about as much emotion. Pride restored, he was magnanimous and drove her to the airport. Aside from that horrible memory, which she would expunge as soon as she could, she knew in her heart that Pedro was right. *What would a General want with someone like me? A mere geologist? What had I been thinking? Why am I so bad at reading people's motives?*

It was another disaster, and she wasn't sure she could trust Pedro to keep it to himself. She didn't want to imagine the sort of fit that Black would have if he found out. He might have a stroke and die. Unfortunately, there was not much hope of that. Pedro needed to be manipulated and kept at arm's length on her next visit to Mondongo, with the likelihood that he might again demand payment for his silence. This job was a bloody nightmare and getting worse and worse.

The only person in the country that she could trust was Jorge, and maybe Black, because in a strange way, Sam thought she might grow to like Black despite his despotic ways. She shifted in her seat, trying not to focus on her bruised pride and nether regions. At least things couldn't get much worse and with the one hundred per cent bonuses that were available, she could afford to cut the contract short if things got any worse.

They arrived at Kardo with a big thud that almost wrested the fuel tanks out of their bindings. Sam imagined being hit in the back of the head by one of them. A driver appeared out of the gloom and ferried her home.

Chapter XII

The next day, the handover of duties between Jim, who was going on leave for two weeks, and Ewen Mackenzie, head of the Gali project, took place. Ewen was a tall taciturn Scot with white-blonde hair and blue eyes in a well-used face. Jim had told Sam that he was a big hit with the ladies but he didn't try charming her. In fact, he didn't direct a phrase her way all day.

Ewen took over Jim's radio and his car, which Sam had been expecting to do, even though he already had a car and a radio from Gali where he was general manager. Sam had been looking forward to bombing around the project without having to hitch a lift with someone who had a pickup, checking on things and hanging out. Now, she had to stay in the office or go with dour Ewen. *Why couldn't he bring his own car? What am I going to do while Jim is away? Worse still, what was going to happen when Black arrived?*

Sam dreaded Black's arrival, and she wasn't alone. She cheered herself up by giving the horrible pink bear that Pedro had gifted her to the little boys begging for food outside the canteen. They were so excited it almost made it worth the ordeal she went through to obtain it. The smaller boy hugged it close, his eyes bright with tears. Sam had to look away when she felt her own eyes swelling.

Jim left the next day, looking forward to his holiday and taking another large haul of diamonds to the bank. The pothole had produced epic numbers of high-value stones. Sam felt bereft. Jim had been good to her and generous with his experience. No one else had thawed yet. She rang her father using the satellite phone in the Kardo office. Most of the precious thirty minutes allocated were spent repeating what had already been said but not deciphered.

She complained about the crap satellite telephone in the canteen at lunchtime. To her surprise, Bob muttered, 'There's a landline in the office.'

'A landline? Can I make international calls on it?'

The other senior managers glared at him but he ploughed on.

'The landline can receive international calls. There's a roster in the evenings. You can book half an hour of phone time by writing in the roster book.'

'But how do people know what time you've booked?'

'That's where the satellite phone comes in. You phone your family on the sat phone and tell them when they should call you, and hope they remember.'

'Thank you.'

He looked sheepish and stared down at his plate. Sam wondered if he was trying to mend some bridges with her.

After lunch, Sam dug out the landline roster and used the satellite telephone to book a slot with her mother, which she wrote into the roster. *Why has no one told me about this before?* Murphy and his spy story had a lot to answer for.

On the positive side, the handover turned out to be far better than she had imagined. Ewen had changed tack since Jim had left and involved Sam in his decision making. Maybe Ewen had been waiting for Jim to leave before letting her take on some of the work. He didn't seem to realise Sam was a pariah, or maybe he didn't care. He just wanted to share the responsibilities of running the mine with someone who was competent, and he had read her résumé.

He discussed production with her in great detail and asked her opinion on how to spread the bounty over the next couple of months to increase people's bonus payments. It was great to be treated as one of the team. There were glares from the others, but no one wanted to try to include Ewen in their clique. She didn't know why, but he also seemed to be excluded.

To her relief, Jorge was the same as ever and even gave her a big hug. He never mentioned the bet or the consequences. Sam was glad she didn't have to discuss the near debacle at the party. No one had asked her about her weekend, so she didn't have to invent any lies.

'Why isn't Ewen one of the boys? Did he do something wrong?' she said.

'I'm not sure. It's quite strange, really. Did you know that he was one of the hostages taken by MARFO during the civil war in 1992?' said Jorge.

'I had no idea. What happened?'

'They were force-marched a thousand miles before being handed over to the Red Cross. They weren't fed on the trip and suffered unbelievable hardships. I heard rumours Ewen had killed a snake on the trip and hidden it up his sleeve for three days before he could eat it in secret, by which time it was putrid.'

'That's incredible. I can't believe they still give him the cold shoulder after that ordeal. It's weird.'

'I'm not sure what it's about. Ewen is a bit odd. He

doesn't care if people don't like him.'

Later, Sam asked Ewen why he came back to Tamazia after what had happened to him, and he squirmed about on his seat before answering.

'I know it sounds odd but Tamazia is addictive, and I love working here.'

'Aren't you afraid that the MARFO rebels might attack?'

'Oh, I doubt it. We have excellent security here. There are easier places to attack.'

She went out with Ewen and Jorge all morning checking out the river diversions and showing Ewen all the works that were going on. She sat in the back of the car, while Jorge prattled on, telling stories and trying to make Ewen laugh, which was quite a challenge. She sensed hidden depths in his reticence to join in, but they stayed that way.

After lunch, she went to Jim's house to get his radio, which Ewen had decided that he didn't need after all. Ewen came to the door in his socks with the radio and the charger and handed her the car key.

'Off ye go then with Ramos,' he said.

She must have beamed as she got a wee smile back.

She went with Jorge in Jim's death-trap Nissan, which still didn't drive in a straight line but danced down the gravel roads with its bum swinging wildly from side to side like a dancer in the Rio Carnival. It was fun and liberating to be given the chance. She could get to like Ewen. He was as hands-off as Jim was hands-on. Chalk and cheese sprung to mind. She realised she had been influenced by Jim's jaundiced view of Ewen, just like many people appeared to have preconceived notions about her.

She tried to get Fred, the geologist, to come with

them to see the river diversions, but he refused on the grounds that he was 'busy.' Fred's geology room was often locked while Jim was away. He had taken up with one of the local village girls who offered herself for sale. Sam was sure she was only about fourteen, but like most of the men who thought they were 'helping' by paying underage girls for sex, Fred couldn't see anything wrong with it.

He didn't get to bed most nights until dawn, so Sam guessed that he often sneaked off for a sleep at lunchtime. He would always pitch up late in the afternoon, sighing and flopping about like a beached catfish and talking about being down at the terrace, which was being mined at the time. Sam was sure he was lying. She would have spotted him at some stage if he had ever been there at all. He was very large and not easy to miss.

It was becoming obvious that he didn't bother with the truth at the best of times. He wasn't too pleased that Ewen had put her in charge of production. *Maybe he had expected a temporary promotion?* She couldn't help that. She really tried to get Fred to work with her. She showed a lot of interest in his work and tried to get involved. Despite what Black had said in Johannesburg, it was the expatriate males who didn't want to work with her, not the locals. It had always been her problem. She wasn't surprised, but she was disappointed that things had changed so little.

At lunchtime, Sam heard the news that MARFO had shot down a military transport plane, killing twenty-four people to the north of Kardo. She hoped that they could tell the difference between a military plane and a TransTamazia flight, as she was due to fly a lot in the coming weeks. *I should have bought a parachute before I left the UK.*

Her call home had been scheduled for three o'clock. She shut herself into the office with the phone and waited. True to form, her mother rang on time. Sam grabbed the receiver and thrust it to her ear.

'Hello?'

'Hello,' said her mother. 'Can I speak to Sam Harris?'

'Hi, Mummy. It's me.'

'Hello darling. How's Mondongo?'

Sam hesitated.

'Oh, busy, you know. I don't really have any news.'

'The line's not very good. It was clear as a bell last time.'

'Nothing around here works consistently. I expect it's just static.'

'Have you been to the tennis club yet?'

'No, it's the rainy season here and the clay courts are quagmires. I'll just have to wait.'

'But you are all right? Your voice sounds funny.'

'Yes, I'm fine. Just tired. We work long days.'

There was a pause.

'I saw on the news that MARFO shot down a plane in Tamazia,' said her mother.

'Don't worry about that. It was nowhere near our mines. It's perfectly safe here.'

'Okay, but you should come home if it gets worse.'

'I promise. Give my love to Daddy.'

'I will, sweetheart.'

Sam put down the phone. She felt bad lying to her mother, but she didn't want to worry her. She would come clean when she got home. What they didn't know couldn't harm them.

While Jim was away, Sam had to learn the radio codes so that she could contact all sections of the mine.

She was 'Office Two' or production manager, until Jim got back. All day, she could hear people talking on the radio with the ubiquitous 'over' at the end of every sentence. She did a lot of coordinating and went with Ewen to the diamond recovery plant to check on the progress of the Tunde material that was being processed.

'How do they decide which materials to process?' she asked Ewen.

'All three mines, Kardo, Gali and Tunde, share the processing facilities, so there is intense competition for picking time at the end of the month. All the mines are trying to fill their quotas of diamonds and win bonuses for good production.'

'Doesn't that cause disputes?'

'Oh, yes. There is a tendency to process any old material in the vain hope of reaching the bonus figures before cut-off day. This causes resentment between the mines who have good material to process and those that are scrambling around in the dirt and tying up the recovery plant with low-grade material.'

Black was due to arrive from Mondongo at any time and there was an atmosphere of dread in camp.

'Black should arrive any day now.' said Jorge.

'Yes, I'm a bit nervous,' she confessed.

'He likes to drink,' said Jorge. 'And he likes his management to drink with him. We don't get to lie in the next morning like he does, more's the pity. His visits can be a bit of an ordeal.'

At midnight, the doorbell rang. Drugged by sleep, she threw on some clothes and went to the door. Jim's car was parked right up close to the outside door. In the moonlight, she could see Marybelle, Black's girlfriend, on the steps to her house, swaying like a reed in the wind. Out on the road, Sam could see the figures of Black and Ewen talking to the occupants of another jeep. Black looked like a pantomime bumblebee in profile with a yellow and black striped rugby shirt on his rotund body, balanced on tottering legs in shorts.

They didn't talk to her at all, leaving her standing at the door in her pyjamas. Finally, Sam said, 'Good evening, gentlemen. Did you come in on the flight tonight?

'Yes, we did, last minute,' said Marybelle.

'Is this important? Can I do anything for you?'

'Oh, no, we're all just drunk. We thought you might like a drink too.'

'No thanks. Night-night, then.'

Sam went back to bed before they could protest, and she fought for sleep for far too long before drifting off.

She had to get up before dawn to go to the diamond sorting plant, so her midnight visitors were not popular. Since Jim was on leave and the chief metallurgist wasn't back yet due to illness, she had her first go at taking the diamonds out of their envelopes in the recovery cabinet using the leatherette gloves. It was like picking up a needle with tweezers. She knew how astronauts felt about working in space with their huge gloves. The diamond recovery area was dark and dank and full of mosquitoes.

It was difficult to work in those conditions. She could sense people enjoying her discomfort. She was sweating like the proverbial pig when she finished. Sweat was dripping off her nose onto the cabinet, and her shirt stuck to her back. The diamonds were put in acid, and she cadged a lift to the office where the production meeting had just started.

***

Black was on his way out of Mike's house when he was waylaid by Brian Lynch. Brian did not notice his employer's foul humour and forced him into conversation.

'Boss, it's good to see you. Did you have a good flight?'

'Is that a joke? No, I didn't. What do you want, Brian? I'm in a hurry.'

'Boss, I'm worried about that new woman you hired. Did you know that she is running production while Jim is away? I think that it's a really bad idea.'

'Who asked you? You should mind your own business. I don't tell you how to run security.'

'Now, boss, don't take it the wrong way. I'm just trying to give you some good advice. That woman is trouble. I don't know what she's doing in a mining camp.'

'For your information, I'm the one who hired Sam and I'm the one who makes decisions about what she does or doesn't do. You can stuff your advice where the sun never shines and I'll thank you to keep your opinion to yourself from now on.'

Brian flinched.

'Sorry, boss. It's just—'

'Didn't you hear me? Now fuck off.'

***

After the customary glare from her cohorts, Sam sat down at the table. Fred looked in a bad way. He had an exaggerated tic in his right eye when he had had no sleep, and he still looked drunk. Another dawn finish with Dina, his local squeeze. Fred weighed about three times as much as Dina, and Sam couldn't help lurid pictures of their congress from intruding into her thoughts.

Sam stayed with Ewen in the office until Black turned up. He was in a filthy mood.

'Who told you that you could get involved in production? I told Jim that you weren't to touch it. Didn't he fucking tell you? Whose fault is this?'

Sam winced but she didn't reply. She could hear the nasty edge in his voice.

'I wasn't expecting insubordination from the new bitch on the block. It's a fucking liberty.'

Sam hung her head and looked apologetic enough to take the sting out of Black's attack. She wasn't stupid. Black was throwing his weight around like she'd been warned about in London. It was similar to watching the alpha male ape thumping his chest when she knew it was all show.

Once the harangue was over, they piled into the car with Black smoking cigarette after cigarette. The ash blew back in her eyes and combined with the red dust to make her contact lenses feel like sandpaper. They went from site to site as Black asked Ewen questions about the work. Ewen was driving, and it became obvious that he wasn't familiar with the terrain. *And why should he be, he's only here when Jim goes on leave.* Black started to direct questions at her, which to her relief she had adequate answers for. Also, she got consulted on the radio to coordinate various things. It was obvious people thought that she was in charge of some aspects of the production.

When Ewen was wandering about on some gravel, Black turned to her.

'I didn't want you to do production. You've no training as a production manager. You haven't got the experience. What if something goes wrong?'

'You're right. It's just that the best way for me to get a feel for the way projects work is by trying to run production, so I can use the knowledge when I am looking for new projects. After all, I am working with an experienced staff and I have two project managers within half an hour's drive if anything goes wrong.'

'You aren't supposed to think, Sam. I do the thinking around here and I don't want you to run production. End of story.'

She had been well-warned about Black's autocratic management style, and she didn't want to start off on his wrong side.

'Okay,' she said. 'I'm sorry I jumped the gun.'

On that one trip, Black changed his mind about the mine plan five times. He was a true 'ideas man,' leaping from theme to theme like a bee in a bunch of fuchsias. He left out stages in his plans, assuming people followed his logic, when often they just looked miserable and kept saying yes. Sam did not want to be one of them.

'Can you give me a list of your priorities so I don't get confused?' she said.

Black smiled at her innocence.

'That would be a complete waste of my time, as the plans will change again often before I leave.'

He was a man who knew himself pretty well.

Chapter XIII

They got back to the office in the early afternoon. Sam was absolutely starving. Her stomach grumbled in protest. Jean brought in a few small, dry bread rolls with some unidentifiable cold, dry salty meat in them. Sam ate two but couldn't drum up enough saliva for a third.

'Where's the tea?' said Black.

Jean turned white as marble and looked as if she was having a panic attack.

'But there's no tea left. It ran out last week. Can I make you a nice cup of coffee?' she managed to get out.

Black's face indicated that he would rather drink cyanide. The infamous Mondongo customs were to blame. They had been holding out for a bribe to let the Gemsite food container from South Africa out of the shipping port. None of the projects had any tea left, and the food was running out fast. Even the meat soup at lunch had been full of fat maggots, which the other management staff members didn't seem to notice. Sam knew grains of rice didn't have one black end. She hadn't got thin by mistake. She got a real thrill from watching them all gobble the soup. When they finished, she said innocently, 'Nice soup, lads?'

'Not that it's any of your business, but it was delicious,' said Brian.

'Oh, so you like maggots in your soup, do you? I'm not very keen on them myself.'

Brian's face was a picture.

'What do you mean?'

'You should look closer at the grains of rice in the soup.'

She smiled smugly and left them inspecting the soup with expressions of disgust. Revenge could take many different forms.

Most of the senior staff survived on alcohol and coffee and hadn't really noticed the lack of tea at the site. This was a massive failing where Black was concerned. When he wasn't drinking alcohol, he survived on a diet of tea and cigarettes and was quite indifferent to food, eating anything that he found in front of him. He had to have tea. It was not an option to tell him that there would be no tea until next week. He worked himself into a tantrum. He went bright red in the face and the veins on his neck stuck out like cables under his mottled skin.

'What do you mean "there's no tea"? How can there be no fucking tea? I don't fucking believe it. What the fuck is Pedro up to? Where is the fucking tea?'

Jean stammered.

'I don't know. I'm sorry. It's not my fault there's no tea. We've been waiting for weeks.'

'Weeks? Weeks? How can you survive without tea for weeks? I'll fire that fucking Pedro! I need tea now.'

Jean cowered, and looked defeated as Black fumed. When steam started coming out of Black's ears, Sam innocently mentioned that she had some tea in her room.

'So go and get it,' muttered Black, holding the edge of the table with both hands.

'That tea has to last me for my whole contract,' said Sam, allowing a note of doubt to creep into her voice.

'I must have some.'

'I don't know if I have enough. Maybe you could have some coffee.'

'Don't fuck with me. Give me tea now. Now!'

'We could negotiate if you like.'

'You bitch. Who the fuck do you think you are?'

Sam took a gamble.

'I'm the bitch with the tea,' she said, and winked.

Black looked astonished at this display of cheek, and he started to guffaw.

'Well, I wasn't expecting pushback from you,' he said, laughing. 'Get me some damn tea, or I'll fire you right now.'

Jean had been standing in the office with her mouth open for so long that it had gone dry. She rushed off to boil a kettle. As she later told Bob in the bar, 'I've never seen the like. Talking back to Black! She's like a tea bag herself. I guess you have to put her in hot water to find out how strong she is.'

Jean made a big pot of tea, which Sam and Black drank in silent appreciation, both deep in their own thoughts. Sam's feisty reaction had impressed Black. She had shown him her gutsy side and made him see that she could come in useful. She watched his jaded reactions to all the sycophantic staff at Kardo sucking up to him all the time. It was his fault that they were terrified of him, but it was obvious that he needed someone a bit less afraid of losing their job to contradict him when he was wrong.

When he asked her to sit in on his afternoon

production meetings, Sam remembered to be diffident. She had no idea what to expect, but she wasn't going to turn down the opportunity to support her mercurial boss. She had made a breakthrough with the tea, and she was not going to waste it.

'I'm not expecting you to speak,' said Black.

'I wouldn't dream of it.'

Was that a grin? Sam couldn't believe it. Finally, finally! She wanted to jump up and down. She contented herself with a couple of fist pumps in the toilet where no one could see her.

The production meetings followed a pattern Sam grew to recognise. Everyone who came to a meeting was humiliated, harangued and dismissed from the meeting room to go and lick their wounds. There was a prolonged session for one of the engineers who was responsible for only about five per cent of what Black was ranting about, having only been at Kardo two weeks. That was company policy. The incumbent in any position took the flak, even if the issue was the direct responsibility of their predecessor or they were replacing someone on leave.

Ewen hadn't had to take any flak. The sun was shining out of Jim's arse with great brilliance at the time due to the high production figures, and Ewen was basking in the reflected glory. Finally, Black let fly at Bob, shouting until he had one of his turns. They were famous. All the veins stood out on his neck, and he looked in danger of having a seizure.

'I'm amazed he hasn't had a stroke or a heart attack yet,' she remarked to Jorge.

'The doctors gave him eighteen months to live a few years ago, as he only has half a liver left and it is riddled with cirrhosis,' said Jorge.

'How has he lasted this long? He must smoke forty

cigarettes during his marathon meetings.'

'I reckon he smokes about three or four packs a day. He gets raging drunk most nights of the week, and, as far as I can make out, he never eats proper food,' said Jorge. 'And he's been doing that as long as I've known him.'

By the end of the afternoon, she had watched a continuous train of people get bullied and intimidated by Black. He loved to humiliate people, and doing this in front of her inflated his ego even more. By doing this, he had ensured she would be even less popular. No man likes to be belittled in front of a woman, especially one he has been rude to. Sam could see that for some of the victims, being belittled by Black was normal, but in front of her, it was unbearable.

She had not anticipated the results of the meetings to be a further drop in her standing in Kardo and felt deflated. Her head dropped and she sighed.

'What the fuck is wrong with you now?' said Black. 'Stop procrastinating and get over to the bar. It's time to have fun.'

If she wasn't popular, at least she was protected by her status as teacher's pet for the time being. She decided to enjoy herself. By midnight, the whole crew was plastered. Sam had managed her intake with great ease, as they were all trying to outdo each other in drinking ridiculous amounts and didn't notice that she drank tonic by itself without the gin. The barman was complicit in this, having had a soft spot for Sam ever since the night that they had excluded her from their circle.

Black looked remarkably sober. They played a couple of close games of pool, which Sam was careful to lose by very slender margins, giving Black the chance to crow about the victory but not to feel sure about it until the last ball had gone in. She wondered if he knew that she was letting him win. Black wasn't stupid by any means, but he loved to bask in the adoration of his team when he had a few drinks. He beckoned her to the door of the bar. 'Come, come. Bring your drink.'

He started off to the office. Sam had the barman put gin in her tonic just in case. She scampered over to the office and found Black in Fred's room.

'What kept you, woman?'

'Sorry, forgot my ciggies.'

'Give me one. Come over here.'

Sam wasn't sure where here was, but he was indicating Fred's desk. Jim had forbidden her to approach Fred's desk. She wasn't allowed to touch the computer if Fred wasn't there, but Black gestured for her to sit down.

'Start it up,' he said. 'I hate these things. I want to see the production data for this month.'

Sam did as she was told. It wasn't hard to find the records that Black was looking for. Fred was methodical, and there weren't too many files on the computer that weren't to do with diamond production in one way or another. Sam opened the file and stood up so Black could sit in front of the screen.

'Now that's what I call beautiful.'

'Sparkling figures,' said Sam, and immediately regretted it as Black glared at her like an owl woken up during the day.

'Okay, turn it off. Go on with you.'

Black dismissed her from his presence and staggered off in the direction of the bar. Why did Black show me the data? Perhaps it was a demonstration of his growing trust in her. She considered herself lucky to escape another ordeal by alcohol and poured her drink onto the roots of the mango tree outside the door of the office on her way out. She went home and lay awake for a while on her bed, reflecting on the way a small incident can change the whole complexion of any situation.

***

The next morning, she waited in the office at six-thirty for an 'early' meeting with Black. When he arrived at midday, he apologised for being late. She looked so startled to receive an apology that he asked her what was wrong, and she had to mutter something about women's problems. After procrastinating for an hour and drinking two large mugs of tea each, Black stood up.

'Can you drive?' he said.

Sam nodded.

'I'm teaching Marybelle to drive,' he said. 'She's pretty good.'

Sam stifled a laugh. A vision of Marybelle at the wheel with her hair flying in the wind and her eyes half-closed loomed large in her imagination.

'Oh?' she managed.

'It's a pity she can't come today. She could practice.'

Sam managed another nod.

'Well, let's go then. Tom's busy so you can drive,' said Black.

He did not need to ask twice. Sam grabbed the keys and headed for the pickup truck. The road to Tunde had originally been tarmacked but now it was mostly gravel pitted with huge potholes, most of which were unavoidable. The way was deserted. Sam counted only six vehicles on the half-hour drive. The locals knew when MARFO had been out laying mines and avoided the roads. Sam avoided the ditches beside the potholes. *Better safe than sorry.*

Black was in a good humour for once, chatting and telling stories. Sam did not say much, unwilling to break the mood.

'Have you heard the story about the phantom Filipino?' he said.

'No, I haven't.'

'Well, in 1989, during one of the many cease-fires in the civil war, MARFO rebels launched an attack on Kardo, and a Filipino mechanic disappeared. Local people said that he had been kidnapped and taken away. Three days later, Greys security men found the bottom half of a rotten torso on the riverbank. Fearing the worst, they got a doctor to examine it. He told them it didn't appear wholly African or European in origin, but it was mixed race, possibly Asian.

When shown the remains, one of the missing man's colleagues said that he had helped sew up the wound that caused a scar found on the left calf. With this confirmation of the death of the poor unfortunate man, Gemsite collected contributions for his widow from his workmates, and an insurance payout from Lloyds, and sent the "body" back for burial. The widow declared the legs to be those of her beloved and accepted the thirty-thousand-dollar compensation with tears of gratitude.'

'Wow, that's a lot of money in the Philippines.'

'Quite so,' said Black. 'Most people assumed that the story ended there. However, twenty-two months later, the missing Filipino turned up in a Red Cross convoy that arrived in Namibia carrying prisoners released by MARFO. It turns out that MARFO leaders were embarrassed to admit they had taken a hostage during a cease-fire, so they hid him for two years.

Meanwhile, his "widow" had remarried and spent all of the thirty-thousand dollars that she got as compensation in his absence. She was astonished when he arrived home demanding she get rid of her new husband.'

'Oh my, that's awkward.'

'The Filipino mechanic ejected husband number two, moved back into his house and started suing Gemsite for unpaid salary over the two years. Can you believe it? Cheeky bastard.'

The story finished there, as Sam didn't dare ask who won the case, but she had to admit it was a good yarn, even if it wasn't entirely true. She never could tell with Black.

They got to Tunde in good time. Black discussed pressing matters with the production manager and the head of metallurgy, chainsmoking his way through half a packet of cigarettes, and jabbing the air with his finger. Then he pushed back his chair and pointed at Sam.

'Truck,' he said.

With Sam driving, they visited the terraces being exploited at Tunde. As usual, Black was full of ideas, hopping back and forth across the mining areas like a demented leprechaun. At one point, he was unable to go any further, as his bad knee seized up. He got stuck halfway across a ditch and had to be helped back across. He needed an operation to fix it, but like many bullies, he was also a coward, so he preferred the daily pain. Sam made sympathetic noises anyway, as she knew on which side her bread was buttered.

When they got back to the offices, Sam stayed in the truck, engine running, staring ahead at the road home. Black came to the window and peered in.

'And just where do you think you're going?'

'Back to Kardo,' said Sam, crossing her fingers.

'But we're going to have a barbeque. Don't you want to be one of the boys?'

Not really.

'I have to go to the diamond sorting plant to do the export tomorrow. I want to be sharp, just in case.'

She let the last three syllables hang in the air. Black frowned and rubbed his arm. He puffed his cheeks and blew the air out, his breath rank with cigarettes. Sam struggled not to grimace, keeping as neutral an expression as possible.

'Hm, well, okay. Go home. I'll get a lift tomorrow. I've a busy evening ahead.'

Sam bit her lip.

'Thanks, boss.'

'And don't look so fucking pleased with yourself.'

'No, boss.'

Before Black could change her mind, Sam pressed the accelerator and steamed out of camp. The radio crackled but no demand for her return came over the airwaves. Relieved not to be stuck at Tunde with nowhere to sleep, Sam shot home at full speed. Black would just be given the best room as a matter of course, but she had a funny feeling that the back of the truck was reserved for lepers like her.

When she pulled up outside the house, lights were still on in the communal sitting room. Surprised, she steeled herself for whatever ordeal awaited inside and opened the front door. The sitting room had been transformed into a girly heaven. Scented candles and patterned throws had turned the basic furniture into an inviting nook. Marybelle and her friends were draped around the chairs or cushions on the floor, drinking wine from the kitchen mugs and beer glasses.

'Hello. Would you like a glass of wine?' said

Marybelle.

Sam wanted her bed more, but there didn't seem to be a polite way of refusing.

'That would be lovely. Thank you,' said Sam, wavering on the edge of the group, uncertain.

The other girls made a space for her on some cushions and gave her a jam jar with white wine in it. Sam sat down, her back against an armchair and sipped the cool wine which tasted of elderflower. Since she didn't offer any comments, the girls soon forgot that she was there, or maybe they didn't care. They were discussing their boyfriends in camp.

'Oh, it's not so bad. I make him buy me dresses. Anyway, he can't get it up so I don't have to do anything.'

There was a chorus of tittering behind manicured hands. Marybelle swished her hair.

'What about you, Suzie? Have you found someone yet?'

'I was thinking about Jim.'

Sam froze with the jam jar halfway to her mouth. This was not a conversation she wanted to hear.

'Don't waste your time. Jim's not interested.'

'Is he gay?'

'No, he's weird. He loves his wife.'

'Who do you suggest?'

'I think Matt is free but, ugh, gross.'

'Ew! He's repulsive. He looks like Jabba the Hutt.'

'He's no worse than Black,' said Marybelle.

Sam held her breath and shrank into the floor, terrified her presence would prevent any more chat. *Maybe it was the wine, or maybe they didn't consider her a threat, having heard that she was toast from their boyfriends.*

'How do you stand it?' said a girl with fake blonde

hair.

'He'll be dead soon. The doctors have told him to stop smoking and drinking or he won't last the year. I can wait.'

She smiled and pushed her hair back, twirling it into a bun and sticking a swizzle stick in it. Her smug air alarmed Sam. *Where was the sweet, soft-spoken Filipino girl she had met in Johannesburg?* This was the smile on the face of a tiger.

Sam waited a little longer, then she drained her glass and stood up.

'Thank you for the wine. I'm off to bed.'

Marybelle gave her a vague wave and slumped back on the sofa with the other girls, who were plaiting each other's hair. Sam sloped off to her room.

She got up before dawn the next day to go to the diamond recovery area with Ewen and do the diamond export for Mondongo. She expected to do Jim's job of weighing and checking the diamonds, but Tunde's chief sorter stood in for her which was just as well. Sam was so tired that she couldn't get the inner safe to open despite knowing her combination off by heart. Ewen did it for her, and she could feel the disdain of the watching crew.

'That's your street cred down the drain,' said Ewen.

Not that I had any before.

The rest of the Tunde management arrived for their weigh up, and then both exports left on the flight to Mondongo. Ewen and Sam went back to the office. Black had scheduled the daily production meeting at lunchtime, and Sam had not eaten breakfast. She approached Black, who talked in low tones to Ewen.

'Do you mind if I go and have lunch now?' she said, during a pause in their conversation.

'Can't you wait an hour until we have driven around the production sites?' said Black.

The canteen would close by then. She wasn't going to eat lunch yet again. *No wonder I'm losing weight.* Misery swamped her as she slumped in the backseat of the car without protest.

To her surprise, they stopped outside the canteen on their way to the diamond terraces.

'I suppose you're still hungry?' said Black.

'I'm about to eat my own arm.'

'Grab something from the canteen and bring it with you.'

Sam went into the mess hall searching for something portable, and, as luck would have it, scotch eggs were on the menu. She grabbed four eggs and an armful of apples and walked outside, dropping a couple of them at the feet of the two boys begging outside. She winked at them, eliciting some excited giggles and went back to the car.

'Those look good,' said Black, who hadn't noticed the contraband change hands, as he had been lighting a cigarette.

Sam smiled to herself and divided the spoils, two scotch eggs and an apple each. Black's indifference to food was caused by living with a girl who ate only lettuce so she could stay stick thin. Sam suspected he had a healthy appetite if he was allowed to eat but, after what she had heard the night before, it was not in Marybelle's interest for Black to eat well. His big paunch and puffy face were the result of heavy drinking. *Did Marybelle ever tried to swap some of the drink for food? Probably not.* She wouldn't mourn long after his death with all that money to comfort her.

Sam and Black spent a couple of hours blundering around the terraces and came back in the failing light.

Night really did crash down like a shutter in Tamazia. They saw two tawny eagles that drifted along in front of the truck, a large flapping guinea fowl, an iguana and some quail. The wildlife was extraordinary, especially at sunset. Black was pretending to shoot everything and wishing he had his gun. Not that the animals would have been in any danger. With Black's shaky hands, he couldn't hit an elephant hiding in a Ford Fiesta. Black was all hat and no cattle in lots of ways.

They drove to meet Ewen at the river diversion which had had the water pumped out. There was a big crocodile in the drying-out riverbed, thrashing about in the gloom and fishing in the remaining pools of water. Black insisted on going for a walk in the dark bush growing on the bank of the river diversion. Crocodile prints were everywhere in the gathering gloom, but Sam was more uneasy about the possibility of meeting a hippo on its way to feed. Hippos killed more people a year than crocodiles, snakes and all African predators put together.

They went back to camp and had drinks with Jorge, Bob and Jean. Jorge's wife brought out plates of chorizo sausage and cheese and raw onion and bread that the starving entourage wolfed down. They all had a glass of wine and chatted over the plates of food. Then, as suddenly as he had appeared, Black left with Marybelle on the plane to Mondongo.

Sam staggered back to Jim's house where she reviewed the visit in her head. She had without a doubt made inroads with her recalcitrant boss, and with patience she could make the job work in her favour, and learn everything she needed to succeed. She just needed to get some more of the management working with her. *How on earth do I do that?*

Chapter XIV

In the days that followed Black's departure, it was made clear to Sam just how much she was despised at Kardo, but she didn't care. She smiled at everyone no matter what they said to her, and she avoided the bar so as not to cramp their style. *Talk away, boys.* She was plotting a coup. Now that she had all the production information from Ewen, she was determined to get another one hundred per cent bonus for Kardo.

No matter what the management team thought of her as a person, she wanted a tiny bit of respect for her professional abilities. If she could reach the elusive target of doubling the baseline monthly production without Jim on site, she would show them what she could do. It would take some planning, and she might have to adjust Black's orders a little bit, but who would notice that? Black changed his orders every other hour, and Sam was the only one present at all the meetings, so she was the only one who knew what the final orders were.

She assumed that he wouldn't even remember his own orders after all that change. She knew what mix of material to use and where to get it from. The only person who might notice what she was doing was Jorge, but he didn't know what Black's instructions were either. Black wanted to spread the good material over a couple of months to keep production down to prevent the government boys at SDM from taking an interest. They might try and change the terms of the agreement if they thought that Gemsite was making too much money. However, a spike in production was normal from time to time when they hit potholes in the riverbed.

Ewen was quite happy to let her run things at Kardo, as he needed to keep an eye on production levels at Gali. He left her in charge for several days in a row, while he spent time in the diamond recovery plant and chose terraces for clearing in the north of the area. Sam started to adjust the plans put in place by Black just enough to have the desired effect on production.

Since Jorge didn't see the production figures, he was not aware of what Sam was doing. He knew that some terraces were richer than others, but he didn't know the fine details involved. He was content to work with Sam on an equal basis, and they had a fine time together organising the mining and production to fit in with the availability of machinery and manpower.

Sam started to feel like she was settling into her job at last. The management team were realizing she did know something about mining and the production was looking good that month. She even managed to have a short but embarrassing talk with Dirk, who came to apologise when no one else was around.

'I wanted to tell you how sorry I am about, well, you know.' He stood staring at his feet as if unable to look up. 'I never wanted to take part in the bet. I'm new too, you know. I got bullied into it.'

'That's okay,' said Sam.

'Honestly, I wasn't pretending. I do like you, quite

a lot.'

'Okay, don't tell me, please. I don't think I could deal with it right now.'

They were interrupted by Bob's arrival. He looked surprised to see Dirk consorting with the enemy. Sam had good news for Bob, which she hoped would persuade him that she was on his side.

'Bob, just the man I wanted to see.'

'Oh yes? Why's that, then?'

'I thought you might be pleased to learn that there is a big consignment of spare parts coming from South Africa for your machinery.'

'That's brilliant news. How do you know that?'

'Oh, I suggested to Black that we needed to get the diamonds out before the civil war broke out again. I tried for new machinery but he said that MARFO rebels would only come and steal or sabotage them.'

'Jesus, that's pretty great. Thank you.'

'No problem. I get a bonus too, you know.'

She had not made any progress with Fred, who was still flopping around like an overweight catfish, harrumphing and sighing every time he was asked to do anything. Sam couldn't understand how he remained so overweight with the quality of food on site. She was getting thinner and thinner and had to ask one of the mechanics to use an awl to make some more holes in her belt.

She spent a lot of time in the recovery facility monitoring the production, which was relayed to Fred. He wasn't happy that Sam had been given access to his precious data. She did her best to cajole and flatter him into cooperation, but she had to put up with his grudging compliance and mediocre work rate.

'I'm not happy about you being given access to the diamond production data,' he said.

'I know, but Black wants me to get more involved. I can't direct production with Ewen if I don't know what's going on with the grades.'

'I still don't feel comfortable.'

'I know you are used to being the only one who can access the data, but someone else needs to do it when you are away. What if you leave?'

'Who said I was leaving?'

'No one. Just saying.'

Fred relied on his ability with computers to lord it over the administration department. There were very few staff with good computer skills, and he wasn't going to share his knowledge with anyone if he could help it. After all, if someone else could use the computer, it would soon become apparent that Fred took ten times longer on any minor job than was necessary. Sam knew this, but she also needed access to the data to make her plan work, so she didn't comment on his lack of application.

After a couple of weeks of elevated production, the number of carats of diamonds in the safe again approached danger level. This was a nominal value at which it was thought the camp became too much of a temptation for the MARFO fighters to ignore. Diamond shipments to Mondongo were always organised at this point to reduce the chance of attack. Sam called security on the radio and told them to arrange an export. There was a long silence on the other end.

'Coming to you. Your location? Over,' said a voice.

'In the office. Over.'

Five minutes later, a red-faced Brian Lynch arrived puffing at the office. He sat heavily down on one of the desks in the middle of the office. Sam brought him a glass of water, which he gulped down so fast that water ran down his chin and dropped on his pristine uniform. Oblivious to the gathering storm, she went to get some more water. She wondered how many rosters Brian had left in him, as he was heart-attack material. A ticking bomb.

She sat on a chair opposite him, waiting for him to start talking. Brian composed himself and snarled, 'Are you fucking mental? You'll get us all killed.' Sam was taken aback. She tried to imagine what on earth he was talking about, but nothing came to mind.

'I'm sorry,' she said. 'I've no idea what you are talking about. Have I done something wrong?'

'Something wrong? Did you hear that, lads? Sam wants to know if she's done something wrong.'

The other people in the office, who up until then had not paid much attention to the arrival of Brian, turned around in their chairs and listened.

'She's only gone and talked about the export on the radio, that's all.'

None of them needed any encouragement to stick the knife in where Sam was concerned, and they laid into her with gusto.

'For fuck's sake, how stupid can you be?'

'Jesus, woman, don't you know MARFO listen to the radio? There are dozens of stolen radios out there.'

'Fucking typical. Black must have been out of his mind when he put you in charge. Did you sleep with him, or what?'

'Well, Sam,' said Brian, enjoying the effect of his tirade. 'You've put us all in danger now.'

Jorge, who had been making himself a coffee, walked over and stood beside Sam, who was speechless with panic. She felt a horrible chill run up her back, which came out in a cold sweat. Jorge shook his head at her.

'Don't be ridiculous, Brian. Every village picker who works in the recovery house knows how many diamonds are being put in the safe and what quality they are. They can all tell MARFO any time they like. Sam didn't know the rules because she's only just been issued a radio and this is the first time that she has been in charge of an export. I don't think you can accuse her of putting us in danger.'

'Why are you taking her side? Did she sleep with you too?'

'My wife is on site, Brian. I don't think she'd like that.'

Jorge smiled to reduce the tension.

'I'll be reporting this to Black,' said Brian. 'The bloody woman is a fucking liability.'

He stomped out of the office, leaving Sam and Jorge with a sea of glaring faces. Jorge took Sam's arm and pulled her into one of the cubicles. He shut the door.

Sam was shell-shocked. No one had told her not to mention the exports on the radio, but it was something she should have known instinctively. She had been too cocky and overconfident. *What a fool.* Her big chance was missed, and now she had put everyone in danger by breaking a cardinal rule. She wanted to sink into the floor and disappear. She felt like crying, but she couldn't produce any tears. She was numb with shock. She hadn't even noticed that Jorge had left the cubicle and was re-entering with a large mug of coffee, which he handed to her. She drank it without thinking. It was very sweet and strong, and it shocked her back to the present.

Jorge was watching her, waiting for her to recover her composure. She could almost feel his empathy willing her back to normality.

'You okay?' he said. 'It's not true, you know. All the locals know how production is going. It's not a secret. Anyway, it's my fault, not yours. I should've told you about the radio codes. I forgot you don't have anywhere to get your information from. I'm supposed to be your friend. I'm sorry I dropped you in it.'

'I thought Brian was going to have a heart attack,' said Sam.

'Ah, you don't know about Mr Lynch? He went to Black, while he was here on his visit, and made it clear how horrified he was that you had come to Kardo to work. He also complained that you were running production while Jim was away. Black told him to mind his own business, which didn't go over very well because he isn't used to having his advice ignored. He's been looking for his chance to prove that he was right and that you are a liability. So far, he's been disappointed by your grasp of operations and obvious flair for the job. He was just waiting for this opportunity.'

'But what has he got against me?'

'Don't you know? Lynch is a misogynist. He hates you. He was one of the instigators of the betting pool, placing a large bet on Dirk to be the first one in your knickers. To his chagrin, you weren't taken in by Dirk's advances, despite spending a lot of time with him. Brian told the others that you were a lesbian. What normal woman works in a mining camp after all?'

Sam managed a smile.

'I hope you're feeling better because we need to go and look at the stockpile at the DMS plant. Come on.'

Sam did feel better. She knew that what Jorge said made a lot of sense. The MARFO leaders were being fed a constant stream of information by the pickers all the time. She wasn't going to collapse in a heap. Not now, when she was so close to success. She stepped out into the main office where everyone glared at her. She felt the need to apologise.

'I am sorry about the breach of radio conduct. I had no idea that mention of exports was prohibited. I feel like an idiot. It won't happen again.'

No one responded, and she left with Jorge following behind.

After the incident with the radio, Sam felt as if all her hard work on making better relationships on site had been undone. She had not anticipated giving Brian the upper hand. She was losing more ground in the oppressive heat as she struggled to get things done against a tide of indifference and obstruction. Fred was thrilled to have a weapon.

'I heard that you told MARFO when to attack us. Way to go, Sam.'

He turned a self-satisfied, sweaty back on her.

Worse was to follow. Two days later, Jorge's father had a heart attack, and he got permission from Black to leave the site for a week. There was plenty of stockpiled material to wash, so Jorge being away wouldn't affect production.

'I don't want to leave you alone here with these bastards, but I have no choice.'

'That's okay. Jim will be back soon. I'll manage.'

Despite her show of strength, when Jorge left for Mondongo with his wife, she felt bereft. *How will I survive without any support?* Ewen hadn't noticed that she was being bullied, or if he had, he didn't do anything about it. He wasn't very observant at the best of times, and he didn't mention the radio incident. Sam didn't know if he was even aware of it.

The loss of Jorge hit her hard, but she couldn't help noticing that Jorge's tragedy was an excuse for her to high-grade the material going through the plants by using the stockpiles of rich material instead of diluting it with lower grade material dug by Jorge on a day-to-day basis. Jim was due back at the end of the week. She could survive until then and complete her mission before he took over the reins again.

Sam sat out on the steps of the office for a long time after Jorge had left for the airstrip. Smoking one cigarette after another, she mulled over the events of the last few weeks. She could smell the red earth and hear a million insects competing for a chance at love. She looked up at the sky with its carpet of stars and marvelled again at the difference compared to London skies. The moon was full and yellow and loomed large through the mango trees. She could see the man in the moon, and he was laughing at her.

So much for her office job in Mondongo. That turned out to be a big fat lie. In a funny way, she thought it was better to be at Kardo. A life in the field suited her and she didn't miss the home comforts much. If the other residents of Kardo would only give her some credit, she might even start to enjoy her job. Only two more days were left before Jim came back from leave. Two more days to hit the target.

Chapter XV

The attack started in the light of a full moon, which threw fat shadows around the mango trees lining the roads. The MARFO rebels overcame the local security forces with ease, as most of their expatriate superiors had gone to a meeting in Mondongo to negotiate a new contract. The local men who worked for Greys security were well-trained, but they lacked structure without their leaders. Some of them ran away rather than face the ferocious rebel fighters.

The MARFO fighters spread out through the compound, searching for management staff who could be used to access the diamond recovery plant. They found several people in their houses who had not had the time or initiative to flee, but they didn't locate a sufficient number of the keyholders to get into the diamond safes.

Sam woke from her exhausted sleep to a peculiar popping noise. *What the hell is that? Could it be gunfire?* She sat up in bed hyperventilating with fright. An attack on the mine had always been a remote possibility but like most people, Sam had assumed it would happen to another mine, not Kardo. *Could I have precipitated the attack with my radio announcement about the export?*

Jorge had assured her the sorters already knew how many diamonds there were in the safe in the sorting plant but was he right? Guilt and fear almost overwhelmed her. She made herself think rationally. The attackers had to be members of the rebel movement. MARFO fighters had used the light of the full moon before, for their attacks on the isolated compounds of the diamond mining companies.

In the past, they had been driven away from Kardo by the army who formed the outer ring of defence by patrolling the surrounding countryside, but this time, it looked like they had evaded that first line of defence and were engaging with the private security force. People might die because of her ignorance.

Groggy, she swung her legs out of bed and fumbled about for her clothes. She put her dirty socks on, shoved her feet into her working boots, grabbed a scrunchy from the rough wooden table beside the bed and bundled her hair into a tangled bun. She sat back down on the bed. It was hard to think clearly, but she knew she wasn't dreaming because she could feel every thread in the rough blanket under her fingers. Her heart thundered in her chest.

Her emergency backpack was hanging on a hook on the door across the darkened sitting room. She forced herself to review the contents in her head; the malaria tablets, insect repellent, mosquito net, full water bottles, tins of tuna, penknife, hat, underwear, socks and towel all jostling in the bag. Water purification tablets! She felt around in the drawer of the bedside table. She grabbed the bottle of tablets and a large bag of chewy sweets that were also there.

Trembling with fright, she inched across the floor of her house on her hands and knees to the window facing the road that ran through the compound and looked out. The stars were still visible through the window and bright moonlight illuminated the compound. The shooting had stopped and an eerie silence reigned. The moon shadows on the dirt surface of the road looked like monsters. She unhooked the backpack from the door and unzipped it, thrusting the sweets and purification tablets into the front section.

She sank to the floor, clutching her pack close for comfort. *Now what?* She knew that it was safer inside her bungalow than out on the road risking a stray bullet. *Where were the security forces? Where was Frik?* The fat, bald security man carrying an old Kalashnikov had been assigned to look after her in case of trouble when she first got to the site. His large gut had not inspired her confidence at the time. He didn't look like someone who could run away at any speed. The only time Sam had seen him since was in the canteen carrying an overloaded plate of food. Given the circumstances, he was sure to be too busy to look for her right now.

A blast of gunfire split the night and she hugged her knees tight trying to control the cold fear rising up her spine. She wondered what had happened to the others. They were all capable of fleeing Kardo to hide in the bush if they got the chance. *I hope Ewen got away.* She couldn't bear to think of him having to do another long march. It was even worse to think that this could be her fault. They had been right. She was a liability. *I should have gone home when I had the chance.*

Sam almost jumped out of her skin when the shooting started again, much louder. Suddenly, there was shouting outside, the sound of people running past her house. The smell of cordite wafted under the door into her room, making her stifle a cough as it caught the back of her throat. Someone rattled the padlocks outside her house. She hoped that it might be her plump saviour come to whisk her out of danger, but no one knocked or called out for her.

A sharp snap reverberated around the sitting room as bolt cutters severed the padlocks, and the outer door was breached. She held her breath, and pushed herself against the wall, trying to melt into it. The shadow of a large pair of feet in an old pair of boots appeared through the gap below the inner door. Sam let out an involuntary whimper. The padlock was wrenched off the door, and it burst open. A huge black man stood blinking in the gloom. He felt for the light switch with a massive hand.

Sam gasped as the strip light flickered to life. The thick tribal scarring on his face stood out in stark relief. His dark eyes fixed upon her huddled against the wall holding on to her backpack with white knuckles. A nasty smile spread across his face but he did not hurt her. He gesticulated at her to stand up and come with him. Sam was not about to protest. She staggered to her feet, hanging on to her rucksack as if her life depended on it.

Her massive captor led her out of the house. Once in the street, he took her by the hand. It was oddly reassuring. *Surely he doesn't intend to shoot me if he's holding my hand?* Perhaps he took pity on her because of her obvious terror. He carried her CD player, which he had picked up on his way out, under his other arm, holding his AK-47 and crowbar awkwardly in his big hand.

The shooting had stopped. The mango trees dripped onto the road, and dark pools of water sat in the road wells and gutters. They walked down the middle of it, Sam now carrying the player and her captor smoking a cigarette.

'What's your name?' said Sam.

'Ha! You speak Portuguese?'

'Yes.'

'My name is Thiago. Yours?'

'I'm Sam.'

'Sam?'

'Yes.'

That was as far as Thiago's interest in his captive went. They headed for the canteen in silence. They arrived outside where several large black armed men, their skin gleaming under the street lights, were congregated. They all stuffed themselves with food. Loaves of bread, bananas, ham, anything edible disappeared down their throats. Bags of rice and other contraband looted from the larders and freezers were sitting in the road.

Sam glanced around trying to spot who else had been captured. She caught a glimpse of Brian, Bob and Fred in the group on the side of the road that included most of the Filipino mechanics and heavy machinery operators.

There was no sign of Ewen, but then Sam remembered that he had slept at Gali. She had forgotten to put a loo roll in her rucksack. She approached Thiago.

'I need to go the bathroom.'

'You can go in the road.'

'Please, I have women's problems.'

He looked alarmed. She signalled that the toilets were inside the canteen and he shoved her inside, before standing guard outside the door. Sam had a quick pee for authenticity and stole both loo rolls from the cubicle. She started to wash her hands and then stole the soap, too. She stuffed them into her rucksack.

Suddenly, she heard a noise from the end cubicle. She froze.

'Who's there?' she hissed.

'It's me, Jean. Please don't tell them I'm here. I've got children at home.'

'Don't be ridiculous. Why would I tell them? You stay there, and don't come out until morning. Please make sure my family knows what happened to me.'

'Okay, sorry. You're right. Thanks, and good luck, Sam. You will make it. I've seen you in action.'

Thiago banged on the outer door of the toilets, and Sam came out so he wouldn't go in and find Jean too. He grabbed her rucksack and looked inside it. Dismissing most of the contents, he took some of the sweets and handed it back to her.

Outside, she found the captives and fighters organised into a convoy. The fighters carried booty looted from the camp and had loaded bags of rice and grains and other foodstuffs into crude wheeled carts. They co-opted the Filipinos to pull them, one between the shafts and two others pushing on either side. The British captives were sullen, staring at the ground or smoking.

Sam tried to approach the group of Kardo captives but was prodded with a gun towards the women at the back of the convoy. They were the camp followers, wives, girlfriends and cooks. They were accompanied by a scattering of excited children who gazed at Sam but did not approach.

As they walked out of camp, Sam noticed some bodies on the side of the road. Some of them were wearing Greys uniforms. Sam had never seen someone dead up close before. She wondered if she knew any of them, then she let out a gasp. Dirk! That lifeless bundle with a big hole in his chest was Dirk, his head thrown back and a look of surprise on his face. She tried to go over to him, but the women grabbed her arms and pulled her away. *What if he was injured?* They couldn't leave him there. But they did.

'He is dead,' said one of the women, as if that explained everything.

'But he is my friend.'

They pulled her away. She acquiesced, looking back over her shoulder at his dead body. It was pointless to make a scene. If they had shot Dirk, they would shoot her, too, if she slowed them up.

It was still dark when they set out along the road that went through the village. The doors of the huts remained shut as they passed through, even though the villagers must have been aware of what had happened. No one wanted to be recruited forcibly by MARFO. *Ewen had survived his long walk with MARFO.* They were taken hostage for cash and released when Black paid up. *Would she be fit enough to last until then?* If she fell behind, she'd be disposed of. Whatever happened, she would keep going. One foot in front of the other.

Dirk's death had shocked her. It made the nightmare real. Until she saw his body, she had still been hoping she was having a bad dream. She would get through this somehow; she just didn't know how yet. Being alive was a good start.

Something touched her hand, and she jumped with fright. She looked down to see one of the small boys who hung around begging outside the canteen. He gazed up at her and smiled. His small grainy hand reached up and insinuated itself into hers. His brother appeared at her other side, and although he didn't take her hand, he walked close to her, bumping into her thigh. She almost burst into tears with relief.

'Hello,' she said. 'Are you coming with me?'

'Yes, our mother is a cook for the valiant fighters of MARFO. I am Edison, and my brother is called Pibé,' said the older boy.

'Like Valderama?' said Sam.

'Yes. My father liked football, but he is dead now.'

'I'm sorry to hear that.'

'He fought for MARFO. He is a famous hero.'

'I'm sure he was very brave just like you.'

The little boy gave her a radiant smile that would have melted a glacier, and they all walked on into the dark night of the Tamazian bush.

They walked in the moonlight for about four hours on the first night. The gravel road crunched underfoot, and Sam stumbled into several puddles despite the brightness. The cicadas sang their hearts out, and big fruit bats swooped close to the convoy, catching the mosquitos attracted by the hot sweaty bodies. Her colleagues trudged ahead of her, but no one looked back to see how she was coping. Their backs accused and ostracised her.

Sam remembered again what Jorge had said about the pickers knowing about every export, and refused to take the blame for the attack. *Where was Jorge?* She hadn't seen him amongst the hostages taken by the rebels. But Jorge had left for Portugal with his wife. She smiled in relief. His sick father had saved his life. Every cloud.

She kept walking at an even pace, hoping they would soon stop for a rest. Finally, they arrived at a river with several stepped banks of alluvial gravel with rounded quartz pebbles glinting in the moonlight, the kind of geology that shouted 'diamonds' in this part of Tamazia. Definitely the sort of place that made Black's balls itch. The rough agates littered the ground, their beautiful banding obvious in the moonlight. She resisted the temptation to collect them, even though there were no security guards now preventing her from picking up any stones. She didn't know how far she would have to walk, and she suspected the agates would get thrown away again if it was far.

The women set up fires and mixed up the *funge* for cooking. Funge was the staple diet of the local population in Tamazia. It was made from the cassava root, which was sliced thin and left to dry in the sun. These dry chips were pounded into flour and then mixed into a paste, which was cooked in a pot over the fire. As Sam could testify, it had the consistency of wallpaper paste and tasted awful. It had a way of sticking in her throat that made her worry she might choke. Not that she had a chance to taste it. The hostages were not offered any food.

Sam sucked a sweet and decided to save her cans of tuna for the time being. She was grateful that Thiago had not bothered to take them from her. She assumed that he had bigger booty in mind, considering all the food they had stolen from the storehouse. She drank some bottled water and sat on the edge of the cooking area. She heard movement behind her and looked around to see Pibé standing there holding out a banana. She beckoned him over and made him sit beside her on the bank of sand. She peeled the banana and broke it in half. She gave half back to the little boy.

'Thank you.'

'You're welcome.'

Pibé looked exhausted, and he leaned against her with heavy eyelids drooping. Sam patted her lap, and he swivelled around as if it were the most natural thing in the world and put his head in it. She scratched his dirty head. She felt his dusty curls springing back under her fingers. Pibé sighed, a big, tired sigh. He shrank as the air left him and became even smaller and more vulnerable. She was also very tired, so she swung her legs up on the bank, lowered her torso onto the ground, moved the little boy up to her chest and put her arm around him. She put her rucksack under her head and tried to fit her body to the contours of the terrace. The round pebbles slid over one another, creating a hollow for her hips.

She lay listening to the chirping of the crickets. The noise was deafening but also comforting. She was struck by the fact that she now fulfilled her wish to have a man to sleep with, although this was not quite the scenario she had in mind. She fell asleep soothed by his soft breathing.

Not long afterwards, she was awakened by someone shaking her sleeve. It was a skeletal woman wearing a worn-out T-shirt with the logo 'She's got to have it.' Sam looked around to see if they were leaving again.

Nobody stirred. The fires were dying, and the cooking utensils had been cleared away.

'Are you Pibé's mother?' said Sam.

'Yes, my name is Tereza. What is yours?'

'My name is Sam.'

She shifted around so she was sitting up, and Tereza sat beside her on the bank.

'Thank you for looking after Pibé. He is still too small for such a big walk, but don't tell him I said so. I cannot leave them at home, but I must cook for MARFO when they need me. It's my duty.'

'Edison told me your husband fought with MARFO.'

'Yes, when the western powers were on our side. The government troops shot him in an ambush.'

'Oh, I'm sorry. I don't really understand the war at all.'

'Don't worry. We women don't ever understand why men must fight and die.'

'They don't even care who they are fighting.'

'Was that your friend who was killed? The one who was with you when you were fishing?'

'Yes, that was Dirk.'

'I'm sorry too.'

Sam shrugged. As if by mutual agreement, the two women lay down with the little boy sandwiched in between them and were soon joined by Edison, who curled up to his mother's back. Sam pulled her towel over the group as best she could. Pretty soon, they were all asleep.

Chapter XVI

The next morning, they were woken at dawn by shouting and the crunch of river gravel underfoot. Sam filled her water bottle in the stream and added an iodine tablet to it. She had forgotten the neutralising tablets, so she would have to put up with the taste. She wasn't too sure iodine killed all the germs in the water, but she had to drink it. If she wanted to keep up with the marchers, she had to stay hydrated. She swallowed a malaria tablet and sucked on a sweet while she waited for the column to move off.

She glanced over at the male captives from Kardo. The British men looked pretty exhausted. Brian looked rougher than most, with his far from immaculate shirt hanging over his huge belly and one of the epaulets dangling from the shoulder. There were several Filipino mechanics she vaguely recognised, and she felt guilty for not knowing most of their names. The rebels were using them as mules to carry the booty from Kardo. The mechanics were tough little men, and even now, they were all chatting and laughing as if nothing had happened.

One of them wandered over and offered Sam a cigarette, which she accepted without thinking. The Filipinos had salvaged their stashes of duty-free cigarettes from their rooms during the raid. They would use them as currency on the walk to buy food and water from the MARFO fighters, who didn't seem to realise that they could take the cigarettes from the Filipinos by force if they wanted to.

The smoke hit her lungs like a vice, as they tried to cope with the unexpected assault of an unfiltered full-strength Filipino-brand cigarette. Sam coughed and coughed, and bent over double with effort. The mechanic laughed at her, and she recognised him as Marco, her rescuer on the night of the washing machine leak. She grinned back.

She looked up to see Fred and Brian glaring at her, but she wasn't too bothered. She had the upper hand now physical fitness was going to come into the equation. Fit and strong, she was proud of her muscles and stamina. Fred and Brian carried another man in excess weight between them, and it was bound to affect them sooner or later.

Bob sat apart from the main group on one of the terraces, gathering and inspecting pebbles, and then skimming them across the river if they were found to be flat enough. His lanky frame concentrated on the task of getting the most skims he could out of the flat quartz pebbles. He looked unconcerned. He had his crew with him, and that was reason enough for Bob to feel serene.

The Filipinos admired and liked Bob. His laconic humour went right over their heads, but they appreciated his expertise and light-handed management. Sam had to admit that Bob had grown on her since the bar incident. He had made an effort, which was more than any of the others had done. They had wallowed in the success of their trap. Sam had no sympathy for them now.

Had news of the attack reached Mondongo yet? What would Black do? What did MARFO want anyway? She could find out. Being a Portuguese-speaker was going to be a big advantage in this situation. No one else spoke enough to communicate anything other than their need for another beer.

She didn't try to walk with her colleagues this time, and joined the women at the back of the column. She walked along with her hat on, keeping the sun off her face. She wore a long-sleeved shirt and khaki trousers, which were loose enough to allow the air to circulate so she didn't get too hot.

Pibé and Edison soon found her again, and Pibé walked alongside Sam talking in a continuous stream about how good he was at football, what a great fighter his father was, how his mother was the best cook in the village and how his brother was the best fisherman. Sam didn't understand half of it, given that it was a very strange mix of local patois and Portuguese. She made all the right noises in the right places, which was enough to encourage the little boy to keep talking. His brother interjected every now and then to correct any gross errors, but he appeared used to these streams of consciousness, and didn't try to stop the flow.

The column wended its way cross country until midday when a halt was called beside a deserted village. The heat was overpowering. Sam had rationed her water with care, but she only had a tiny bit left at the bottom of her bottle. She had to keep drinking if she wanted to keep walking. She took a chance and handed it to Edison.

'Edison, please, can you find me some water?'

He nodded and disappeared behind the mud huts. While he was gone, the captives were herded inside a hut together. Sam was dismayed to be included with them. She had been avoiding contact with the others since the attack, and she didn't fancy being trapped in a small space with a belligerent Brian Lynch. She sat on her rucksack amongst the Filipinos with her back to the wall and her head down, trying not to draw attention to herself. It was almost dark with the door closed, and like being in an oven.

Rivulets of sweat ran down her back and soaked into her shirt. She could sense the hostile glances from the Kardo captives.

'What's that dirty little snitch doing in here with us?' said Brian.

'She's the reason we're here. Don't forget,' said Fred.

'Why don't you fuck off, Sam? We don't want you in here.'

Sam bristled.

'Do you really think I want to be in here with you lot? After all the friendship and help you have offered me in the last three months? Fuck off, you complete wankers.'

'Now lads,' interjected Bob. 'We should stick together here. Let bygones be bygones.'

'Not fucking likely. She deserves everything she gets. Filthy feminist lesbian,' said Brian.

There was a short silence and then, despite herself, Sam guffawed. Even Bob laughed. Incensed, Brian lunged forward at her, tripping over a rucksack and almost falling into the huddle of Filipino mechanics. They looked startled at this turn of events and huddled closer together, glancing around with incomprehension. Brian stumbled backwards, quivering with resentment. Fred's blank face showed that he couldn't imagine why Sam and Bob were laughing. He put his hand on Brian's shoulder to indicate his solidarity with the security man.

Sam caught Bob's eye, and he winked at her, something observed by the mechanics, who closed ranks around Sam. *Those spare parts were earning their beer now.* She relaxed against the cool mud wall, shut her eyes and fell asleep in the sauna-like atmosphere surrounded by her new allies.

All too soon, the door opened again, and the captives were ushered out, blinking into the bright afternoon sunlight. From the position of the sun, Sam estimated that it was about five o'clock. She didn't need any prompting this time, and joined the women and children at the back of the column. To her relief, Edison was carrying her water bottle, which he offered her, smiling. Sam gave him a sweet, which he bit in two to give half to Pibé.

She decided to keep the sweets as currency. Her stomach growled. She would have to eat some tuna if she wanted to keep going. There were six tins of tuna in her rucksack, so maybe she could walk for twelve days. After that, she didn't know what she would do. There was always the chance of finding something to eat, but she didn't think it was very likely.

The MARFO fighters would have priority over any foodstuffs found en route. They set off cross-country following a well-worn footpath with the setting sun on their left, heading for MARFO headquarters to the north. The pace was relentless but anyone who lagged behind got prodded with the butt of a Kalashnikov, reminding them of the consequences of slowing down the column.

That evening, Tereza came to see Sam and the boys, who were sitting under a tree playing a throwing game with pebbles. She had managed to obtain a tin cooking pot half-full of funge. Sam had never imagined she would be so glad to see that beige, tasteless paste. Tereza made it clear that Sam should share their food and was about to divide it between them when Sam stopped her. She fished around in her rucksack and pulled out a tin of tuna. She indicated to Tereza that she wanted to mix it into the funge and was rewarded with a vigorous nodding of the head.

She used her penknife to open the tin and was careful not to let any of the oil spill on the ground. She tipped the tuna and oil into the pot and Tereza mixed it into the funge. Tereza made greasy balls with the mixture and handed it out to the hungry group.

'Mmm. Very good,' said Edison. 'I like this meat a lot.'

Pibé had a trail of fish oil down his chin, and his eyes were shining. The tuna made the funge almost edible for Sam, who was amused by the boys' exclamations of ecstasy. It hit the spot in one sense, and the hunger pangs were defeated for an hour or two, enabling Sam to snatch a few hours' sleep before they were back on the road again.

***

Jim Hennessy arrived at the Gemsite office in Mondongo, back early from his leave, to deal with the fallout from the raid. He soon located Black, who had commandeered the boardroom and was sitting in the chairman's seat, the table in front of him littered with dirty teacups and full ashtrays. The smell of the ashtrays was overpowering, and Jim, who didn't smoke, tried to open the windows, which were stuck fast.

'Jesus, Adrian, it stinks in here. Can't we go somewhere else? Why don't we go to the café around the corner and have a nice custard tart?'

'They don't have tea or anything I recognise as tea.'

'We can bring a teabag with us. Let's go. I need a decent coffee to wake me up.'

Despite his reputation as a despot, Black was pretty good at taking instructions from people brave enough to issue them. Shuffling along with his head down, as if he were being taken against his will, Black followed Jim out of the office to the café.

Jim ordered a selection of tarts and some coffee and hot water and sat outside with Black, who was making short work of his latest cigarette. They sat in the sun without saying anything until the order arrived at their table. Black launched into the tarts without preamble, making Jim smile. He knew that his boss was a beast when it came to sweet things.

Once the tea and coffee were poured and stirred, Jim asked Black to tell him what had happened at Kardo. Black leaned forward and lowered his voice. Jim had to lean forward, too, to hear him.

'It was a train wreck. The expats in charge of security had come to Mondongo to negotiate a pay rise. The poor fuckers that were left behind got massacred. I hear they were all running around like headless chickens.'

'Did we lose anyone?'

'We lost three men. Two mechanics and a diamond sorter called Dirk.'

'Dirk? Poor bastard. He didn't deserve that. I hear they took captives?'

'Yes. Thirteen in total. They took Bob and his mechanics, Fred, Brian and Sam. They have walked them out of camp and may be heading to MARFO country up north near the Zambian border. I expect they'll ask for a ransom of some sort.'

'They took Sam? Oh, no. Poor Sam. How is she going to survive?'

Black smiled and looked smug.

'Don't kid yourself. That woman is tougher than all of the others put together. She'll make it. Remember Filiberto who turned up two years later? They don't have any reason to maltreat them.'

'Did they get the diamonds?'

'No, one of the keyholders was in Mondongo at the security negotiations. Don't worry; you'll still get your bonus.'

Jim looked at Black in stunned amazement. *Did Black really believe that his motives were financial?* Black was sucking on a cigarette and blowing unconcerned smoke rings into the Mondongo air. He didn't notice the effect his statement had on Jim. Oblivious to people's feelings and with no normal reactions of his own, Black was a man apart.

'What about her parents?' he said. 'Someone will have to inform them about what has happened to Sam.'

'We don't need to tell them until we know what's going on. I don't want them interfering.'

'Yes, we do. We can't pretend this hasn't happened. People are dead. Dirk's parents are on their way to pick up his body. It's all over the newspapers, and on the radio that a female geologist has been kidnapped. Who else could it be?'

'Okay,' said Black, stubbing out his cigarette with ill-concealed fury. 'Enough fucking about. Let's go back and deal with the train wreck. You call the parents. Don't go into detail. Tell them we will sort it out as soon as we can. I have a meeting with General Fuego this afternoon to discuss tactics.'

Jim shook himself to remove the taint of Black's remarks, and followed his boss back to the office. He dreaded making the call, but Black had abdicated responsibility and someone had to do it.

***

Black arrived at the offices of General Fuego in central Mondongo just after the hottest part of the day. He was shown into the cool inner patio where abundant foliage caressed the walls and joists. A small fountain bubbled over into a dark pool containing small coloured fish at its base. Black sat on a wooden bench smoking a cigarette and blowing smoke up through the gap beneath the raised roof. The afternoon breeze blew the smoke back into the atrium, making swirls of smoke and dust, which caught the sun that was low enough on the horizon to sneak under the roof in places.

Particles of dust danced in the sunlight, mesmerising Black, who was miles away by the time the General came out to see him. The General had to stand in front of Black for several seconds before Black realised that he was standing there.

'Mr Black. I was expecting you.'

'Ah, yes, General. Forgive me. I was daydreaming.'

'Counting your money, no doubt.'

Black smiled sheepishly. A remark not so far from the truth. He moved sideways on the bench, making more room for the General to sit down. The two men sat alone for a minute or more, contemplating the rays of sunlight hitting the walls of the atrium.

'So,' began the General, 'I was sorry to hear of the attack on Kardo. I offer you my condolences on the losses suffered by your workforce.'

'It is kind of you to say so.'

'I understand it was a MARFO attack. My sources tell me that the rebels were unable to open the safes.'

'That is correct, General.'

'Do you have any information on the captives?'

'Yes, sir. I believe that twelve men and one woman were taken captive.'

The General turned to face Black, a strange look on his face. He took a deep breath before he asked the next question.

'A woman? Was she a local?'

'No, sir. She's a geologist, one of the new members of staff, Sam Harris.'

The General turned away and leaned forward with his forearms on his knees. He sat very still for a minute, contemplating his ultra-shiny shoes. Black waited for a comment, but since none was forthcoming, he decided that protocol would allow him to ask a question.

'Do you have any news on the whereabouts of the rebels?'

The General looked up and directed his gaze at Black.

'We have a pretty clear idea where they are headed. The main MARFO camp is about thirty kilometres from the border of Zambia. It will take them about a week to get there if they walk all day. Once they get there, we're sure to hear from them. I expect they'll have demands.'

'What sort of demands?'

'They'll ask for a ransom since they couldn't open the safe and didn't get any diamonds. They don't often take captives unless they want to do a swap of some kind. I was in charge of negotiations with MARFO many times, so I have my sources. I expect I will hear from them before too long.'

Black digested this information without mentioning the fabled case of his Filipino mechanic.

'I have taken enough of your time, General. I will await news from you, and we will proceed as you suggest once we know what they want.'

'Thank you for coming. I know you must be worried. We will endeavour to keep you up to date with all news as we get it.'

Black left the General sitting on the bench in the atrium still looking at his shoes. He appeared deflated, and Black imagined he was disappointed at the performance of his security troops.

***

News of the raid on Kardo had been broadcast on the television. No journalists could access the area due to the fact that General Fuego vetoed their travel papers but speculation was rife. Rumours of a white woman among the MARFO captives had spread like wildfire and was picked up by the news channels.

Sam's parents were having lunch in the kitchen when they heard the news on Radio 4. Matilda Harris gasped and dropped her fork back into her spaghetti, splattering its contents on her dress. Brushing it off with her hand, she stood up and ran to the sitting room to switch on the twenty-four-hour news channel, Sky News, followed by her shocked husband.

They sat watching with horror as the story unfolded, their lunch forgotten and congealed on cold plates.

'Oh my God, we shouldn't have let her go,' said Matilda.

'Now, darling, stay calm. We don't know it's her,' said Bill.

'But how many women can be working there?'

'She rang us from Mondongo. I'm sure she's fine.'

But the tremor in his voice gave him away. They

sat watching the news on a loop, tiny details being added every hour. The doorbell rang, making them both jump. Hannah, Sam's sister, stood at the front door, white-faced with panic.

'Have you seen the news?' she said. 'Could it be Sam they've taken?'

'Yes, we just watched it,' said Bill. 'They haven't mentioned any names yet.'

'But she's working in Mondongo, sweetheart,' said Matilda. 'It must be someone else.'

'But Mummy, how many female geologists are going to be working in Tamazia? It's not exactly safe.'

'She took her tennis racket,' said Matilda, as if it was a talisman.

'Have you tried ringing Gemsite?' said Hannah.

'We can't get through. The lines are terrible,' said Bill, rubbing his hands through his sparse hair. 'We can try again shortly.'

'But we have to do something.'

'Let's have a cup of tea,' said Matilda.

Tea, the universal panacea, but what else could they do?

They were sitting at the table absorbed in their own thoughts when the phone rang.

'You get it, Bill,' said Matilda. 'My hands are shaking.'

Bill Harris took a deep breath and lifted the receiver.

'Hello, Harris residence.'

'Hello, Mr Harris? This is Jim Hennessy, Sam's boss at Kardo.'

'Kardo? Isn't she working in Mondongo?' he said.

'She came to me for work experience but…'

Jim's voice tailed off.

'Have they taken our girl?' said Bill.

'I'm so sorry. The security forces were massively outnumbered.'

'What are you doing about it? Can we help?'

'No, there is nothing you can do. General Fuego, the head of the armed forces is in talks with the rebels about a ransom. He has done it before and the hostages were all freed unharmed.'

'How long will it take?'

'Days, maybe weeks. She'll be okay. Your daughter's a tough young woman and she speaks Portuguese so they'll need her for communications with the other hostages.'

'Thank you for calling us. Please keep us in the loop. It's hard to hear stuff like that on the news.'

'I'm so sorry. We needed to confirm the facts before we rang you. We'll be in touch.'

Bill Harris replaced the receiver and turned to face the devastated faces of his wife and daughter.

'It's her.'

Chapter XVII

After eight days, the now exhausted MARFO fighters and their captives arrived at their main camp in the north of Tamazia. Sam had remained in pretty good shape thanks to the food and water provided by Tereza and her sons. She had lost a lot of weight, something that would have cheered her up under normal circumstances, but it didn't top her list of priorities at that moment. She was marched through the camp with the other staff from Kardo, generating curious looks from the inhabitants and some cheering.

The camp consisted of about twenty mud huts with palm leaf roofs surrounded by a thick hedge of thorn bushes. The largest hut sat at the edge of an open area, which looked as if it might serve as a football pitch. There were a few light bulbs strung around the camp at eccentric intervals, indicating the presence of a generator. A cooking area contained two girls naked from the waist up who were using large blunt-end poles to pound the cassava in the mortars into flour. Sam half-expected her colleagues to make some sort of childish comment about the young breasts swinging free, but Brian and Fred had shrunk in stature and bravado during the walk, and both walked by without noticing.

Bob and his mechanics still had enough energy left to make wisecracks about the state of the camp, including inquiring where the pool was located. She was just glad to take off her boots and socks, and sit in the shade under a mango tree. The captives were left with one guard, whilst their fate was discussed in the main hut. They considered overpowering the guard and running away, but they had no idea if the border was close or whether their captors would come after them with guns. Maybe they would be better fed now that they were in what looked like a well-run camp with an obvious cooking area.

The arrival of the foreigners caused quite a stir amongst the children in the camp. When they first arrived, the children scattered, screaming in terror. Some of the toddlers burst into tears and had to be comforted by their mothers. Edison started to giggle.

'Why are they crying?' said Sam.

'When we are small, our mothers tell us that if we don't go to sleep, the white man will come and eat us. Most of those children have never seen a white person before, never mind a blonde one like you.'

She knew her light brown hair was considered blonde but not that she was also terrifying to small children. It was quite funny to see their little faces screwed up in terror.

'Tell them not to worry. I'm not one of those white people,' she said.

She sat under the mango tree, and little by little, the children overcame their terror and came to touch her hair and her face. As long as she didn't move, they were quite brave, but if she lifted her arm, they ran away screaming and laughing. Pibé was determined to show that he wasn't afraid and sat himself in Sam's lap, lording it over the others.

There was a commotion in the main hut, and several loud voices could be heard. This went on for several minutes, but then the voices were silenced and the door opened. A tall, muscular man with a wispy beard on his chin came out and approached the group. He surveyed the group with something approaching sympathy.

'My name is Joao Contes. I am in charge of this MARFO unit,' he said in Portuguese. There was silence for a few seconds, and then Sam greeted him back.

'Nice to meet you, sir,' said Sam.

'Do you speak Portuguese?' he said her.

'Yes.'

'Translate this please: the council of MARFO is grateful for the help of the Filipino workers in carrying our goods back to camp. They are not involved in this white man's war, so they will be allowed to go home. I have instructed my contact in Mondongo to have them removed as soon as possible. That should happen in a few days' time. We will be keeping the white people for ransom. Do not worry. As soon as the ransom is paid, we will release you too.'

He turned to Sam. 'Do you know if there is an electrician amongst the Filipinos?'

'At least one, if you include Bob. I think there are three.'

Sam indicated Bob, who was sitting amongst his mechanics smoking a cigarette. Sam guessed the supply of cigarettes would be running out soon and could imagine the panic that would cause. *Worse than being captured?* Maybe not. It looked like they wouldn't get the chance to smoke them all.

'Good. Can you inform them that in return for their freedom, I want them to fix the generator?'

'Of course.'

She was sure of getting a positive response from the group, who hated not having anything to do and loved to show off their skills. She approached them and translated the news. The Filipinos all cheered and set off with one of the rebels to look for parts amongst the tools and electrical goods stolen from Kardo.

Brian and Fred were nonplussed.

'What about us?' said Fred.

'I told you,' said Sam. 'He says we are being held for ransom. Don't worry. I'm sure Black will sort something out.'

'That shows how much you know. Black would rather die than pay a ransom. We are fucked.'

Fred moved back into the shade of the mango tree and started talking to Brian in a low voice.

Sam shrugged. In a strange way, she felt liberated in the MARFO camp. Being the only Portuguese-speaker gave her a power that she didn't have at Kardo. She wondered if Black would really abandon them. *Had the General heard about the raid? What would he be thinking? Was Pedro right and was she just a source of easy information?* Sam had been so sure that she had made a genuine connection with the General. She was usually right about these matters. One thing was certain: the connection had been much stronger than the one Pedro tried to make with her. She shuddered.

***

Soon after the captives arrived in the MARFO camp in the northeast corner of Tamazia, the General set out to see the President. Having received the news of their arrival and of the imminent release of the Filipinos from his sources, he was keen to discuss the delicate issue with his brother-in-law with whom he had a certain amount of influence. He entered the palace and was shown into the inner sanctum where he was kept waiting a good hour and a half before the President came in.

He gazed at the marble walls and floors, which were the best Italy could offer and cool to the touch even in this infernal heat. The swirling patterns in the rock told stories of ancient orogenies and of heat and pressure under the earth. A large chandelier, with hundreds of bulbs, hung from the domed roof, and the walls were covered in paintings of women with implausible robe slippage. It was obvious where the oil money was going. In truth, he was getting his share. Being the brother-in-law of the President had its perks.

He heard the tall doors swing open and turned to face the person who had entered.

'Good morning, Mr President.'

'Cunhado, good morning. How are you today? And your family, are they well?'

'Thanks be to God we are all fine, sir. And your family?'

'Thanks be to God everybody is well also. Have you any news for me?'

'Yes, sir. We have had news that the Filipino hostages are to be released as soon as practicable. I have instructed Eduardo to go to the north and hire a bus to take them to the nearest airstrip where we will have a helicopter waiting. He will be given safe passage by the rebels.'

'That is good news. One less ambassador to worry about. What about the others?'

'I have heard that MARFO will ask for a ransom for the other foreigners. I suspect it will be a considerable amount.'

'Do you have a view on the likelihood of it being

paid? I would prefer that we did not start paying ransoms. It might be a slippery slope as far as MARFO is concerned.'

'There is no law against ransom payments, sir, but I suspect that Mr Black will not pay. He is more likely to give away his children than his money.'

'What will MARFO do if the ransom is not paid?'

'We do not know, sir. This is the first time they have asked for a ransom. In the past, they just shot any captives after they served as mules for the booty from raids on mining camps. I suspect the captives will be murdered if the ransom is not paid. I would like permission to rescue them if they are in danger.'

'Let us see how the situation develops. I don't want to give any permission right now until I get a clear idea of how things will play out.'

'But, sir, a rescue operation needs forward planning. I cannot send people in at a moment's notice. Please, let me organise a raiding party just in case.'

'No, not yet. Have patience, Fuego. MARFO rebels do not kill their hostages if they think they can get money out of it. They use them to play games. Remember the Filipino who turned up after two years? The captives might be killed in the rescue, and I don't need to generate an international incident just now.'

The President turned away to indicate that he was finished with the discussion. Under normal circumstances, the General would have left it at that, but he hadn't finished yet.

'Sir, please. There is a woman amongst the captives. We cannot let them kill her.'

The President spun around in fury.

'Fuego, your peccadillos are not my concern. I have heard that your failure to obtain information from that woman was due to your infatuation with her. I am not risking an international incident so you can rescue your crush. Don't try my patience. If we need to act, we will. Come and see me when you have news.'

The President swept out of the room and left the General standing by himself in its marble opulence. Arguing with the President would just harden his resolve not to interfere. He resented the insinuation about Sam, but he knew in his heart of hearts that she had touched him in a way that he wasn't expecting, and he had been unprofessional because of it. When he thought of Sam, it was his heart and not his head that provided the canvas.

What made it worse was that he considered the attack on Kardo to be his fault. If only he had agreed to a reasonable pay raise for the security staff, they would have been in Kardo and not in Mondongo. The raid succeeded because some of the senior officers were missing. MARFO headquarters must have received the news from one of their spies and known that Kardo was vulnerable. The MARFO chiefs hadn't realised that the keyholders for the diamond recovery plant would also be in Mondongo.

All too late now. Sam was a prisoner and might be murdered, and he felt responsible. He got into his car and told the driver to take him home.

***

Life in the MARFO camp soon settled into a routine as nerves became less frayed and it appeared less likely that the rebels were planning on harming their guests. The Filipinos had fixed the generator on the first day and had continued to find ways of making life more comfortable as was their wont. They had made some stands for the cooking pots and a rudimentary barbeque for the kitchen. Bare light bulbs now hung in almost every hut and at six-thirty every night, the generator was called into action, making the whole village shine like a diamond on the pitch dark plain.

Sam took advantage of the goodwill created by the Filipinos' actions to improve their living accommodation in camp. The empty huts had been cleared out and shared among the hostages. Bob and the Filipinos slept together in the largest hut and Brian and Fred shared a hut near the centre of camp.

Sam had been allocated a small scruffy hut beside the hedge surrounding the compound. It contained a single bed made of branches raised above the mud floor and a couple of hooks made from twigs thrust into the mud walls. Her mosquito net was hanging from the roof over the bed. Her precious rucksack hung on a nail over her bed, which was covered in a hemp sack, serving as a mattress. She still had iodine tablets, repellent, malaria tablets and her precious penknife. She had mourned her supplies of tea, and now forced herself to drink the hot, sweet coffee served in the morning.

She spent her days with the women, walking down to the river in the morning to wash herself and her clothes. There was intense interest in her bra, which was often passed around the group and examined. Tereza had managed to borrow a T-shirt from somewhere, which Sam wore whilst her shirt was drying on the hot stones on the river bank. When the washing was finished, it was time to harvest the cassava and tend to the plantations. Sam was delegated to child watching, which was easy for her. She spent many happy hours joining in the games and rolling around in the dust.

They were always hungry but not starving, so Sam continued to lose weight but at a slower rate than before. She fantasised about food a lot, mostly dairy products like cream, butter and cheese. Funge was not growing on her, but she forced herself to eat it and any meat that was offered. Edison was a champion mouse catcher, and Tereza toasted their little bodies on the barbeque for the children. Sam found them only just worth eating, but she remembered tales of Auschwitz and inmates eating insects to survive. If she were ever to escape, she had to keep her strength up somehow. She told herself that they were just meat and made Tereza cut the heads off so the incisors and bulging eyes didn't accuse her of mouse-icide.

She did not mix with the men at all if she could avoid it. There was a lot of curiosity about having a white woman in camp, and she had to be very subtle about going to relieve herself as she had twice been aware of men trying to spy on her. The other women kept her safe from most of it, but at night, she preferred to pee in a bowl rather than leave the relative safety of her hut.

Fred and Brian spent their days sleeping in the sun and talking. They could not communicate with anyone in camp and were not interested in helping out. Both had lost a lot of weight and Fred was unrecognisable now that his frame was uncurling from his computer-related hunch. They both had beards, and Brian was beginning to look like an aging hippie.

Bob, on the other hand, was always busy, running around fixing things and in his element. He couldn't speak Portuguese, but that didn't stop him from having animated discussions with the MARFO fighters about all things fixable in the camp. He used a twig in the dirt to illustrate most of what he was saying, and that worked very well most of the time. Sometimes he roped Sam in to translate when no one could understand, although she couldn't translate what she couldn't understand either. Bob could be seen in the evening drinking cassava beer with his mechanics and the MARFO fighters as they sat around the football pitch under the stars.

The bus arrived for the Filipinos on their fifth day in camp. To Sam's immense surprise, Eduardo stepped off the bus. She was playing with the children at the time, and they all ran towards the bus in excitement. She waved at him, but he affected not to see her and was shepherded into the main hut by Joao and the other fighters before she could approach him.

Meanwhile, the driver of the bus opened the luggage compartment under the bus and called the women over to help him unload the contents. There was great excitement as sacks of rice and sugar and boxes of cooking oil and biscuits were unloaded. Sam spotted some boxes of UHT milk and tinned tuna. There were even crates of live chickens, which were worse for the wear and needed to be revived with water. The booty was taken to the kitchens and stored away from sight. Fred groaned as the precious biscuits disappeared into the store.

'I'd kill for a biscuit,' he said.

'You're not the only one,' said Brian.

The Filipinos had assembled their paltry possessions and were loitering near the bus. Marco came over to shake Sam's hand and gave her two packets of cigarettes 'for emergencies.' Sam hid them in the shin pocket of her cargo pants. Eduardo emerged from the hut and went over to the kitchens where he was engaged in an earnest conversation with Tereza. As Sam watched them, Eduardo gave Tereza something that she put in her pocket without looking at it.

He turned to go. Sam was sure he had seen her, but he didn't approach her. She couldn't understand it. And to make matters worse, Bob was getting on the bus. He waved sheepishly at her. He looked relieved and tired, like an old man after a party. *Why aren't I on the bus, too?* Sam couldn't believe it. *What about women and children first?* She looked left and right trying to find someone who could help her get on the bus with Bob. She saw only the devastated faces of Fred and Brian, who looked as if they might collapse with chagrin.

'Why is that useless old fucker leaving first?' said Brian.

'Because he's a useless old fucker, I expect,' said Sam, without irony.

The comment was not received well by Brian and Fred, but Sam had worked it out by then. Bob wasn't worth very much ransom because he was a mechanic. Brian, on the other hand, was head of security and could provide important information about the security arrangements in the Gemsite mines. Fred had all the statistics for the diamonds in his head, including how big, what quality and where from. *But why had they kept her?*

Sam suspected that someone had suggested to the rebels that she was Black's new pet and could be used to turn the screw on him. Something she doubted very much, considering how much he loved his money. It was all going wrong, and she was powerless to stop it. *Why hadn't the General told Eduardo to get her out?* She couldn't understand why he pretended not to know her. She stood in mute horror as the bus pulled out without her. She felt abandoned, and she had only Brian and Fred for company. *Could it get any worse?*

***

Hannah started to cry. Her mother Matilda stared mutely at the television, blinking as if to wipe the image from her eyes.

'It's good news,' said Bill. 'If they are releasing people unharmed, that's a positive development.'

'But why release Bob Norton? It doesn't make any sense. Surely they should be releasing Sam first? She's a woman,' said Hannah, blowing her nose and sniffling.

'I think they released the low-value hostages first,' said her father.

'I can't bear to think of her all alone in the camp,' said Matilda. 'What if she gets ill? Or injured?'

'Bob Norton said the other hostages were doing well. We have to hope for the best,' said Bill. 'Don't distress yourselves. Sam's a fighter. She'll get through this.'

But no one answered.

Chapter XVIII

A deep depression hit Sam over the next few days. She found it hard to eat, despite the luxury of rice and tuna for the evening meal instead of funge. Tereza even smuggled her out a packet of biscuits, which she put in her rucksack instead of eating. The children picked up on her despondency, and Pibé was quite affected by it. He spent a lot of time sitting with her and refused to play with the other children.

Even in her depressed state, Sam became concerned with his lack of energy, and she invited him into her lap for a cuddle to cheer them both up. She put her arms around him and held him close, crooning into his ear. She was alarmed to feel how hot his skinny body was to the touch. The little boy was like a furnace. She could barely tolerate him on her lap, as it was like holding a hot water bottle in that heat.

'Are you all right, Pibé?' she said. 'You feel very hot.'

The little boy nodded, but his eyes were yellow. He was drenched in a cold sweat. His eyes rolled up into his head, and his body went limp. Sam only just managed to catch him as he fell backwards off her lap. She lifted him onto her chest and walked to the cooking area. She soon spotted Tereza, who looked up and dropped the large spoon she was holding. She ran up to Sam and took the boy from her. She noticed the heat he was giving off.

'What's wrong with him?' said Sam.

'Malaria,' said his distraught mother. 'He is so weak. How will he survive?' She ignored Sam and took Pibé into one of the huts near the kitchens. Sam entered the hut too. Tereza was wiping the boy with a damp cloth.

'Will you give him medicine?'

'I do not have any medicine. He must survive without it.'

'But he could die.'

'Yes, I lost a daughter to malaria two years ago. Life is hard, and God takes away your children when he wants to.'

The mention of God infuriated Sam. She thought the death of so many children from disease and famine was pretty good proof that there was no such thing as God. She had malaria tablets in her bag that could save the little boy, but she wasn't sure she wanted to give them away. *What if I'm captive for months? What if I get malaria and have no medicine left?* She wasn't like the local people, who were inured to the effects to a great extent. If Sam got cerebral malaria, she would die for sure.

Pibé moaned and sank into the bed, becoming thinner and frailer in an instant. Sam's conscience worked overtime. *Surely they would be rescued soon?* She would make sure to put repellent on all the time. She cursed her goodness. *Why can't I be a shit like Black or Brian?*

'Tereza, are you sure that it's malaria?'

'Oh, yes, we have all had it many times. I am worried about Pibé because he is so thin and tired.'

'I have some malaria tablets in my rucksack. I'll bring them now. Wait here.'

Without waiting for a reply, Sam headed for her hut and rooted around in her rucksack for the tablets. She found them with ease, and then she sat on her bed, considering the box and the consequences of giving it away. She tried to form an argument for keeping them for herself, but it was hopeless. She was too well brought up.

At that moment, she hated both her parents and their honesty and bravery that she had been immersed in from an early age. No lying was tolerated. Everyone else came first. She was forced to play with the unpopular children at parties because being kind was important. Now, she was going to risk her life for a little boy who was bound to die of something else even if he survived the malaria. *How bloody annoying.*

She slipped out of her hut and walked across the camp to Tereza's hut. She stopped outside, reading the instructions in the bright sunlight before she went in. Brian was passing by.

'What's wrong with the wee lad?' said Brian.

'Malaria.'

'That's him dead then,' said Brian, in a matter-of-fact way.

Sam almost punched him, but he made her mind up for her. She entered the hut and helped Tereza dose the boy with tablets. Tereza grasped Sam by the hands.

'You're an angel; I don't know how to thank you.'

'Just look after Pibé for me. He's the only reason I survive from day to day.'

Sam had said it to make Tereza feel less beholden, but she knew it to be true even as the words formed in the stifling air of the dirty hut. She looked down at Pibé on the bed. She saw Tereza had given him the pink teddy bear to hold. The teddy was not pink at all now but dirty and matted. Tereza smiled.

'He loves the teddy,' she said. 'I could never afford to buy him any toys.'

Sam felt so ashamed the teddy wasn't even from her, but a cast-off from Pedro. She earned a fortune compared to anyone from Tamazia and couldn't imagine living in that sort of poverty. She leaned over and caressed his cheek with her finger.

'Come on, Pibé. Don't leave me here alone,' she murmured.

Despite the medicine, Pibé lingered for three days between life and death before turning the corner. Sam stayed by his side when Tereza couldn't, and Edison often sat with her. Pibé lay still in his bed, fighting the invasion in his small body. Sam was still very depressed by her predicament, but sitting beside the almost lifeless boy gave her a sense of perspective. She knew her mother and father would have been informed about what had happened to her by now. Her flippant comment that she could leave if she wanted to came back to haunt her.

As Pibé recovered, Sam started to try and build bridges with Brian and Fred. As much as she hated them for the way she had been treated, she knew there was often strength in numbers. Kardo seemed very far away, both in distance and in time. None of them had been party to the negotiations with the capital, so the uncertainty of their position made them desperate to discuss the possible scenarios of their incarceration.

'We should try to escape,' said Brian.

'To where?' said Fred.

'I'm pretty sure the Zambian border is close,' said Sam. 'We walked north from Kardo. I was watching the sun.'

'But how do we get out of the compound? We're locked in at night,' said Fred.

'What do we do if we reach the border? Will the guards let us cross without a bribe? The rebels might hunt us down in a day, and their treatment might not be so benign as a result,' said Sam.

'It's safer to stay in camp until we are given news by Joao about the payment of the ransom. We should know next week according to him,' said Fred.

'It's certain to take a while to settle on the exact amount, but I don't doubt that it will be paid, as Black has taken a shine to Sam,' said Brian.

'I don't know what you did to him,' said Fred. 'I suspect that even the Filipino girls are less skilled at getting what they want.'

'Maybe he'll only pay for me, then,' said Sam.

'For fuck's sake, woman, why can't you quit when you're ahead?' said Brian, but he couldn't help smiling.

The relaxed atmosphere in the camp even had its effect on him, and he could be spotted playing chess with the MARFO commander in the evenings. Even Fred had started to thaw, helping people with their mobile phones and trying to scrounge food from the women in the kitchens.

Whilst it was true that there was no violence directed at them, there was a certain menace surrounding the closed meetings that sometimes took place in the meeting hut. Afterwards, the fighters would emerge red-eyed from the smoke and glare at the captives with something approaching loathing.

***

Back in Mondongo, Black was getting ready to meet the General who was coming to the Gemsite office with news of the ransom demand. He called for some tea, and Pedro put his head around the door.

'The secretary is at lunch, boss. Can I help?'

'Yes, you can get me some tea.'

Pedro could see that he was in a good mood. He knew that Black was buoyed by the news from Ewen of near-record production from Kardo. The ransom was sure to hurt, but with this sort of production, it wouldn't make much difference to the bottom line over the quarter.

The tea in the Gemsite office in Mondongo had also run out, and no one had dared tell Black yet. Pedro was not fazed, though. Sam kept some tea in the Villa Alice for her visits to Mondongo. He drove there as fast as he could to keep his boss in a good mood. He found Sam's supply stashed in a box hidden behind the sofa. These British people and their tea. He could never understand why they wouldn't drink coffee like everyone else.

He grabbed a handful of bags from the container and shoved them in a plastic bag he found in the kitchen. He also stole a packet of biscuits that was hidden in the box. She wasn't going to need any of this stuff now. He spotted the floral dress rolled up and shoved into a corner of the box. He smirked as he remembered Sam's panic when she realised that she would have to sleep with him to keep him quiet. He didn't even like her that much. He was just pushing his luck. Mind you, she was worth it. If she ever got out, he would make sure he got some more of that.

On his way back into the office, he met Eduardo, who was loitering beside the General's limousine smoking a cheroot. Never one to miss the chance of picking up some high-level gossip, Pedro took out a cigarette and approached him for a light.

'Good afternoon, Eduardo. Are you here with the General?'

'Pedro, good afternoon. Yes, my boss is inside with your boss.'

'I hear there is news on the ransom demand.'

Eduardo nodded and rubbed his thumb against his index and middle finger.

'Well, I guess the hostages must be worth that much to Black.'

'The General would pay that much for only one of them,' said Eduardo and winked.

'Really,' said Pedro. 'I had no idea.'

Eduardo, who liked to make himself look important by affecting knowledge that he did not have, winked again.

'Oh, yes. I have it on good authority that, well, you know, Sam stayed the weekend with him on the island.'

He made an obscene gesture with his hands.

'Is that so?' Pedro struggled to remain calm and neutral. 'You never can tell. I'd better get these tea bags inside before Black gets withdrawal symptoms. Not a pretty sight.'

'Of course. Good to see you.'

Pedro was by now quivering with rage. The bitch. He knew she was lying about the General. She was spying for him. Black was being led up the garden path by that lying cow, but he would never allow it. He must tell Black the truth. His honour was at stake. He went upstairs to the boardroom. Black was alone, smoking a cigarette.

'Here is your tea. Shall I make you a cup?'

'No, not yet. I shall wait for the General to come back. He is making a call downstairs in the office. Leave the teabags in the kitchen.'

Pedro did not leave. He stood hovering in the doorway; despite the very obvious dismissal he had received from Black.

'Was there something you wanted?' he asked Pedro.

'I think there is something you ought to know. About Sam. Sam and the General.'

'Sam and the General?'

'My sources tell me they were having an affair.'

'An affair? Are you mad? What makes you think that? How on earth has Sam had an affair with the General in Kardo? The General lives in Mondongo, and he has not visited Kardo since last year when we invited the government to the inauguration of the new plant.'

Pedro stuck to his guns.

'I have good information that Sam has been meeting the General in Mondongo and that she has been passing him production information about Kardo.'

'Now that is ridiculous! Sam didn't have any access to that sort of information until I went there on my last trip. I had to wait until Fred was drunk before she could access his precious information. She couldn't have passed any information about that night to the General. She was kidnapped straight afterwards.'

Pedro faltered, doubting his own certainty, but he couldn't back down now. That would be fatal.

'The General's man, Eduardo, told me. He is very close to the General. He should know.'

At that moment, the General stepped back into the room and caught the last volley from Pedro.

'What has Eduardo been telling you?' he enquired. 'He is the most terrible gossip. I wouldn't believe half of it.'

***

Black needed time to think.

'Pedro, go and tell the girls to make us some tea. General, you will have some English tea?'

'Yes, thank you. I hope that Eduardo has not been spreading more false rumours. I am tempted to cut his tongue out.'

This was said in a weary tone of voice that suggested this was not the first indiscretion committed by Eduardo but one in a long line of similar leaks and fibs. The General had a fearsome reputation. He was more than capable of cutting out Eduardo's tongue if he was in the mood. Black decided to proceed with caution.

'So, General, I presume this is not a social visit?'

'You're correct. I've had news from the rebel camp. They are asking for one million dollars for the hostages. I can't tell if this is a final demand, but I don't recommend pushing them too far, as they are quite capable of killing the hostages if they don't get what they want.'

'One million dollars! Holy fuck! Even my mother's not worth that much. Are you sure they won't negotiate?'

'They might, but they might not. Their leader, Joao Contes, is a bit of a hothead. And remember, they're holding Sam. Who knows what they could do to her?'

To Black's immense surprise, he heard the General's voice break when he said this. It was almost imperceptible, but he had not imagined it. The girls arrived with the tea, giving the General time to compose himself. Black affected a relaxed demeanour as he said the next question.

'Have you met Sam, General?'

'Yes, several times. She is a special person, don't you think?'

This was said with a total lack of guile, but Black didn't notice. His brain went into overdrive. He had been taken in by Sam. How could he have been so stupid? The woman was playing both sides. He should have known. Sam was just another lying, duplicitous, two-timing bitch. But he held the cards now.

'Yes, very special indeed. It would be a shame to lose her. Let me talk to my people about our finances. We have a diamond sale coming up. I hope we can raise the money before it is too late. Meanwhile, ask your sources to inquire about the ransom. I need to know if it is a fixed price or if there could be some movement.'

'That could be very dangerous.'

'I'm not paying a million dollars to a bunch of terrorists. Get the price down, and I'll think about it.'

The General looked taken aback at the tone, but he nodded. He had expected Black to ask for a lower ransom. Everyone was well aware how much Black loved his money, even the General.

'Very well. We'll talk tomorrow. I'll call you.'

'Thank you for coming, General. I know how busy you are. Please give my regards to the President.'

'I shall. Have a good day, Mr Black.'

After the General had left, Black worked himself into a fury. He was a primitive man, and the only two colours he acknowledged were black and white. He had by now completely forgotten that Sam could not possibly have been feeding the General information before she had access to it. His pride was hurt, too. He had imagined that his relationship with Sam was special and had even considered taking it further.

Now, he felt betrayed. Why should he pay a ransom for a traitor? And that buffoon Fred? Did he imagine that Black didn't know what a useless, lazy, lump of lard he was? Pretending that no one else was clever enough to use the computer? Cheeky fucker. The only person worth a fig was Brian, but was he worth one million dollars? Brian was always disagreeing with Black and talking back. His attitude betrayed his lack of respect for his boss.

The rebels were unlikely to murder the hostages. MARFO would throw the hostages out to fend for themselves if no ransom was paid. The Filipino had managed to survive, after all. Sam could talk to the locals in their own language. They would get home alive. No doubt. Would serve them right if they didn't. Traitors.

He poured himself a large whisky from the tray on the cabinet and went into the kitchen to get some ice. He would have to pretend that he was going to pay the ransom and then refuse at the last minute on some pretext or other. He swirled the whisky around in his mouth as he stared into space. No one from Gemsite needed to know what he had in mind.

***

A couple of days later, the General arrived for lunch on the island at his favourite restaurant on the beach. He was sitting at a table for two in the corner of the patio that had been built out over the sand. It was a breezy day, and the seagulls were being buffeted from side to side as they scoured the beach for scraps. The General was sheltered from the breeze by flimsy wooden walls painted in a faded pink. He could feel the coarse sand scrunch under his shoes. He had the impulse to take them off and enjoy the warm boards on the soles of his feet, but before he could do so, he was joined by Eduardo, who had the air of someone bringing important news.

'Good afternoon, my General.'

'Good afternoon, Eduardo. Won't you sit down? I took the liberty of ordering us some fried squid to pick at with a cold beer. I hope that is okay?'

'Perfect. Thank you, General. I was dreaming of a beer when I was stuck in traffic on the way here. I apologise for my lateness, but you know how it gets at lunchtime.'

'No need to apologise. We both know all about the traffic jams in Mondongo. Do you have news for me?'

Eduardo sat forward, preparing himself to impart the news. At that moment, the waitress approached the table with the beers, and the General raised his hand to stop Eduardo from starting his report. The two men sat back as the waitress fussed around their table, putting out the beer mats and the tankards, which were frosted with ice. She took out a novelty bottle opener in the shape of a diamond and opened the beers. They were already cold, and when poured into the iced tankards, they were just too tempting in the heat of the Tamazia midday.

Eduardo's news was put on hold as they took deep draughts of the icy liquid. The fried squid were also delicious, and there was an appreciative silence as the two men enjoyed their crunchy heat washed down by the arctic beers.

'Fantastic.'

'So, Eduardo, what news have you of the rebels?'

'I have heard from my source that they have agreed to lower the ransom to five hundred thousand dollars on condition it is paid next week. The rebels claim they will kill the hostages if it is not paid on time.'

'Next week? That doesn't give us much time. I will have to speak to Mr Black as soon as possible. By the way, I forgot to ask you what you and Pedro talked about before my meeting with Black last week. He rushed upstairs and repeated it all to Black, you know.'

He saw Eduardo freeze with a piece of squid halfway to his mouth and go pale. The General could always tell when Eduardo wasn't telling the truth. Eduardo wouldn't dare to lie to him about what he said to Pedro.

'We were talking about the ransom. I told him that you wouldn't have a problem paying for Sam if it was your choice. Because she's nice.' He faltered and stopped.

'Jesus Christ, Eduardo, don't you have any sense at all?' said the exasperated General. 'Did you tell him that Sam was on the island?'

Eduardo's miserable face told him the truth. The General was shocked by this revelation. No wonder Black was cross. He was not a stupid man, and he must have guessed why Sam was being courted. The chances of Gemsite paying the ransom were receding by the minute, and he felt responsible for the debacle.

'You have put Sam in grave danger. I don't know if we can save her. Did you leave the phone with Edison Sousa's widow in the MARFO camp? My sources were right about her being there?'

'Yes, General. She was grateful that you remembered her. I gave her money for her children. She likes Sam and will keep an eye on her.'

'You'd better be right, for your sake.'

'I'm sorry I'm such an idiot. I'll do whatever you say to get Sam back.'

Eduardo looked like he might burst into tears.

'Okay, don't take it like that. We're warriors, are

we not? We'll find a way to rescue the hostages, especially Sam. Just promise me to keep your phone charged and in your possession day and night. We may need to move fast. I've talked to General Bruiser, from my old brigade. He has a helicopter available day or night if I give him word that I need it. We will get into big trouble with my brother-in-law, but it can't be helped.'

'I don't care. I will go anywhere with you, my General.'

'Fine, you might have to. Let's order some good fried fish. I'm still starving. Waitress?'

Chapter XIX

Pibé was getting better every day and had started following Sam around like a puppy. She had to shoo him away when she wanted to go to the toilet. When he was strong enough, they walked down to the river, and she used some of her precious soap to wash the pink teddy. It was a thankless task, but Sam was sure the soap would at least kill some of the bacteria adhering to the pink polyester fur.

She was running out of repellent and had taken to spraying it on her clothes and not washing them for days. Her hair had begun to clump up until Tereza and her friends dragged a plastic comb through it and plaited it close to her head in cornrows. She hadn't looked in a mirror for weeks, but her clothes told her that she was rake thin.

Sam's inner steel core had become more apparent as she fought to keep her spirits up. The deadline for the ransom payment was fast approaching, and the atmosphere in the camp had become tense. The hostages were shut in their huts at night, and the games of chess and shared beers had become a thing of the past.

Sam spent many hours in her hut lying on her uncomfortable bed wide awake with fear and anticipation, running through possible scenarios in her mind. She was aware that not all scenarios had happy endings, and she kept trying to imagine herself being brave if worse came to worst. It kept her awake, but she couldn't picture it. She was a glass-half-full girl, and all stories had happy endings, just maybe not quite the way one was expecting.

The next day, Sam was summoned to the main hut in the centre of the compound by Joao Conte, the rebel leader. He was sitting on a stool made of an upright piece of log polished by the sweat of many posteriors. He was wearing a rather fetching pink T-shirt with a picture of a kitten on it. Sam couldn't help smiling at the contrast between the bloodthirsty rebel leader and his less than terrifying attire. What he said next put the kitten right back in its box.

'The committee of the Santos unit of MARFO have made a decision about your future, you and your companions from Kardo.'

He paused to examine a scab on his leg, which he was picking and rubbing while he was talking to her. A small drop of dark blood oozed out and ran down his shin towards his battered trainers. He stopped it with a finger and cleaned his leg with spit.

'We've asked for a ransom of half a million dollars for you. We have given the authorities one week to pay the ransom. If the ransom is not paid, we'll put you on trial, charged with stealing the diamonds of Kardo from their rightful owners, the people of Tamazia. If you're found guilty, you will be shot. You'd better hope the ransom is paid on time. I can't guarantee your safety if my men don't get their money.'

Sam sat in stunned silence, trying to process this information. Their lives were hanging in the balance, and Black was the only one who could save them. She wondered if it was worth arguing that Gemsite had a contract from the government to exploit the diamonds and that they paid close to half their income in taxes and royalties to the ministry, which were supposed to be spent in the Kardo district.

She remembered the dusty road and the battered huts along it. It was pretty obvious that no government money had ever reached Kardo. The local people had lost their only form of income when Gemsite had begun the commercial excavation of the diamond gravels. They had been shot for trying to take gravel at night. Sam knew there was no argument that would change Joao's mind, and that any protests were likely to antagonise him.

'I understand,' she said.

'It's nothing personal,' said Joao. 'MARFO needs to force the western companies to leave before they take all our diamonds. We need the income to buy weapons to fight the government. Killing a few foreigners worked the last time we took hostages. Asking for a ransom means that if we don't get the diamonds ourselves, then at least we get the money earned from them.'

Sam couldn't fault his logic. She felt his total lack of sympathy for their fate in his tone. They were at war; people died. Sam went to tell the others.

There was a shocked silence as Sam explained what she had learnt from Joao.

'Jesus,' said Brian. 'That's us fucked.'

'Couldn't you do something?' said Fred. 'After all, you speak Portuguese.'

'I'm sorry,' said Sam. 'I don't think that anyone is listening. We'll have to rely on Black. Half a million dollars is peanuts to Gemsite. We just have to wait.'

'Rely on Black? That's a laugh; he wouldn't pay

for his mother. We have to escape.'

But escape was not in the cards, as the rebels now kept a very close eye on their captives, and from that time on, didn't let Sam near the others at all. The days passed very slowly. The rainy season was almost over, and the heat and humidity in the small huts was unbearable.

Sam used the last of her repellent on her clothes and decided not to wash them again until she was free. She would smell terrible, but malaria stalked the camp. She had no tablets left. Tereza brought her food in the evenings, but the portions were shrinking again, as the rebels didn't want to waste food on the hostages. Tereza smuggled in bananas to Sam via Edison and Pibé, but then the little boys were banned from going to see her after one of the rebels caught them giving her a tin of tuna.

Sam lay on her bed to conserve energy and tried to remember how to speak French. She conjugated irregular French verbs on the ceiling and the walls, forcing herself to pry them out of her memory. She ran through relationships she had in the past, dwelling on every good moment, every concert and every walk on the beach. *Would she ever see Yannis again, or Fergus?* If she got home, she would never take another geology job. She was finished.

Sometimes Tereza would sneak in for a few minutes when she delivered the contraband food, and ask Sam about living in England.

'Do you know Princess Di? Have you ever seen her?'

'No, I'm afraid I don't. I have only seen her in newspapers. You do know that she is dead now?'

'Yes, it is sad. The princess came to Mondongo to support the landmine trust and everyone in Tamazia knows about that. A real princess!'

Sam tried to imagine the distance in realities between Tereza and Princess Di and gave up. If Di had come from the moon, she couldn't have been from further away.

'Tell me about Edison, Tereza. Was he handsome and funny? How did you meet him?'

'He was from my village. He was not tall, but he was strong and brave, like Pibé. We met at school and we fell in love. I got pregnant with Edison junior at seventeen.'

These little interludes kept her sane while she waited for news of the ransom and lay on her bed, imagining the worst and listening to the noises of people going about their daily lives in camp as if nothing was happening.

***

In Mondongo, Black was sitting in the meeting room waiting for the general. He looked even more dishevelled than usual, and the sore on his forearm was weeping. He had been on a serious binge the night before, and he could only just keep his head up. He was still quite drunk. He was lighting a cigarette with great concentration, unaware that there was already a lit one that was balanced on one of the ashtrays with a long piece of ash hanging from the end. The air in the room was thick with smoke, and there was a rank smell of sweat and bad breath. There was a knock on the door.

'Come.'

Black drew deeply on his cigarette, composing himself for a confrontation. He had made up his mind days ago to make no attempt to raise the money for the ransom payment. *What sort of example would that be to his workforce?* Traitors didn't deserve any sympathy. If anything, Black was more determined to punish Sam than ever. He didn't care that two more people would die to make him feel better. Sam had betrayed him. That was unforgivable.

The General entered the room and waited to be addressed, wrinkling his nose in mute protest at the fug. Black looked up, and gave the General a malevolent glance.

'General, was I expecting you? Oh, yes. Yes, I was,' he muttered. 'I don't have good news, I'm afraid.'

General Fuego looked startled, but he did not say anything.

'We couldn't raise the money in time. The diamond sales have not gone through yet. Can't we persuade the rebels to wait?'

The insincerity of his tone surprised even the General.

'To wait? You want the rebels to wait. Don't you realise that the hostages will be murdered if you don't pay now? How will you sleep at night knowing that you have, to all intents and purposes, signed their death warrants?'

Black knew damn well it was a final demand. He was going to leave the hostages to their fate because he imagined he had been betrayed by one of them. Something approaching a smirk crept across Black's face, and he cocked his head at the General as if daring him to say something. There was a tense silence.

'I see,' said the General stiffly. 'I suppose it can't be helped. The President will be most disappointed.'

Black was not fooled. He knew as well as the General did that the President wanted diamond revenue at any cost, and if he had intended to do something about the hostages, he would have done it weeks ago.

The President would only be disappointed if production stopped because of the raid. In fact, everyone had carried on as if nothing had happened. Brian had been replaced by his deputy and Black had interviewed replacements for his technical staff already. He had sent Jim straight back to Kardo to reorganise the staff so that diamond production would not cease or be diminished by the raid. He already forecasted another bumper month of production following the hitting of the double production target this month.

'I'm sorry, General, but I'm pretty busy this morning. Was there anything else?'

***

Black started shuffling some papers that happened to be on the board table and soon appeared to forget that the General was there. General Fuego managed to get his limbs moving and left the room. He was already miles away, thinking about Sam, scared and alone in the rebel camp. He was so absorbed in his thoughts that he tripped as he descended the stairs. He flailed around and made a grab for a non-existent bannister. Luckily, one of the office gophers was coming up the stairs and managed to grab his arm and steady him to prevent him from crashing down the stairs headfirst.

The General was shaken. He realised that the only chance that Sam had of escape was now in his hands, and he had almost ended up in the hospital. He waved the gopher away and sat on the stair for a moment, his breathing agitated. He could feel his age. Every old wound, every broken bone was telling him that it was too late. *Was it hopeless to waste his time trying to do something?*

Black appeared at the top of the stairs alerted to the near-accident by the gopher. He was concerned enough to stagger from the boardroom when he realised that the national hero of Tamazia had almost died in his office. He was amazed to see the General still sitting on the stairs with his head in his hands. *Could he really be in love with that woman?* Black was bemused.

'Leave her to her fate, General. She is only a spoilt white bitch,' he shouted down the stairwell.

Black's total lack of humanity stirred the General into action. He stood up and straightened his uniform. His dignity returned with the rush of fury that flooded his body with adrenaline. Without looking back, he left the Gemsite office and went to call his friend General Bruiser.

***

In the rebel camp, Joao Contes had received the bad news about the non-payment of the ransom. He called a meeting of the fighters and told them that Gemsite had refused to pay. There was a lot of shouting as they worked themselves into a group fury. Joao had provided a ten-gallon plastic tank full of strong local beer, which he poured into plastic cups and passed around the hut. He announced that it was his intention to try the prisoners for stealing the diamonds belonging to the people of Kardo. He appealed to their patriotism and their machismo.

He was a good public speaker, which was the main reason that he had taken over the unit when Edison de Sousa had been killed. He didn't have any trouble persuading his frustrated men that the foreigners had to die. No one even mentioned that one of them was a woman and that it was against their rules to kill women. Despite their status as illegal rebels, MARFO had military roots and strong discipline, which had enabled them to keep fighting for years on very small means. Joao had been able to prevent them from raping because of this, although he had no real appreciation of the fact that many of the fighters wished they could drag her into their huts for an hour or two. She had strong novelty value, even if she was not young anymore.

Joao was jealous of the strong attachment Tereza and the boys had formed with Sam at a time when he was hoping to move in on Tereza himself. Getting rid of Sam would clear the way for the final takeover of Edison de Sousa's life, which he so craved. The other two men were roadkill to him: expendable, soft, foreigners. He encouraged his men to drink up. They would need Dutch courage for the task ahead.

Chapter XX

That night, two rebels appeared at the doorway of her hut, and Sam was dragged roughly outside without time to put on her boots. As she emerged, she saw Fred and Brian also being manhandled and pulled to the meeting hut on the main square. They were thrown through the door onto the floor in front of two rows of improvised seating, which were occupied by the hierarchy of the rebel group.

A strong smell of alcohol permeated the hut, and a few of the soldiers had bright red eyes and looked stoned. Loud jeering accompanied the hostages' undignified arrival into the hut. Joao sat in the middle of the front row of seats wearing his kitten T-shirt. This time, it wasn't at all amusing.

'You'll translate for the lawyer,' Joao told Sam, indicating a small wizened man without a tooth in his head. The little man slipped off his chair and dropped to the ground. Standing, he looked even smaller. He had what looked like a pair of shorts tied around his waist with a piece of string, and what remained of a waistcoat covered his bony chest. Sam wondered if he was a pygmy.

The lawyer started to speak with an authority belying his small stature, his voice quavering and spittle flying out of his mouth onto the dirt floor. Sam struggled to understand his antiquated and flowery Portuguese, asking him several times to repeat himself. Addressing the hostages, he said, 'You have been called to a people's court convened to deliver justice for the people of Tamazia. You are on trial for stealing diamonds from the village of Kardo, the execution of local villagers and the violation of local women. I have witnesses from Kardo who will testify against you.'

He paused as Sam struggled with the legal terms.

'MARFO, being a just and fair organisation, gave the company, Gemsite, the chance to pay reparations for the damage done to the village, but the company has refused to pay, despite the amount being reduced by half.'

Sam translated this in a shaking voice. Fred and Brian looked stunned. *Oh my God, the bastard has hung us out to dry.*

'This being the case, MARFO has decided to put the captives on trial for the wrongs of the company.'

Sam translated this, realising as she did that their last hope had gone. As she looked into the crestfallen faces of her fellow captives, she felt the cold chill of reality mix with the suffocating heat of the communal hut. They were going to die. It was only a case of when and how, but not if anymore. Sam felt her knees give out, and a short time later, she was surprised to find herself propped up against one of the central posts in the hut. Tereza was forcing her to drink water.

'Sam, you have to translate. Wake up.'

Sam got groggily to her feet. Faint with hunger and fear, she stood swaying on her weak legs. She couldn't stand for long, and slid to the floor again, so Joao made her sit on a chair placed beside the lawyer. The trial began.

Tereza stepped outside the hut into the cool night air. Despite her status as the widow of a war hero, she had not been allowed to participate in the trial because she was a woman. The captives had no hope of redemption in a court in which all the jurors were drunk and aggressive. There was nothing she could do for Brian and Fred. They would have to fight their own ground, and she didn't like either of them much anyway. They always excluded Sam. She couldn't understand what Sam had done to be treated in such a way. The woman she knew was kind and brave and loved her boys like an auntie or a second mother. She had never seen Sam be horrid to anyone, even when she was depressed.

Tereza remembered how Sam had saved Pibé at great risk to her own life, and she knew that she had to try and save Sam in return. It would mean the end of her life in Tamazia, but she could make a new life with the money she had received from Eduardo for looking after Sam. She felt no loyalty to the rebels, who had used her like a servant since her husband died. Sam had shown her how it felt to be equal, and she wanted that for herself and her children no matter what the risk.

Her mind made up, she ran back to her hut and dug under her bed until she found a small tin box. She opened it up. The unused mobile phone was still there, accusing her of treachery with its shiny black case. She took it out and sneaked over to the generator hut where she plugged it into a row of sockets placed along the wall. She rang the only number in the contact list. After five rings, the phone was answered by Eduardo, who was panting.

'The hostages are on trial,' she said. 'They will kill her. You must come early in the morning, or it will be too late. I will direct her to the house that you told me about. She is weak. You must come now, or she will die.'

***

Brian was on trial. A woman from Kardo was talking about the time her husband went out to pan the gravels on a strip of diamond-bearing gravel that had been exposed by the company machines, under the cover of night with twenty other men. They had been spotted, and her husband had been shot dead trying to run away by some of Greys' security men. Brian was charged with being responsible for the murder because he was head of security.

Brian looked confused as Sam translated the charges. Then, he smiled as the misunderstanding of his role at Gemsite became apparent. He was too arrogant to realise that whatever he said, he would still be guilty. Trying in vain to explain the difference between the mercenaries and the internal security guards, he told the jury he was not a member of Greys but head of internal security.

'My job was to prevent stealing of the diamonds once they were mined. I never carried a gun in Tamazia and I have certainly never shot anyone,' he said.

No one was listening. He was shouted down by the drunken rebel fighters who had been getting tanked up well before the trial started. Sam couldn't make herself heard above the jeering.

'We know you were a soldier. You are a killer. We don't believe you.'

Brian managed to stay standing despite some of the rebels jumping up and shouting in his face and shoving him. He was muttering to himself. Sam could hear him saying, 'It's not true, it's not true,' again and again.

The fighters started shouting, 'Guilty, guilty, guilty!' Brian was drowned out, but he kept trying.

'A security guard looks after things, not people. I didn't ever use my gun.'

Sam tried to shout the translation over the drunken roars.

'Silence!' Joao shouted at him. 'You have been found guilty of murder, and you will be executed by firing squad. Take him outside and carry out the sentence.'

Sam's throat constricted so much it almost closed over, and she could not—would not—translate. An eruption of cheering was followed by a nasty change in atmosphere. More rebels had come over to Brian and had started to push him back and forth between them. Sam started to protest over the clamour of angry voices. Brian shouted at her.

'What did he say, Sam? What did he say?'

But Sam couldn't look him in the eye. Suddenly, several large men grabbed Brian; one of them got him in a headlock and took him away. His eyes bulged with terror as they dragged him through the door. Sam, who was standing up in protest, sank to her chair as her blood sugar betrayed her, and she feared she would faint again. She couldn't take it in. *After all this time, the rebels were just going to shoot them? People they had laughed with and drunk beer with?* She was sure she had translated the tense wrong. *Maybe they were just taking him back to his hut?*

There was a lot of shouting outside, which faded as the rebels moved away from the door. There was a moment's silence and then a loud retort of what could only have been gunfire. All the men in the hut cheered. Fred had started to cry. He was sobbing on his knees, his over-large clothes hanging in rags around his diminished frame. Sam looked at the floor. She couldn't bear to catch his eye and humiliate him further. He didn't have much dignity left, but he had to defend himself. Their only chance was to stick up for themselves.

The rebels stumbled back into the hut and slumped on their makeshift chairs. There was a smell of cordite in the hut. Joao silenced the back rows by pointing his AK-47 at them. Fred was the next to be judged. He hauled himself to his feet and stood on the sandy floor of the hut, scratching his thigh for a non-existent itch. Sam couldn't imagine what he had done to be on trial and had hoped to help him by judicious translation. She now knew what would happen to them both barring a miracle. She was not expecting the next development.

The lawyer reappeared from outside the hut, where, from the marks on his shorts, he had been urinating in some corner in the dark, and stood at the front of the rows of fighters. In a loud voice, he proclaimed that Fred would be tried for rape. Sam had to get him to repeat it three times. Fred stopped sobbing and looked bemused. He looked at Sam for guidance. Sam shrugged at him. She had no idea what this was about, either.

Then, from a dark corner of the hut, a young woman was pushed forward. She was weeping and covered her face with her hands when she saw Fred. It was Dina, Fred's girlfriend from Kardo. The rebels were baying for blood.

'Do you know this woman?' said the lawyer.

'Yes, I do,' answered Fred. 'We're friends.'

'Friends?' said the lawyer. 'Have you had relations with her?'

'Yes, we have been together for four months.'

'Four months? Have you no shame?'

'I'm sorry. I don't know what you mean. I love her.'

'She's thirteen. That is rape in your country, is it not?'

Sam flinched. From where on earth did he get that piece of information? Fred looked astonished and then horrified.

'Thirteen?' he stammered. 'Thirteen? She said she was sixteen. I swear.'

The lawyer turned to question the girl, who appeared to have been coerced to appear, as she did not want to answer the questions of the lawyer and stood looking at Fred with a pleading expression on her face. As he started to sob again, she ran forward and wrapped her long limbs around him, weeping too. A couple of the less drunk rebels came forward and dragged her away.

'It wasn't rape,' said Fred. 'I paid her. I wasn't the first. She's a prostitute. How can that be rape?'

Sam did not translate, but she could tell from the expression on the lawyer's face that he understood far more English than he was letting on.

'You have raped a thirteen-year-old girl. And then insulted her by giving her money. How would you feel if that happened to your daughter?'

Fred realized that he had made things worse. He started pleading.

'But I love her. We were a couple. I gave her money because she asked me for it. I gave her the dress she is wearing. I didn't know she was thirteen. I swear I didn't know.'

Sam had to translate over a sea of jeers and insults, and she knew the lawyer had already made up his mind about the verdict, as Joao stood up to silence the tribunal, who had taken up their chorus of guilty pleas again.

'Take him outside,' he said.

'No,' screamed Fred. 'No, I don't want to die.'

The girl freed herself from the soldiers and launched herself at Fred. She was wailing and screeching and clung on to him like a leech. She had to be slapped hard to make her let go this time. Fred howled in fear. The sound went through Sam like a knife. The soldiers prevaricated, uncertain of what to do.

'Didn't you hear me?' said Joao. 'Take him outside and get on with it.'

Fred had to be dragged along the ground, as his legs would not carry him. His awful howls of fear could be heard through the walls of the hut. There was a thud, and he went quiet. This was followed by a single shot and the sound of a body being pulled over the sand.

The dreadful scenes had knocked the stuffing out of the tribunal, who had sobered up. Fred had become a favourite with the fighters and could often be seen trying to fix a mobile phone or explain something in sign language. They made fun of his skin, which got bright pink at the least provocation either by the sun or embarrassment. The execution of such a gentle being diminished the effects of the drink and affected the atmosphere in the hut. Joao appeared uncertain how to proceed.

Sam sat on her chair, wondering if she was brave or not because up to this moment, she had always assumed that she was a courageous person. People had called her brave for coming to Tamazia, and she had accepted it. Of course, she must be to work in a war-zone. But now, she was pretty sure that she, like Fred, would have to be carried out howling, and she envied

Brian, who hadn't known what was happening until it was too late.

Joao pointed to a spot on the floor, and Sam managed to walk to it without help. The tiny lawyer stood up again and accused Sam of stealing diamonds from the village of Kardo, causing starvation and penury. Sam did not answer. She could not think of anything to say that she could remember how to translate into Portuguese, and she knew that nothing she said would make any difference to the verdict.

'Have you nothing to say in your defence?' roared Joao.

Sam looked him in the eye, forcing a defiant look onto her face. She drew herself up to her full height and tried to spit on the floor in defiance, but her mouth was dry. She waited for the verdict she knew was coming. She was another expendable foreigner, and her time had run out. She wobbled and almost fell. There was an air of expectancy as Joao worked himself up to pronounce sentence.

Just then, the door of the hut opened, and Tereza came into the silent room. She stood in front of the tribunal and beckoned Sam to stand beside her. Sam tottered across the room and stood hip to hip with her. Joao came to life and roared, 'What are you doing in here, woman? You know it is forbidden for women to interfere with the decisions of the tribunal!'

'I'm a witness for the defence. I have a right to be in here as the widow of your most beloved war hero. You don't tell me what to do. I have borne the children of Edison de Sousa.'

There was a muttering of assent in the hut. The lawyer stepped forward and pointed a bony finger at Sam.

'This woman has stolen the property of the state of

Tamazia. She has worked for the killer company Gemsite. She deserves to die.'

'This woman has fed my children when they were hungry. She has brought them gifts from the capital. How many of you have helped the children of Edison the Brave? I have almost starved since he died. You, who are such big men, who judge people and shoot them for no reason, what have you done for the children of your biggest war hero?'

'This is not a defence.'

'And who saved Pibé from malaria? Did you know she gave up her own medicine and risked death that Pibé might live? I claim her life. She is mine to do with as I wish. Under our laws, she may not die until I have repaid her. You do not have the right to take her from me.'

'I cannot agree. The woman must die, like her colleagues. They are all vermin and must be exterminated.'

'I claim my right to get the judgement from the leader of MARFO. I know he is due here tomorrow. Let the woman live until then.'

'Don't be ridiculous. He will not save her. Let's get this over with.'

Tereza stepped in front of Sam and shielded her with her body.

'Don't come any closer, or you will have to kill me too.'

There was a definite shift in the mood of the room. The drunken fury had been replaced with a maudlin apathy. No one stepped forward to remove Tereza from the hut. No one touched Sam, who was in a catatonic state of fright and stared into the distance with her mouth open. Joao stood and held up his hand to calm the room, as he felt he was losing his audience who were moved by the presence of Edison the Brave in their midst, personified by Tereza, her eyes blazing.

'Very well,' he said. 'We will wait until tomorrow, but that is all.'

He addressed one of the rebels. 'Take her to her hut and guard it well.'

Sam was by now in an advanced stage of shock. She was unaware of what had happened. Her legs would not move when the man grabbed her arm and tried to make her move. When that didn't work, he slung her over his shoulder and, pushing Tereza aside, he marched outside. He took her to the hut she had been living in where he dropped her lifeless on the bed. He positioned himself outside the door, but Sam wasn't going to be awake again that night. He made himself comfortable against the door frame and fell asleep.

Sam lay on her rough bed. She moaned with fear in her confused sleep. She was close to death with shock, exhaustion and hunger. She had lost all hope of survival and was just waiting for the end. *Let it be quick. I would do it myself if I had a gun.* She was shivering with fear.

Suddenly, she felt a small grainy hand take hers in the darkness. She squeezed the hand, but it did not disappear. She opened her eyes, convinced she was dreaming.

'Sam, drink this now.'

It was Pibé, and he held a battered plastic mug with dark liquid in it. She blinked twice, but he was still there holding her hand and proffering her the mug like a little gnome in the dark. She hauled herself up in the bed and took the mug. She sipped the contents. It was sickly sweet. Some sort of juice with added sugar.

She sat for five minutes with Pibé, while the magic

juice sent sugar coursing through her veins. Pibé saw her inflate with new vigour and whispered, 'Come on, Sam. You must follow me.' He slipped onto his hands and knees and vanished. Sam was now sure she was dreaming, but with the sugar rush taking effect, she got off the bed and crawled after Pibé, who had disappeared into the dark at the wall of her hut. She felt his foot for an instant, and then it vanished into a hole at the bottom of the wall. The hole was pretty small, but Sam was thin now.

To her surprise, she glided through it with no effort. This was explained when she realised that Edison had grabbed her hands and pulled her out, sliding her over the damp, dew-covered earth. Tereza was there too.

'For God's sake, follow me.'

Sam was unsteady on her feet, but if this was a dream, it was a good one. She staggered after Tereza, trying not to fall flat on her face. She was aware of the soft, cool earth under her feet and the small sharp stones that penetrated the soles, but she didn't feel any pain. Her boots were left behind in the hut, but nobody noticed, least of all the boys who never wore shoes of any type. She saw the bats swoop beneath the bulbs in the village square, and she could hear their calls. She looked up at the starry sky, and she ran straight into Tereza, who had stopped at the village fence.

'Shh. They will kill me if you are found now. Go through this hole and run out to the road. When you get there, you must run to the south, down that way.' She pointed. 'Do you hear me? Run fast, and don't look back. You'll be safe in the dark. No one will see you. Don't stop running until you get to an old stone building on the left-hand side of the road. It has a few tiles still on the roof. It's the only one like it. You can't mistake it. Go into the building and hide. The fighters will kill you if they find you, but they will look for you to the north, as Zambia is only thirty kilometres away. Stay until someone comes for you. God bless you, Sam, and keep you safe.'

Tereza pushed her through the fence before she had a chance to say goodbye to Pibé and Edison. She was left with the feel of Pibé's grainy hand in hers and the taste of sugar on her tongue.

Chapter XXI

Sam stumbled out across the terrain separating the village from the road, trying to run, trying to be brave. She couldn't see her feet and stumbled and fell into a ditch that marked the side of the road. She was winded but uninjured. She climbed out of the ditch and started running down the road to the south from whence they had arrived all those weeks ago. 'Run,' she told herself, 'run, run, run.' The terror got her legs moving. Somehow, she started to trot down the road. Only a couple of hours were left until daybreak so she had to keep going.

She fell over several times, but each time she did, she could hear Fred howling and the baying of the tribunal. She got up again and again. There was no way she was going to give up. Finally, when she could go no further, an old stone building with a damaged roof loomed into view. She swerved off the road towards it and crumpled to the ground as she tripped into another ditch. She was not conscious of falling, she just folded into it when her legs gave way. Lying there in the dirty shallow water, her head cushioned by the mud, she fell sound asleep.

Sam was woken by the sound of a helicopter nearby, but she was too far gone to recognise the sound. She covered her ears. She was surprised to find herself in what appeared to be a stream. Her feet hurt like hell, and she was wet through. She froze at the sound of voices coming towards her and lay still, hoping to be camouflaged in the ditch.

They would shoot her now. Would it hurt? She was afraid, and she started to cry into her hand. She shut her eyes. If she didn't see the gun, it would be okay. Just like vaccinations. She tried to make herself smaller holding her breath and waiting for the darkness. The voices got nearer.

'Where did you see it, Eduardo? Are you sure it was a body?'

'Yes, my General. It looked like a body. I saw it when we were landing. It was over here.'

Footsteps crunched on the road and stopped right where she was. She was confused. Was she already dead and dreaming? She did not breathe.

'Sam? Oh, my God, Eduardo, it's Sam! Come quickly. Help me. Sam, Sam, are you okay? Is she dead? Is she? I can't bear it. Tell me. Have I killed her?'

Sam felt herself being picked up by some strong arms, and when nothing horrible happened next, she dared to open her eyes. She thought she recognised her saviour. *Was this a dream too? Had she died and gone to heaven?*

'Eduardo?' she said in a tiny frightened voice. 'Is it really you? Am I safe? Am I really safe?'

'Yes, Sam, you are safe. We are here, and you are safe, and no one's going to hurt you anymore.'

Eduardo placed her upright on a wooden bench at the back of the ruined house. He moved aside, and to Sam's amazement, the General's kind, round face peered into hers. He was crying.

'How are you, my Sam?'

Sam gathered all the strength she had left and smiled and said, 'Not too bad. Quite hungry. I really need a lobster right now.'

She sank back along the seat. Eduardo covered her with a blanket and helped the General sit down on a nearby tree stump. General Fuego was overcome with sobs of relief, and sat with his shoulders heaving while Eduardo stood guard over Sam. He managed to pull himself together by the time General Bruiser approached them and told them they had to get back into the helicopter and leave right away.

They woke Sam and gave her some lukewarm coffee with lots of sugar that was better than the nectar of the gods. They carried her over to the helicopter and had to lift her on, as she was too weak to climb up and her feet were in ribbons. The General almost cried again when he saw how thin and weak she was. They had to get her back to Mondongo.

'Bruiser, get us out of here. Those bastards would shoot me if they found me in their terrain.'

Bruiser laughed. They were all in for a rocket on their return to Mondongo when the President discovered his Chief of Staff had stolen a helicopter. Fuego had a way with his brother-in-law that would ensure minimal punishment. He liked an adventure from time to time. They took off, avoiding flying over the rebel village where the hungover jury had not yet woken up. Then the pilot headed for the capital.

***

Back in the rebel camp, Tereza de Sousa was long gone. She took her sons and left when dawn broke, taking with her the mobile phone and the money that Eduardo had given her. She had a sister in Zambia, to the north along the main road, who would take her in. They could build a new life, far from Tamazia. She walked briskly holding Pibé's hand. Edison marched alongside, a big stick on his shoulder.

They caught a local bus and sat in the back. Tereza snuck a few looks through the back window but no one followed them to the border. A quick bribe was all it took to drive straight through. Her shoulders sank as she realised that they were safe.

'Do you think Sam got away?' said Edison.

'Of course she did. Sam is a heroine, like your father. She never gives up.'

'Will we ever see Sam again?' said Pibé, tears in his eyes.

'No,' said Tereza. 'Sam is not coming back. She has gone to live with Princess Di.'

***

The news was bad. The ransom had not been paid in time and the rebels had executed the hostages. Bill, Matilda and Hannah Harris had been mourning for a couple of days when the man from the foreign office turned up at the house. He stood on the doorstep in his grey suit with a briefcase in his hand.

'Send him away,' said Matilda. 'I can't bear to get the official confirmation. I need more time before I let hope die.'

'Darling, we can't send him away. We have to deal with this.'

Bill Harris let the man in, and Matilda made them a pot of tea. Her face was etched with grief, and she did not speak.

'I'm so sorry,' said the official. 'It happened so suddenly. We didn't have time to react. But there's scope for good news. That's why I'm here.'

Matilda Harris gasped and choked. 'Good news? How can it be good? Sam's been murdered.'

'Um, look, I'm not saying it's definite. We don't have all the information yet but—'

'But what?' said Hannah, animated.

'The Tamazian troops went into the MARFO camp the day after the murders. The MARFO rebels had abandoned the camp, but the troops found two bodies, both male.'

'They didn't find Sam? Have the rebels taken her with them? I don't understand.' Hannah stood up in her agitation.

'We don't know, but the newspapers have permission to print the story tomorrow so I'm here to tell you what we know.'

'But where is she?' said Matilda.

'We're trying to find out. I promise you'll know the instant we do.'

'Can we go out to Tamazia?' said Bill.

'I'm sorry. We really don't recommend it. Sit tight. I'll be in touch.'

***

Sam woke up in the only private hospital in Mondongo, in one of the few expensive private rooms. The throbbing pain in her feet and the drip in her arm stopped her moving, but she was aware of someone sitting beside her holding her hand. She smiled and slipped away again, moaning in her sleep as the nightmares hit.

She took almost a week to find the energy to sit up in bed and survey the room. There were some tropical banana flowers in a vase, and she was wearing a clingy nylon nightie that wrapped itself tighter and tighter around her the more she moved, giving off sparks in the dark recesses of her bed. *Soon get rid of that.*

To her amazement, she noticed Jim sitting across the room talking to the General. He had a bag on his knee that looked like hers.

'Sam,' he said, when he noticed she was awake. 'How are you? We've been so worried about you.'

He had the grace to look embarrassed, and Sam knew that not everyone was that worried. He came over to the bed and put the bag on the end, being careful to avoid her feet.

'The General tells me you'll be fine now. I brought you some clothes from Villa Alice. I'm afraid you won't see the other clothes again. The women from Kardo looted all your underwear before we could rescue it. Anyway, I can see that none of them will fit you anymore. You're so thin. You look like one of those stick-insect models.'

'Thanks a bunch, Jim. I think I look pretty good, actually.'

Sam had no idea what she looked like but could see her stick-thin legs poking out of the nylon nightie.

'I came to tell you that Gemsite can't take you back after what happened,' said Jim. 'It would be too dangerous for you in Kardo. The rebels would hunt you down. Anyway, I don't expect you want to go back after all you've been through.'

He paused, looking at her with real concern.

'Jesus, Sam, you look like you had a holiday in Auschwitz. I'm so sorry about Brian and Fred. The General told me that they didn't make it. I didn't know that Black wasn't going to pay the ransom. I swear it. He's an evil bastard.'

Sam tried to deflect his apology.

'I've wanted to be this thin all my life. Be careful what you wish for, that's what I say.'

'I got you your bonuses,' Jim blurted out and then looked horrified at what he had said. 'Not that you care about the money, but I didn't want you to miss out. You'll receive all your pay to date, including the time while you were kidnapped, but I couldn't get you any holiday pay as you won't be coming back.'

Jim looked at the floor, and Sam let him off the hook.

'That's great, really. I appreciate you coming. I know you didn't have to. Give my regards to Jorge, please. I'm going to miss him.'

'Bye, Sam. You're a real trooper. Black said you could look after yourself. I guess he was right.'

'Where is Black, anyway? Does he know that I'm alive?'

'He knows, but he's not happy. He would have preferred Brian.'

He winked to show that he was joking but Sam knew better.

She shrugged.

'Don't worry. It's almost six months' pay and that's a lot. I don't think I want to hang out around here anymore. I know I wouldn't win any popularity contests at Gemsite.'

Jim couldn't bear to stay any longer, and left after kissing her cheek.

The General had been waiting patiently while this happened, pretending to read his newspaper. When Jim left, he sat on the bed and looked at Sam with something approaching reverence. He took her hand and raised it to his lips.

'Sam, thank you for living. I would never have forgiven myself if you had been killed. I am so sorry I got you into trouble. I thought I was doing my job, but I was a fool. Eduardo confessed that because of him,

Pedro told Black we were having an affair. You know what a maniac he is. He actually thought you were feeding me information. It is true that I was supposed to be milking you for diamond data for the President, but you never told me anything. Black thought he had been betrayed. He is slow to trust but quick to abandon if he thinks that trust is broken. You got caught in the middle. I am sorry. Do you forgive me?'

Sam looked long and hard into his round brown face with its age spots and tiny, almost pointless, moustache. She raised a hand and stroked his cheek.

'Hmm,' she said. 'It will cost you dearly. I will require at least three lobsters this time.'

The General giggled.

'My daughters are dying to see you again. Will you come out to the island for lunch when you are able to leave the hospital? We will make you a lovely leaving party.'

'Can I call my parents?'

'Call the moon if you want.'

***

It was a lovely party. Many lobsters were eaten, and many whiskies were drunk. Sam and the General smoked on the balcony and talked about life until dawn. They spent the next day getting over their hangovers and swimming in the sea with the General's family and Eduardo, who never let her out of his sight. She had to stop him from following her into the toilet.

'Eduardo, I'll be all right in here on my own.'

In the afternoon, the General drove her to the airport, 'to make sure you leave.' As usual, he drove too fast and made Sam worry that after all that she had been through, she was about to die in a car crash on the way to the airport.

Being accompanied by the brother-in-law of the President had its perks, and she got VIP treatment all the way to the plane door. The General went with her everywhere and made sure no one delayed her or tired her. Sam wondered if an English general could have done this. As they parted, the General gave her a small black box and told her not to open it until the plane took off. She shoved it into the pocket of her new rucksack, bought from a vendor through the window of the General's car.

He hugged her for a full couple of minutes and got quite tearful again. Sam cried too, but it could have been the relief of leaving. After a last look back at her very own General, she boarded the flight. Gemsite had paid for her to travel business class, so she turned left and found her seat, which was easy to recognise due to the massive bunch of flowers on it. She had them taken away to a cupboard, mourning their certain demise before landing.

She sat in her seat and strapped herself in. As they took off, she grasped the armrests and willed the flight to take off safely. As they banked over Mondongo, she saw Pedro's rocket glinting in the late afternoon sunlight and all the plump citizens like seals on the beach. She lowered her seat for a sleep.

****

Black ground his teeth in fury.

'That bloody bitch escaped, and I lost two good men because of her.'

Marybelle rolled her eyes. She had heard the unofficial version of events from one of the secretaries in the Mondongo office. This placed her husband squarely in the centre of the blame vortex. She had had enough of Black's tantrums. She stretched out a calming hand.

'I'll run you a bath. Shall I make you a nice drink?' she said.

Black subsided and blew out the air in his lungs.

'Okay.'

Marybelle ran the bath and put some incense in the holder, filling the bathroom with an odour of sandalwood. She laid out a couple of fluffy towels and dimmed the lights. Black came up behind her and thrust his pelvis into her backside.

'Want to get in with me?' he said.

'Sure, I've just got to finish something and I'll be back.'

'Is it a sexy secret?' said Black.

Marybelle winked and sashayed her way out of the bathroom. Black threw his clothes on the floor and cupped his balls in his hand.

'It's time you woke up,' he said, and stepped into the bath, sinking into the hot water with a sigh.

The warmth and the soft smells soon lulled him into a slumber. He didn't hear Marybelle as she came back into the room, holding a bucket with a lid on it at arm's length.

Chapter XXII

There were no reporters at the airport. The Foreign Office had respected the wishes of the Harris family, and kept her return secret.

'She'll have to do some interviews,' said the man from the government.

'We'll let her decide what to do when she's ready,' said Bill.

Matilda Harris went to the airport by herself so as not to arouse suspicion. Bill and Hannah waited at home, drinking tea and checking their watches.

If Matilda Harris was shocked to see how thin and wasted her daughter looked when she came out of customs with her bags, she was sensible enough to hide it well. She did allow herself the luxury of a long hug with the daughter who had returned in one piece, albeit a skinny version of her former self. Sam did not fight her, knowing the effort her mother was putting in not to make a fuss and enjoying the rare luxury of a hug from her mother.

'Did you have a good flight, darling?' said Matilda.

'I don't know. I was asleep. They put me in business class.'

Sam smiled to show it was a joke. Her mother

risked another hug and led her out to the short-stay carpark.

Sam found her mother's handbag in the footwell of the car and rooted around for some wine gums, which she knew would be hiding amongst all the change the Bank of England was missing.

'Want one?'

'No, and don't do that without asking. A woman's handbag is her castle.'

The family had a tacit agreement not to mention Sam's ordeal but her mother still asked.

'Do you want to tell me about it, darling? I don't know how you want to cope with it all?'

'I'll talk about it when I'm ready. Don't worry. I'm alive, and it's all that matters right now.'

'What about the journalists?'

'Oh, I had a visit from the foreign office in Tamazia. They gave me a press release to hand out. I can add details, but nothing solid. Relationships with Tamazia are important because of all the oil.'

After being smothered in hugs by her father and sister, Sam told them the same thing.

'After what they did to you?' said Hannah.

'That was the rebels. And they didn't do anything.'

'They certainly didn't feed you.'

But Sam stayed mum and her family respected her privacy.

For a while, it was good to be home where nothing had changed. She hadn't found a flat yet. Nobody talked about her ordeal or commented on her weight. Sometimes Sam wanted to talk about it, but her parents were studiously avoiding the subject and her sister didn't know what to say. Sam thought she knew them well enough to avoid it too. They hated any kind of attention-seeking behaviour, and Sam suspected that getting kidnapped came under this heading.

The truth was that her parents did not want to talk about her traumatic experience in case it upset her. So, in their own very British way, the subject never came up, and life went back to normal. Sam didn't tell them the truth for years and by then, it was almost like someone else had lived through it. She was good enough to gloss over the scenes of the trial, which she felt were too gruesome to recount.

Meanwhile, her mother had assumed that Sam had finished with that phase of her life and would now settle down and get a proper job. Sam had almost agreed with her, but she had a nagging feeling that wouldn't go away.

'We're going to a wedding this Saturday,' said her mother. 'You'd better buy something nice to wear.'

'Mummy, you know how I hate weddings. I would rather eat my own sick than have to sit on another odds and sods table entertaining the black-sheep uncles and cat-hair singles. Can't you say that I am too traumatised to leave the house?'

'Don't be silly, darling. I've told you a million times not to exaggerate. You love telling stories.'

Sam gave her a thunderous look, and her mother repented. 'Okay, but just this once. I don't want people thinking that you're peculiar.'

That particular ship had sailed long ago, but she felt vindicated. Suddenly the doorbell rang. Her mother had probably forgotten her hat. She bounced to the door ready to make the usual jokes about her mother's forgetful nature. She swung the door open, a broad grin on her face, which turned into an open-mouthed astonishment.

There at the door stood Jim Hennessy. He was staggering under the weight of a large cardboard box.

'Aren't you going to invite me in?' he said.

Jim sat at the kitchen table and gobbled a piece of her mother's fruit cake. Sam watched in amusement as he picked all the crumbs off his plate.

'You can have another piece, you know,' she said, smiling.

He flushed.

'No, you're all right. Well, maybe just a small piece.'

Sam cut another generous slice and refilled his cup of tea.

'What's all this about?' she said.

'I brought you all your stuff, well, most of it. Books, CDs, tapes. It was scattered around your room but it seems no one in Tamazia likes Led Zeppelin.'

'That's really nice of you. I thought it was all lost. How did you get permission from Black to bring it to me?'

An odd expression appeared on Jim's face. He bit his lip and rubbed his chin.

'Spit it out,' said Sam, irritated. 'What's the old bastard done now?'

'He's dead,' said Jim. 'Last week.'

Sam blanched.

'Oh, bloody hell. How did that happen?'

'A snake. In his bath. Marybelle found him drowned.'

'A snake? Are you serious? How did a snake get in his bath?'

'They have no idea. He got bitten and the poison rushed around his body in the hot water. He probably passed out and slipped below the water.'

But Sam wasn't convinced, and it showed on her face.

'What?' said Jim.

'Oh, nothing. I guess Marybelle is a rich woman now. She finally got what she wanted.'

Jim's face was a picture of mischief.

'Oh, you're wrong there. She didn't get a penny. Not a farthing.'

'But…'

Sam tried to compute and failed.

'He left everything to his daughters, the triplets. You remember them?'

Sam laughed.

'I do.'

Jim fiddled with his teaspoon.

'You could come back now. We've got rid of all the dinosaurs now that Black's wife is in charge. She asked me to inquire if you would consider taking over production at Kardo.'

Sam didn't hesitate.

'Tell her thanks, but no thanks. My days of roaming the mad back hills of tinpot dictatorships are over. I'm staying home from now on.'

'You don't mean that. You're made for it.'

'I do. Today, I do.'

When Jim had left, Sam realised that she hadn't asked him about the General. *Had he got into trouble for stealing the helicopter?* And, suddenly, she remembered the little black box. *Where on earth was it?* She had forgotten to open it. With great effort, she moved all of her bags around the loft, which was as hot as the sauna in her local health club, and found her travelling rucksack. She searched all the pockets, and out fell the box. It got stuck under one of the rafters and she got sweaty and dusty digging it out again.

Sam took the box down the rickety stairs and into her bedroom. She sat on her bed and turned it over a few times. *Was this Pandora's Box? Would all evils of the world rush out and invade her world?* Not much of a present then.

After procrastinating for a few moments, she pried open the box, peering in. She cried out in amazement. It was a large black diamond. Totally worthless and totally wonderful. The perfect parting gift from a man who, despite living on another planet from her, had understood what mattered in the end.

In that instant, she didn't care how peculiar people thought she was. They would have to put up with her, because Sam had a plan. No more remote sites for her. She would do a master's degree in business administration, and try her luck in the real world. It couldn't possibly be as misogynistic and dangerous as her present career. London was as safe as houses. She would go and see the university on Monday.

Thank you for reading my book. If you enjoyed it, won't you please take a moment to leave me a review at your favourite retailer?

Thank you

The next and last book in the Series is **Concrete Jungle** On Pre-Order soon.

Other Books in this Series

Fool's Gold - Book 1

Newly qualified geologist Sam Harris is a woman in a man's world - overlooked, underpaid but resilient and passionate. Desperate for her first job, and nursing a broken heart, she accepts an offer from notorious entrepreneur Mike Morton, to search for gold deposits in the remote rainforests of Sierramar. With the help of nutty local heiress, Gloria Sanchez, she soon settles into life in Calderon, the capital. But when she accidentally uncovers a long-lost clue to a treasure buried deep within the jungle, her journey really begins.

Teaming up with geologist Wilson Ortega, historian Alfredo Vargas and the mysterious Don Moises, they venture through the jungle, where she lurches between excitement and insecurity. Yet there is a far graver threat looming; Mike and Gloria discover that one of the members of the expedition is plotting to seize the fortune for himself and is willing to do anything to get it. Can Sam survive and find the treasure or will her first adventure be her last?

The first book in the Sam Harris Series sets the scene for the career of an unwilling heroine, whose bravery and resourcefulness are needed to navigate a series of adventures set in remote sites in Africa and South America. Based on the real-life adventures of the author, the settings and characters are given an authenticity that will connect with readers who enjoy adventure fiction and mysteries set in remote settings with realistic scenarios.

Set in the late 1980's themes such as women working in formerly male domains, and what constitutes a normal existence, are examined and developed in the context of Sam's constant ability to find herself in the middle of an adventure or mystery. Sam's home life provides a contrast to her adventures and feeds her need to escape. Her attachment to an unsuitable boyfriend is the thread running through her romantic life, and her attempts to break free of it provide another side to her character.

Hitler's Finger - Book 2

The second book in the Sam Harris Series sees the return of our heroine Sam Harris to Sierramar to help her friend Gloria track down her boyfriend, the historian, Alfredo Vargas.

Geologist Sam Harris loves getting her hands dirty. So, when she learns that her friend Alfredo has gone missing in Sierramar, she gives her personal life some much needed space and hops on the next plane. But she never expected to be following the trail of a devious Nazi plot nearly 50 years after World War II.

Deep in a remote mountain settlement, Sam must uncover the village's dark history. If she fails to reach her friend in time, the Nazi survivors will ensure Alfredo's permanent silence. Can Sam blow the lid on the conspiracy before the Third Reich makes a devastating return?

The background to the book is the presence of Nazi

war criminals in South America which was often ignored by locals who had fascist sympathies during World War II. Themes such as tacit acceptance of fascism, and local collaboration with fugitives from justice are examined and developed in the context of Sam's constant ability to find herself in the middle of an adventure or mystery. Sam's home life provides a contrast to her adventures and feeds

The Star of Simbako - Book 3

A fabled diamond, a jealous voodoo priestess, disturbing cultural practices. What could possibly go wrong? The third book in the Sam Harris Series sees Sam Harris on her first contract to West Africa to Simbako, a land of tribal kingdoms and voodoo.

Nursing a broken heart, Sam Harris goes to Simbako to work in the diamond fields of Fona. She is soon involved with a cast of characters who are starring in their own soap opera, a dangerous mix of superstition, cultural practices and ignorance (mostly her own). Add a love triangle and a jealous woman who wants her dead and Sam is in trouble again. Where is the Star of Simbako? Is Sam going to survive the chaos?

This book is based on visits made to the Paramount Chiefdoms of West Africa. Despite being nominally Christian communities, Voodoo practices are still part of daily life out there. This often leads to conflicts of interest. Combine this with the horrific ritual of FGM and it makes for a potent cocktail of conflicting loyalties. Sam is pulled into this life by her friend, Adanna, and soon finds herself involved in goings on that she doesn't understand.

The Pink Elephants - Book 4

Sam gets a call in the middle of the night that takes her to the Masaibu project in Lumbono, Africa. The project is collapsing under the weight of corruption and chicanery engendered by management, both in country and back on the main company board. Sam has to navigate murky waters to get it back on course, not helped by interference from people who want her to fail. When poachers invade the elephant sanctuary next door, her problems multiply. Can Sam protect the elephants and save the project or will she have to choose?

The fourth book in the Sam Harris Series presents Sam with her sternest test yet as she goes to Africa to fix a failing project. The day to day problems encountered by Sam in her work are typical of any project manager in the Congo which has been rent apart by warring factions, leaving the local population frightened and rootless. Elephants with pink tusks do exist, but not in the area where the project is based. They are being slaughtered by poachers in Gabon for the Chinese market and will soon be extinct, so I have put the guns in the hands of those responsible for the massacre of these defenceless animals

The Bonita Protocol - Book 5

An erratic boss. Suspicious results. Stock market shenanigans. Can Sam Harris expose the scam before they silence her? It's 1996. Geologist Sam Harris has been around the block, but she's prone to nostalgia, so she snatches the chance to work in Sierramar, her old stomping ground. But she never expected to be working for a company that is breaking all the rules.

When the analysis results from drill samples are suspiciously high, Sam makes a decision that puts her life in peril. Can she blow the lid on the conspiracy before they shut her up for good?

The Bonita Protocol is the fifth book in the Sam Harris Adventure series. If you like gutsy heroines, complex twists and turns, and heart pounding action, then you'll love PJ Skinner's thrilling novel.

The Concrete Jungle - Book 7

Coming Soon

Connect with the Author

If you would like updates on the latest in the Sam Harris Series or to contact the author with your questions please click on the following links:
Website: www.pjskinner.com
Facebook:
https://www.facebook.com/PJSkinnerAuthor
Twitter: https://twitter.com/PJSkinnerAuthor

About the Author

PJ Skinner is the author of the Sam Harris Series of adventure-thriller novels. A geologist who has spent thirty years roaming the planet and collecting tall tales and real-life experiences, she now writes fact-based novels from the relative safety of London. She still travels worldwide collecting material for the series and having her own adventures.

The author is working on the seventh and last book in the Sam Harris Series, Concrete Jungle, in which Sam takes on the City of London. It will be published in Q4 2019.

She is also researching two other new books, one of which, Rebel Green, is being written with the help of a childhood spent in Ireland.

The Sam Harris Adventure Series will appeal to lovers of adventure thrillers. It has a unique viewpoint provided by Sam, a female interloper in a male world, as she struggles with alien cultures and failed relationships.

www.ingramcontent.com/pod-product-compliance
Lightning Source LLC
Chambersburg PA
CBHW050837190726
48286CB00007B/2117